A KISS IN THE DARK

They were dancing. In the deepest dark of the night, with no music save for the passion singing in their blood, they were dancing.

She felt a tremor shake him, and then a low, disbelieving laugh as he realized it, too. He did not retreat. He tightened his hold upon her, sure and strong. He spun her and turned with her. She could see nothing but the broad expanse of his chest; she could hear nothing but the beat of his heart pounding the tempo of their silent song.

Perhaps he was right, she thought with dizzy delight. Perhaps dancing did lead to nothing but trouble, for she felt the desperate urge to cast aside all her responsibilities and obligations and stay here dancing in the woods with him forever.

"I told you this wasn't such a good idea," Neil murmured, just before his lips captured hers.

Sabrina did not spare the time to contradict him. She showed him that his kiss was the best thing that had ever happened to her in her life. She twined her arms about his neck, holding him close.

She had craved this from almost the first moment she had met him.

BOOK YOUR PLACE ON OUR WEBSITE AND MAKE THE READING CONNECTION!

We've created a customized website just for our very special readers, where you can get the inside scoop on everything that's going on with Zebra, Pinnacle and Kensington books.

When you come online, you'll have the exciting opportunity to:

- View covers of upcoming books

- Read sample chapters

- Learn about our future publishing schedule (listed by publication month *and author*)

- Find out when your favorite authors will be visiting a city near you

- Search for and order backlist books from our online catalog

- Check out author bios and background information

- Send e-mail to your favorite authors

- Meet the Kensington staff online

- Join us in weekly chats with authors, readers and other guests

- Get writing guidelines

- AND MUCH MORE!

**Visit our website at
http://www.zebrabooks.com**

Prologue

The Irish Border—1298

"My lady!" The maid's usually ruddy complexion had turned stark white, and her voice shook with dread. "'Tis your mother—she approaches this chamber!"

Sabrina almost let fall the precious flacon of scent that had been her husband-to-be's betrothal gift. "You know that is impossible, Bessie."

"I swear it is she."

"Look again."

Sabrina's hands shook so badly that she had to devote all her attention to setting the flacon safely in its place of honor. Dropping the precious glass bottle would be an omen so terrible it did not bear contemplation. The betrothal gift was the only thing from Robert that she could bear to touch. He had often remarked that once she belonged to him, he would teach her to move with more grace, to hold herself with greater elegance. The lessons did not promise to be enjoyable, and would be even less so if he decided she needed to be trained to be less clumsy as well.

Bessie poked her head through the doorway. With a shriek of dismay, she hopped back into the chamber. She wrapped her arms about her head and whirled until her back pressed into a wall, as if she sought to disappear within the chill stone. "It *is* your mother, my lady."

"Impossible!"

She did not know why she felt compelled to deny it—none of her objections had ever changed what had been decreed. Nor did it this time.

"Naught is impossible, Sabrina," said her lady mother from the door. "May I enter?"

"Of course."

Politeness had been so ingrained within her that she instinctively made the gracious response. A handy skill, for her lips trembled with the need to say words like *A mother should not be a stranger requiring permission to enter her daughter's room.*

But she had lived nigh unto twenty-three years without uttering such criticisms. It seemed foolish to begin casting them about now, on this final night in the chamber that had been her sanctuary, her prison, for all these years. Her mother seemed no more at ease; she trod so gingerly that Sabrina had to check the floor, to make sure she had not carpeted it after all with shards of shattered glass.

And thus they stood: two Desmond women, one whimpering maidservant. Silent with the unfamiliarity of strangers, when there was so much to be said.

On the morrow, Sabrina would wed. Robert of Allingham would cast aside his name and claim her birthright as his own, for the privilege of ruling Desmond Muir. She and Robert would occupy their own wing within the great, echoing castle. She would find sanctuary—she would

MY IRISH ENCHANTRESS

Julia Hanlon

Zebra Books
Kensington Publishing Corp.

http://www.zebrabooks.com

ZEBRA BOOKS are published by

Kensington Publishing Corp.
850 Third Avenue
New York, NY 10022

First Printing: August, 1999
10 9 8 7 6 5 4 3 2 1

Printed in the United States of America

be imprisoned—in a new chamber that her mother would also never visit. A new chamber where she would soon know exactly how many stones comprised each wall; her slippered feet would make no mark upon the stone floor no matter how many courses she paced around the perimeter, or how many times she crossed between the floor and the door.

Endless and dull as they promised to be, those days would no doubt be more endurable than the dark hours of the night.

She prayed the window in her new chamber did not admit much moonlight. It would be best if Robert could not see the aversion on her face when he left his own bed to do what he must with her. There would be no avoiding coupling with him; they must ensure an heir for this lonely keep along the Irish Border.

She reddened at the thought of the grunting and groaning and sweaty embraces she would be forced to endure, the wine-slackened lips that would quest over her wherever they pleased, the messy aftermath. Of a sudden, she understood her mother's unexpected appearance—Lady Elspeth no doubt intended to explain Sabrina's wifely duties.

"I have come to convey a sacred trust," said Elspeth, confirming Sabrina's suspicion.

The small portion of her heart that ever yearned for such shows of concern from her mother glowed warm, easily flaring into life despite the long years of disappointment. This unusual discourse between them must be exceedingly difficult for such an aloof woman, and Sabrina impulsively sought to ease her mother's embarrassment. They might dispense with this unpleasantness, and talk instead of other matters.

"I understand what awaits me."

Her hand strayed toward her mother, but missed its mark, for Elspeth had apparently been distracted by a glass flacon gracing its niche in the wall. Elspeth abruptly moved toward it. She glanced about the room with the open interest of one viewing an unfamiliar sight, and so could not have noticed that Sabrina's hand closed upon empty space, and then buried itself in the folds of her gown.

"Bessie explained all to me."

"Of course she did," said Elspeth. "I instructed her to do so."

Sabrina's inner warmth extinguished, replaced by her usual chill. "Then what duty brings you here?"

"This." Elspeth's hand strayed to her bosom, and traced the length of the ancient gold chain she wore. The rough, worn links supported a tear-shaped stone, as large and as milk white as a pullet's egg.

"The Druid's Tear," Sabrina said. Bessie, still cowering in the corner, made a furtive sign of the cross and seemed to shrink even more against the gray stone wall.

Elspeth pressed the tear-shaped gem against her breast, and Sabrina wondered, as she had so often, whether one could feel a difference between the rock-hard jewel and her mother's heart. She could not recall ever being held close enough to tell.

The Druid's Tear always graced Elspeth's breast; when social occasions demanded finer jewels, Sabrina knew she'd tucked the ancient bauble beneath her garment.

"Yes, the Druid's Tear. When this treasure became mine, my own mother told me that the stone has another, very ancient name, which has been lost over time. All that remains is the legend, the legend that has ruled Desmond women for time beyond remembering."

"And now it will rule me," said Sabrina.

"Aye. The Druid's Tear belongs to you now." Elspeth lifted the chain over her head. The cool disinterest that always marked her expression faded for the briefest moment into relief. She seemed to stand taller, as if shedding the stone had removed an onerous weight from her slim shoulders. "May you wear it with better success than I."

"You always wore it well, Mother. With pride and with respect."

Elspeth made a cup of her hands. The chain puddled atop the Druid's Tear, creating a dull, burnished tangle of metal and pale stone. Elspeth's hands shook as she offered the necklace to Sabrina. "Take it. Every day it mocked me with proof of my failure."

"I do not understand." Sabrina moved to don the necklace, but Elspeth's hand shot out and stopped her with such force that a sound like a slap echoed through the room. Bessie whimpered and pressed into her corner.

"No! You must not place it around your neck until tomorrow, just before you begin your journey to take your place at your husband's side. You risk disaster otherwise."

"Mother, 'tis only a stone. A rather plain stone."

"No, Sabrina. Remember what you have been taught. The Druid's Tear represents the Irish people's only hope, and wearing it is your sacred trust." Elspeth's lip trembled. "You must believe in the stone's power with all your heart. You might have little else to sustain you in the years to come."

Perhaps it was Sabrina's disappointment that this visit was not bridging the emotional distance between them; perhaps it was that so many years of only the most necessary conversation between herself and her mother made it impossible for them to understand each other. Whatever the reason, Sabrina could not fathom why her mother seemed so distressed.

"I remember every conversation you and I have ever had," she said. It was no great feat of memory; there had been so few. "You told me time and again that a Desmond woman who wears the Druid's Tear will bring to this land the true champion of the Irish people."

From the moment she had shown the ability to understand, Sabrina had been taught that it was her duty to marry a man whose warlike strength and patriotism would rally the Irish people against the encroaching English.

The Druid's Tear weighed heavy in her hand. Such a dull, milk white blob seemed incapable of inspiring the Desmond legend. More likely, one of her long-ago ancestors had woven the tale to soothe a reluctant bride, to coax her into marrying a man against her will. Just as was happening to her. She had no trouble believing that the stone might be her only source of comfort in the years to come.

Surely it had seemed so for her mother, herself an inadequate female heir who had married for the same reason that Sabrina must marry. Generations of Desmonds had been cursed—only female children had been born within the family for as long as people could remember. The legend of the Druid's Tear promised greatness, and the castle, so strong and rich, was alluring enough that there was no lack of men willing to marry a Desmond woman and claim the Desmond name as his own.

Elspeth had brought her own would-be Irish champion into the Desmond keep, and then spent many silent hours alone with the Druid's Tear while her champion disported himself with kitchen wenches. Sabrina had often noticed her mother sitting by herself, her blank, unfocused gaze hinting that her mind had wandered elsewhere while her fingers unconsciously stroked the ever-present stone hanging around her neck.

"I know Robert does not love me." To her shame, her voice quavered with anguish.

Elspeth gasped. "You hoped for love? Oh, Sabrina, I thought I had done a better job of hardening you against that particular disappointment. From the moment you were born, I knew you would find little joy in your life. I have done what I could to prepare you for a future that must be devoted solely to the cause of others."

Sabrina's throat tightened. "Those years promise to be endless. Could you not have created a few happy memories for me to look back upon?"

Tears glittered in Elspeth's eyes. "You will not understand, but it is worse to have known happiness and lost it than it is never to have been happy at all."

"That cannot be true," Sabrina protested. "If I knew how to love, I might have found—"

Elspeth raised a silencing hand. "You see, the very mention of love rouses all your headstrong tendencies. Desmond women are not permitted such foolish dreams, my daughter."

"Does it not seem unfair to you, Mother, that *all* Desmond women are denied the right to dream, but only *one* Desmond woman will be chosen to bring the legend to life?"

Elspeth did not flinch. "Generation after generation of Desmond women have accepted their duty as decreed by the legend without bemoaning the fairness of their lot. Do not shame yourself by yearning for something that can never be yours. Instead, pray that you, alone of all Desmond women, will be the one chosen to bring to our land the champion who will help the Irish survive England's incessant onslaught. So you see, naught but duty determines the choice of a Desmond woman's mate. Love is a myth. The best you can hope for is a modicum of kindness and respect."

"And you think Robert of Allingham is the champion who will help our people attain true independence? You think . . . you think he will be kind to me?"

Her mother ignored the second of Sabrina's questions. "Robert's ferocity and strength will inspire our people."

"Robert possesses a cruel nature. He looks upon our lands with lust rather than love. The true Irish champion cannot possibly be a grasping, land-hungry man who is so eager to ingratiate himself politically that he would force his betrothed to learn the language of that hated English king."

She had never, ever had such prolonged discourse with her mother. Her breast heaved with the effort of so much talking, and she was astonished at the rancor that had spewed forth from her. She didn't know which she resented more—the English lessons forced upon her by Robert's demands, or her parents' blindness. They were completely dazzled by Robert's warlike demeanor, by the mean-spiritedness that they mistook for determination.

"The gods should have chosen better," Sabrina said. Despair—and guilt at her own inadequacy—settled around her. She could not help but believe that the Irish people's spirit was sure to be extinguished if their only hope was a marriage between a grasping, land-hungry man and a sad, lonely woman who yearned only to be loved.

"We will see, on the morrow, if the gods have chosen well," Elspeth said.

"Tomorrow I marry. Even if Robert is the great champion you believe him to be, he cannot win the war against England in a single day."

"Nobody could," Elspeth agreed. "But we will know tomorrow whether you are the Desmond woman chosen by fate to bring the champion."

"Why must we wait until tomorrow?"

"According to the legend, the Druid's Tear will transform when the chosen Desmond woman begins the journey that will lead her to the Irish champion. When you slip the chain over your head, Sabrina, and begin walking toward your new husband, pray with all your heart. If you are the chosen woman, and if Robert is indeed the champion decreed by the gods, then the Druid's Tear will shed its bland disguise. It will come to life, glittering from within, as if lit by a thousand stars."

"Did it glow on your wedding day, Mother?"

Elspeth turned away. "The stone has never changed," she said in a low, dull voice, pausing in the doorway. "Sleep well, Sabrina. After this night, your life will never again be the same."

But sleep would not come to Sabrina that night. Soft snoring from the maid's alcove told her that Bessie had found blessed oblivion. Just as well—the restlessness gripping Sabrina would not be eased by companionship. She sat huddled in a chair, with a soft wolf pelt clasped about her shoulders for warmth. She stared at the niche where she'd placed the Druid's Tear alongside her scent flacon. A low-burning candle roused faint gleaming from the glass. The Druid's Tear sat dull and nondescript, as if mocking her for believing it held any promise.

Compelled by an impulse she did not bother to explore, she discarded her night wear and slipped on the red-brown kirtle that was her wedding dress. She tied the belt of Desmond yellow at her waist. Something seemed amiss. Her pouch of medicinals, no doubt—she seldom went anywhere without its weight bumping against her hip. But even adding the pouch left her feeling ... incomplete.

She paused, listening to make sure Bessie still slept, and then Sabrina reached for the stone. She turned it in her hand. Such a sacred talisman ought to be capable of granting her the only thing she truly wanted—to fall in love and be loved in return.

"I wish you did possess magical properties." She rubbed

her thumb over the cold surface. "I wish you could truly set me on the journey that would bring a champion to my homeland."

Nothing could possibly make her heartfelt plea come true. But just in case, she invoked a prayer to her Christian God as well as to those ancient Druids who had captured this milk white tear in gold. "One small miracle," she prayed.

Nothing.

Her mother had cautioned that she must wait to don the necklace until just before beginning the walk to her new husband. Who had devised such a ridiculous scheme? It would be difficult enough to place one foot in front of the other, knowing Robert waited at the end of her short journey. If she slid the chain over her head and nothing brought the stone to life—why, the senselessness of her marriage, the ruin of her dreams, would be weighing her down even more, and it would be too late to put an end to it all.

If she knew now, there was some tiny chance she might beg and plead her way out of a marriage that doomed her to misery.

Feeling suddenly defiant, she held the necklace, the chain spread wide, above her head. "Let me begin the journey that will bring home the true Irish champion."

Her voice rang strong and clear against the stone walls. She lowered the chain over her head. The heavy links settled around her neck. The tear-shaped stone slid along her skin and fell cold against her breast and then almost at once grew warm. Beyond warm—within the matter of a few heartbeats, it threatened to burn her.

No doubt the sensation was nothing more than a manifestation of her apprehension over ignoring her mother's warnings about donning it too soon. She reached to pull it off, but a small cry escaped her when it seemed she had tried to pluck free a burning ember. Puzzled, she glanced down and was almost blinded by a flashing, brilliant crystal fire that seemed to glow against her skin.

The Druid's Tear, no longer a bland milk white, pulsed and glowed as if alive.

As if a thousand stars blazed within its depths.

She clutched the stone with both hands, heedless of its burning heat, captivated by the gleaming splendor. Colors swirled, turning her dizzy, creating the sensation that her room had begun to spin around her. Faster and faster . . . spinning until she grew breathless despite just sitting there, and light-headed, as if her wits were about to desert her. She staggered to her feet, and reached to grasp the post on her bed to steady herself.

Her hand closed around the bedpost so tightly that she felt the engraved design cut into her palm. Her toes curled from the chill of the stone floor penetrating her slippers. The soft wolf hair tickled her skin above the neckline of her finely woven wool gown. She felt all those things . . . and somehow felt totally bereft of sensation as well.

She pitched forward, toward her bed, but did not land amid the safe and familiar straw-stuffed mattress and piled wolf pelts. She fell, and fell, whirling in an endless crystal vortex.

Chapter One

Montana Territory—1867

How in hell was a man supposed to *think* while driving a medicine wagon?

Neil Kenyon shifted his hind end on the ache-making board seat, and stared morosely at the perfectly good horse hauling this godforsaken contraption. A fine horse like that ought to wear a saddle instead of finding itself shackled in harness and traces. A professional soldier like Neil ought to be carrying out his last assignment sitting proudly on that broad back, rather than perched on a board bench like some farmer going to market, with his tailbone taking a hit with every jounce of the wagon wheels.

He'd planned on spending the tedious hours of traveling planning his strategy for the most important campaign of his career. His orders, signed by President Andrew Johnson himself, lay folded in the secret compartment hidden under the heaviest crate of patent medicine.

Those orders charged Capt. Neil Kenyon with the task of traveling incognito to Fort Benton, Montana Territory, to determine whether retired Brig. Gen. Thomas Francis Meagher—war hero, Indian fighter, former acting governor of the territory—ought to be arrested for treason.

Men like Meagher, with the instincts of a fighter, could sniff out trouble with frightening ease. Men like Meagher, who inspired an almost fanatic loyalty and blind obedience, could simply make enemies disappear.

Neil knew that if he wanted to survive this mission, he had to concentrate on more delicate problems than the comfort of his wagon. Did he want to survive? Always his thoughts circled back to that little question. Always his mind went blank.

Maybe that was the answer to his question.

Little jumpy quivers in his muscles warned that cramps were on their way. He groaned and stretched one long leg awkwardly to the side, and then the other. Whoever'd designed this medicine wagon ought to be shot. Nobody could possibly grow accustomed to folding himself up like an accordion pleat in order to cram a six-foot-plus body into a space better suited for midgets or women.

But even that physical discomfort was easier to bear than the incessant squealing of the wagon wheels, the grating rub of wood against wood, the creaking made by yards of leather stretched to its limits. Too loud, too annoying to allow a man the peace of mind required to think through all the details he must master for this last mission.

Whomp.

"Son of a—!" Neil, caught in midstretch, almost tumbled from the driver's bench at the booming thud that rocked the wagon. Well, didn't exactly rock it, he had to amend, considering how easily he regained his balance. Such a loud noise had to mean the wagon had struck a hole big enough to dislodge a wheel, but the vehicle just kept rolling on, generating its usual aggravating noises. The horse plodded ever forward with its usual even pace. Birds kept on singing as if nothing had happened.

He must have imagined the sound. Embarrassment heated him when he realized how tightly he gripped the ledge crowding his legs, how hard his heart hammered in his chest. He forced his fingers to loosen, and he leaned back until his head rested against the wall rising behind the bench seat. He swallowed hard, drawing deep breaths, which experience had taught him would help his pulse slow.

It had been well over a year since real cannon fire had shattered his peace of mind. The imaginary kind usually boomed on the rare occasions when he'd managed to fall asleep, waking him with silent screams choking his throat and nightmare sweat slicking his skin.

He'd never heard those phantom shots while wide-awake and supposedly in control.

Perhaps it was better that it happened now, when he could readily dispel the old terrors. It wasn't so easy to regain his equilibrium in the hours after midnight, when darkness made a perfect backdrop for the endless replaying of the memories in his head; when he was utterly alone except for the ghosts who had no reason to comfort him.

He swallowed. Breathed deep. Congratulated himself that he was on the verge of forgetting the entire incident when behind him, coming through the walls of the enclosed wagon bed, came a scuffling noise.

Neil tensed. He tried to concentrate on those soft sounds through the wagon din. The scuffling continued. If he didn't know better, he would swear someone was moving around inside his medicine wagon. Impossible. He'd closed and locked the rear door himself, with a spanking-new padlock. He'd verified that the inventory matched the bill of sale before he'd handed over his life savings to the charlatan who'd sold him the getup. And then he'd locked the door, bending his head to make sure he heard the snick of the padlock engage.

Nobody had been inside the wagon when he'd locked it. He had the only key. Nobody could have broken in without him hearing something.

He heard a muted crash, the tinkling of glass—just the sort of sound one might expect would follow the dropping of a bottle of Ebenezer's Energizing Elixir. Bottles that Neil had personally made sure were packed in their individual protective slots, inside wooden crates securely fastened to shelves that had themselves been bolted to the walls.

Someone *was* inside the damned wagon. And that someone was doing his level best to destroy the patent medicines for which Neil had paid so dearly.

Neil hauled the horse to a stop, but even before the wagon ceased moving, he'd slid from the bench seat and tore around to the back of the vehicle. The wagon swayed a little as it came to a halt, but not nearly as much as Neil's hand shook when he reached for the hasp holding the two swinging doors shut. The padlock, gleaming with newness, not a single scratch marring its surface, was still just as firmly locked as it had been when he'd taken over the wagon the day before. He gave it a yank to make sure, halfway hoping it would split open to prove it hadn't been locked after all. It resisted his tug with all the strength the storekeeper had promised.

He braced his hand against the door while despair trembled through him. He'd learned to live with the night terrors. The past few minutes had proved that hallucinating cannon fire during the day could be borne, provided nobody besides a horse was around to witness his humiliation.

But this—imagining intruders had somehow magically gotten inside a locked wagon—this smacked of insanity.

Insanity that nonetheless provided a physical manifestation. Through his hand he felt the vibration of someone moving around inside. Scuffling. The scrape of wood and the clinking of bottles moving around when the wagon stood still. He heard a soft cry, followed by yet another tinkling sprinkle of shattering glass.

Well, if he was losing his mind, he'd damned well lose it while confronting his demons. And if this wasn't his imagination playing tricks on him, someone was going to owe him money. A lot of money.

Cursing, Neil fished the door key from his pocket. With a quick snap he undid the lock and sprung open the hasp. The right half of the door popped open at once, as if the pressure from the inside was too intense to allow it to remain closed. There was another soft thud, followed by a high-pitched, surprised-sounding squeak.

A dainty, slippered foot poked through the opening.

A woman's foot.

Of all the suspicions that had raced through his head, a female stowaway sure hadn't made his list. Neil stared at the delicately curved ankle for a split second, and then clamped his fingers around it. Whoever was on the other end of that foot let out an unholy shriek and did her best to scuttle back into the wagon.

He braced his free hand against the closed half of the door and tugged in the opposite direction.

It looked, for a moment, as if his superior strength had won with ridiculous ease. The foot was attached to a damned fine leg. It would've taken more than the strange, coarsely woven wool stocking she wore to disguise the elegant, curving calf. The stocking was gathered and tied at the knee, leaving bare her slim thigh up to the point where the hem of her garment fell. A mighty interesting sight. Going insane might not be the hell he'd imagined, if these were the sorts of visions that would torment him. He stared blatantly, hoping the hem would slip a little further.

He thought his wish might be coming true when she bent her leg and her hem slid an inch, and then another. His mouth went dry as he prayed for more slippage.

"Champion?"

Her voice, humming with tension, dragged his attention away from her legs. Her hair spilled down over her front, so thick and lush that he couldn't tell what she wore above the waist. Her chest heaved, betraying a nervousness that her face did not show.

"What?"

"Champion?"

Confusion, fear, and an endearing bravado made such a potent mixture that it took him a heartbeat or two to realize the elegance of her features. A beautiful woman had somehow locked herself in his wagon.

"Champion?" she asked again, more insistently.

"Me? A champion?" He had to shake his head, and knew she wouldn't understand the little laugh that accompanied the gesture. Two minutes ago he'd been thinking himself insane. "I'm no champion."

Disappointment visibly flickered through her, and somehow seemed to latch onto him as well. The brave set of her shoulders drooped. For a minute there, he almost wished he was the kind of man a woman like her could call a champion.

While he was standing there like a gape-jawed idiot regretting the truth about himself, she gave a purely female shriek of rage and kicked him square in the stomach, sending him sprawling backward onto the road.

He lay there staring up at the deep blue Montana sky. Road dust puffed around him and drifted down over his face. He moved to wipe it off and winced as pain shot through his head. That thunk his head had suffered against the hard-packed surface must have temporarily dimmed his thinking capacity. He'd just been felled by a woman. Maybe knowing the humiliation had been caused by a leg fine enough to bring down the house at any dance hall explained why he couldn't summon a bit of anger.

Groaning, he lifted his head and blinked to clear his vision just in time to notice a swirl of auburn hair as she lunged her top half out of the wagon bed. She moved so quickly that he couldn't have stopped her, even if he had been able to move. If she made a run for it, he'd have to let her go. He had to wonder whether he was seeing things when she gripped the open door and scooted backward, pulling the door shut, closing herself back inside the wagon.

Why hadn't she run?

It would serve her right if he snapped the padlock back in place and left her locked up for the next fifty miles or so until he reached Fort Benton. Thirst and hunger would soon have her banging on the walls, pleading for his mercy in exchange for food and water.

Or maybe not . . . maybe she'd just pull the corks on a dozen or two of his medicine bottles and slug down the contents, wiping out his nest egg and destroying any chance of making this mission a success.

His mission. Now, with his head spinning, and a she-devil hiding in the back of his wagon, it seemed even less likely that he'd be able to concentrate on army business. He had to concentrate. He was good at concentrating. He furrowed his brow because that usually seemed to help. Nothing the slightest bit army-related came to mind, because he could only wonder what the rest of her looked like. What shape of body measured up to that enticing stretch of leg?

No doubt about it—the back of his head making inti-mate contact with the road was responsible for knocking his wits six ways to China, Neil decided. A blow to the head. There was no other way to explain why he was lying all sprawled there in the road, smiling like a fool, curious about a woman's looks when he should be madder than hell for the threat she posed to his mission.

He sat up and winced as bands of pain ringed his head. He'd taken one hell of a crack in the noggin. "Hey!" he called. Utter silence answered him.

His hat had gotten knocked off in the fall. He grabbed it and stood, grimacing when dizziness swept over him. He took a small step, didn't fall, and tried a larger one. He stayed upright. He pounded his hat against his uniform trousers, raising a cloud of dust. He probably ought to clean off his medals, and his captain's insignia as well, but the hell with them; half the grit dimming their luster came honestly, from plain old ordinary traveling dust. "Hey!"

The wagon, the source of so many recent noisy distractions, stood silent as a tomb.

He sighed. "So you want to do this the hard way. All right. I'm coming in."

No response.

Well, if the lady wanted him to go after her, then as an officer of the United States Army, he had no choice but to oblige.

He yanked open both of the half doors at once. They banged back against their hinges with a loud thud, making him wince. Impenetrable blackness greeted him. He gripped the roof edge when another, lesser wave of dizziness weakened his legs. He didn't want her to notice his momentary debility, so he leaned forward and fixed his nastiest captain's scowl toward the far wall of the wagon, where he figured she had to be cowering like a trapped rat.

"You!" he barked. "Front and center!"

No response.

He could hear the soft rasp of her breathing. He waited for his eyes to adjust, for shafts of sunlight to pierce the gloom of the wagon. Within seconds he had the vision and the illumination to see into the farthest corners of the closely packed, enclosed space.

She stood like the cornered creature she was, pressed against the wall.

Sunlight poured in from behind him, stretching his shadow the entire length of the wagon. The knock on the head must have turned him fanciful, for it looked as if his shadow arms held her in their ghostly embrace, as though his shadow head bent toward hers.

In fact, his entire shadow self covered her, intimate and possessive, swallowing all her color and light into its darkness except for the enormous diamond that glittered like a beacon against her breast.

A man could follow that beacon, Neil thought, right out of the darkness.

He shook that foolish notion away, but the motion roused a new wave of dizziness. He took a deep breath and willed his legs to steady before she made a run for it. She still didn't seem to realize her temporary advantage. She stayed put. He let go of the roof edge, and felt a brief pang of remorse when his shadow embrace let loose of her. He had to shake that away, too.

"You," he ordered with more authority. "Get your sorry self out here, right now."

She stiffened. Instead of trembling and meekly obeying, she tipped her chin upward a notch and glared at him. Her whole being shrieked outrage that he'd dare try ordering her to do something.

"Who are you?" he demanded. And then again, much softer, "Who *are* you?" when a shaft of sunlight pierced the gloom and the lushness of her penetrated his senses. Her hair, a glorious mass of auburn, tumbled over her

shoulders to her waist. The sun caught green-gold flecks
in her eyes. She wore a slim-fitting gown, reddish brown
as Georgia clay, and her waist was belted with what looked
like twisted rope, only bright yellow. A pouch hung from
her belt. The improbably enormous diamond she wore
hung heavy between her breasts, pressing her simple garment close against a body that curved in and out with such
allure that he knew everything about her lived up to the
promise of her leg.

She took a step toward him. And then another. She
moved with regal precision, picking her way carefully along
the glass-strewn narrow space that separated the shelves of
patent medicine lining both sides of the wagon.

She stopped a handsbreadth away from him and stared
down, somehow inclining her head and looking down her
well-bred nose in a way that made him think she ought to
be wearing a crown, ought to be brandishing a scepter or
whatever the hell it was that queens waved around. Queens
used those things to tap ordinary men on the shoulder,
turning them into knights.

If this one started tapping him—anywhere—it would be
pretty hard to refuse anything she asked of him.

Damn that knock on the head! She wasn't a queen, and
he sure as hell wasn't a knight in shining armor. She was
nothing more than an intruder who'd stowed away in his
wagon, a person responsible for destroying a goodly number of his bottles of medicine, judging by the mess on the
floor. If she had a scepter, she'd dub him all right—she'd
no doubt bash him right on his already addled head and
finish the job of knocking him cold so she could make her
getaway.

"Every cent I've ever managed to save is tied up in this
wagon," he said.

She didn't apologize.

"You don't need to know the whole story, but I'm no

patent medicine quack. I'm going to have to sell this wagon when I finish something that needs doing. I won't get back my investment if you keep on breaking my inventory."

The thing about standing with feet planted on the ground while a woman stood at wagon-bed level was that it put a man's face even with a certain enticing curve. When that man had been without a woman for longer than he cared to recall, and when that enticingly curved woman had the face of an angel and the bearing of a queen, well, it was no wonder the man might temporarily lose his sensibility.

But only temporarily. An officer and a gentleman ought not continue staring where he'd been staring, and so Neil leaned back and looked up at her face. He caught a quickly suppressed smirk that told him Miss High-and-Mighty knew exactly where his thoughts lingered and figured she'd get away free as she pleased after causing him no end of trouble.

The diamond winked as if it agreed with her.

"The hell with that," Neil muttered. Quick as a snake, he snatched up and pulled at the diamond. The gold chain surprised him with its strength, but a quick twist of his wrist snapped a link and the gaudy bauble was his. He swung his arm out and dangled the diamond like bait.

"You'll get this back when you reimburse me for the damage to my stock," he said.

She clapped her hand to her breast. Her fingers searched for the chain, as if she found it impossible to believe it was no longer where it belonged.

Neil swallowed, watching those fingers quest over every inch of her. He was half tempted to put the diamond back so he could help her pat it into place. And then he realized that there was something frantic about her searching, something vital and despairing at the notion of losing her diamond. Well, of course. Diamonds were expensive. Worth more than twenty medicine wagons, fully stocked.

"I'm only holding it for collateral," he said. "You'll get it back. You have my word on it. I have to count the broken bottles and figure out what you owe me. All we need here is a simple business transaction. I'll return your necklace the minute you pay for the damage."

She was trembling a little, and breathing in the heavy way of one trying not to cry. She grew still as he spoke. She looked at her necklace and nodded decisively. He figured she believed him, and that sent an odd little wave of pleasure through him. She believed him. She . . . trusted him.

He'd sworn to turn tail and run if a woman ever showed signs of trusting him. He couldn't very well run away from this situation. But he shouldn't be standing there with a sappy grin plastered on his face, either.

He decided to back away, put a little distance between them. He let his arm drop to his side. She lifted her head when he moved. He took a step backward just as she launched herself off the edge of the wagon with a screech that would've drowned out the loudest rebel yell he'd ever heard. She dove straight into him, her fists flailing, her legs kicking, as she knocked him back down into the dirt.

"Hey! Wait a minute! I told you— Ow!"

She landed a blow on his cheekbone, making his ears ring and sending his already spinning head into a regular hurricane of confusion. She let loose with a torrent of gibberish. Her knees dug into him, and he had to do some pretty fancy twisting to keep her from unmanning him— but that didn't seem to be her intent. She scrambled on top of him, reaching toward the diamond that he still held gripped in one outstretched hand.

"Oh, no, you don't."

He figured the best way to hold her still was to, well,

hold her still, and so he wrapped both arms around her in a bear hug. She squirmed and wriggled, straining against his hold. No doubt at all that he held a firm, long-limbed, very healthy young woman in his arms. He found himself grinning again, until a thrust of her hip brought them into a contact so intimate that she stilled at once, her eyes widening with shock.

Disgust flooded Neil—disgust with himself. "This isn't like me," he said. "It's conduct unbecoming to . . . well, it's not right to be rolling around in the dirt with you."

An officer charged with protecting the people certainly ought not to be wrestling with a female captive and glorying in her scent, her warmth, the tensile strength of her body. He rolled with her once more, pinning her beneath him, but holding his weight off her so she couldn't tell, he hoped, the way his body had reacted to hers.

"I'm going to let you up now. And then we'll talk about this." He dangled the diamond above them.

"Champion?"

"I already told you—no."

She socked him in the jaw.

"Good God, woman—I told you I'll give your diamond back to you. Don't you understand English?"

"Anglish?"

Neil's heart sank. From the way she'd whispered the word, with some weird accent, he couldn't be sure that she'd understood a word of all the explaining he'd done. Just his luck that of all the medicine wagons in this world, some foreign hellion bent on mischief would decide to vandalize his vehicle.

But she knew enough English to ask him if he was a champion.

"Anglish?" she said again.

She lay quiet, unmoving, no longer a physical threat, but somehow a worse threat to his peace of mind. She felt soft and warm beneath him. She gazed up at him with breathless wonderment, her lips parted, her hair tousled and begging to be tucked back behind her ears.

"Not *Anglish*. English. English."

He couldn't get to his feet fast enough to suit him. But eventually he was upright and away from her. She, on the other hand, seemed perfectly content to lie on the road, making that hard-packed clay look more inviting than a silk-sheeted feather bed.

"Get up," he ordered.

She didn't move.

"Get up." He extended his hand to help. She stared at it with such dismay that he wondered if anyone had ever offered her a hand before. Eventually, by slow degrees, she lifted her own hand and inched it toward his. She tentatively closed her grip around the very edges of his fingertips, as if afraid to be contaminated by a better grip.

"Now, that's just plain ridiculous," Neil said. "The minute I pull back, you're going to lose your hold and you'll fall back into the dirt."

She stared at him with blank incomprehension.

"Aw, hell," he muttered.

He shook off her prissy grip with no more effort than it took to chase a fly. Moving fast, to take her by surprise before she could slug him again, he plunged both hands under her arms and hoisted her onto her feet. He almost staggered backward because he'd put more strength than necessary into the effort. There wasn't much to her. No weight to speak of, and she was so slim in diameter that the bases of his thumbs ended up pressed against the lower curves of her breasts.

And she was not as tall as he'd thought when she'd stood on the wagon bed above him. Here, on level ground, the top of her head barely cleared his shoulder. And yet she'd knocked him flat. Well, she'd had the advantage of surprise. It wouldn't happen again.

Although a good coating of dust dimmed her hair, he could smell the lavender and roses that she must have used in her wash water. Yes, she smelled of flowers. Flowers and something else. He sniffed again, and then sighed. Flowers and patent medicine, as in eau de Ebenezer's Energizing Elixir, no doubt from one of the bottles she'd broken.

This reminder of the money he stood to lose helped clear his head. A woman who possessed a diamond like hers no doubt had some money to go along with it. Maybe she kept her cash in the pouch she wore tied around her waist. Though small, the cloth bag bulged, obviously well stuffed with something. All he had to do was figure out a way to explain business matters to a woman who couldn't seem to understand him. A woman who acted as if touching him would contaminate her.

He held out his hand toward her and rubbed his thumb against his forefinger and middle finger. That ought to be some sort of universal code for money, judging by the number of times he'd seen it used.

She watched and then duplicated the motion. He nodded. She peeked at him through the tangle of her hair, as if expecting praise.

"Pesos," he tried. "Gold. Uh, *oro*. No? Greenback. Green-a-back-a." He couldn't think of any other foreign words for money.

The diamond. She understood that well enough. Maybe he could coax her into saying something he could understand. He held it up over his head, letting it sway back and forth to catch the sunlight.

Damn if she didn't start *jumping* for the jewel.

She came a few inches closer with each leap. Her breasts bounced every time her feet left the ground and every time they landed again. He found himself backing away from her. If he didn't, he'd drop the stupid diamond into the dirt and grab her around the waist and let those breasts bounce against him, and to hell with being an officer and a gentleman.

The backs of his legs came up against the wagon, and he hopped up into the bed, to get away from her. He crouched in the doorway. She walked up and stood right in front of him.

Now what?

He couldn't close the doors on himself, now, could he? That would be even more stupid than all the mistakes he'd made so far. She could lock him in, unhitch the horse, and take off.

His boot heel crunched into glass.

"Look," he said. He carefully gathered some of the larger glass shards and made a pile at the edge of the wagon bed. The broken pieces glittered in the sunlight, not as glorious as the diamond, but prettier and sparklier than ruined glass had a right to look. "This is what you've done."

He reached back into the closest bin and pulled free a bottle of elixir. A whole, unbroken bottle.

"Look," he said again, too loud. She wasn't deaf. "This good." He shook the bottle, and then pointed toward the broken glass. "That bad. You. Break." He pointed emphatically from the pile of broken glass to her. "Bad. Break. You."

"Bad. You." She whispered the words, and reached a tentative hand toward the whole bottle. Although he had serious qualms, he let her hold it. She turned it, tracing the lip, running her fingers down its length, all the while shaking her head as if she'd never seen anything so fine in her life. She reached past him and set the bottle carefully in its slot. He barely had time to sigh with relief when she withdrew another, which she examined with the same disconcerting thoroughness.

She pulled the bottle close, cradling it for a moment the way a young girl held a china doll, and then she set it alongside the others in their slots. She gazed from the unbroken bottles to the pile of shards and back again to the bottles with equal measures of wonder and dismay. She moved, as if she meant to fondle the broken glass as well. Neil caught her hand before she could cut herself.

A strange sensation shot through him. Maybe his head was still dizzy. He felt suddenly off balance, as if he'd been walloped by a lightning bolt. Warmth surged through him, from his fingers to his toes. One hand held her. One hand held the diamond. Something sizzled from her to the stone. In his addled state of mind it seemed that the diamond glittered with a more brilliant fire than it had before.

The woman inclined her head toward the broken glass, then toward the bottles. She touched her heart. "Bad, you," she said, her voice quavering.

"Aw, hell," Neil muttered, wanting more than anything to call back those words and tell her she was not bad.

Her hand slipped free. She placed it on top of the diamond. On top of the diamond! He'd left himself wide open to be robbed of the one thing of value that might ensure his financial well-being and yet there he squatted, like a paralyzed lump, regretting that he'd hurt her feelings. He knew in his gut that if she plucked that diamond out of his hand, he wouldn't do a blasted thing to stop her.

"Bad." She rested her fingers against the diamond for a moment, and then she gently closed his fist around the glittering stone. Once he'd completely enclosed the gem, she cradled both her hands around his clumsy paw and squeezed, and then pushed his hand against his heart.

She didn't need to say a single word to tell him she meant for him to keep the stone.

Tears brimmed in her eyes, but none fell.

Chapter Two

Sabrina offered no resistance as he led her to the front of the wagon.

Her head whirled with confusion. The air she breathed did not carry the familiar scents of Desmond Muir. The sky above burned a brighter blue than any she had seen. She did not recognize the trees that burgeoned along both sides of the path that snaked out before her. Desmond Muir's bailiff should have ordered the thinning of such impossibly lush growth. At the very least, the villeins would have hacked down the lowest-growing branches to warm their cottages. The very color of the leaves seemed off—a darker green than the sunlit emerald she loved so well.

A bird called out in a song she had never heard. Deep purple flowers, cone-shaped, unlike any she had ever seen, nodded in the wind.

Nothing grew upon Desmond Muir that she could not name; nothing lived within its boundaries that she could not recognize. Her life had been dedicated to Desmond,

and she knew every inch of it as well as she knew her own
body.

This place, teeming with unusual beauty and riches, was
not her home.

She had somehow been taken away from Desmond
lands. She, who had been told that she alone represented
the hope of the Irish people, had been physically torn
from her duty and given over to a man who said he was
not the champion.

It made no sense.

Her virginity had been more carefully guarded than her
father's gold. No stain must besmirch her honor. Never
would a man be granted private audience with her, let
alone the right to touch her bare ankles and lift her person.
Such a thing would not happen unless . . . unless she had
been determined a failure and handed over to an executioner.

And yet her jailer handed her up onto the wagon seat,
and took his place next to her, and slapped the horse into
motion—all without lopping off her head.

He was not the champion. If not an executioner, she
did not know what he might be.

A king, whispered something inside her. The frantic racing of her pulse slowed as she recognized the sense of this.

A king could claim the right of droit du seigneur: the
right of the sovereign to claim the virginity of any female
in his realm. This man had held her in his arms and
trembled with desire . . . and yet claimed her not.

None but a king would travel about with such a wealth
of precious glass—glass so magnificently crafted that every
flacon was virtually identical to the one next to it. It seemed
such a short time ago, and yet a lifetime ago, that she had
shuddered in fear of breaking a single flacon, and now
she was responsible for smashing many.

This conveyance they rode upon—she had never seen

such a finely built vehicle, with wheels so perfectly wrought that they spared one's bones of the worst of the jolting. The horse, a noble beast, bore harness smooth and supple as a knight's undertunic.

No man but a king would be garbed in raiment so exquisitely sewn that the stitches marched in perfectly even, perfectly spaced rows along each seam, a true seamstress's triumph. She did not recognize the cloth, but it was of such a wondrous, deep midnight blue, with the hue impossibly even from hem to hem, that there could be no other like it. He wore the badges of royalty proudly upon his chest. Embellishments graced his arms and shoulders, crafted of molten gold that had been spun into thread. A king, no doubt.

Save . . . what sort of king drove *himself* about?

He did not seem particularly expert at the task, or fond of doing it. He let loose with a sharp, piercing whistle that goaded the horse into swifter speed, and cursed when the sudden lurch of the wagon jolted them both back against the wall rising behind them.

What sort of king toiled so, that his hands bore calluses? She could still feel the strength of his grip around her ankle, and the rough but pleasant slide of his fingers against her skin. She lowered her head, afraid she might blush at remembering the way his body had flexed against hers. He'd lifted her from the ground with the strength of one who did not depend upon others to shift his hay and grain sacks.

An Anglish—no, he had corrected her—an English king.

She knew of but one English king: Edward Longshanks, the most hated enemy of the Irish people.

She stole a covert glance toward her captor, and found him unlike the descriptions she'd heard of that despicable despot. This man next to her boasted extraordinary height, it was true, but beyond that there was no resemblance. Longshanks was said to have thinning red hair laced with gray, and bulging eyes better suited to an insect. Her king's hair was thick and long, the warm golden brown color of boiled honey, his eyes a richer shade of the same.

And if she had any doubt, she need only study his face. His features were indeed royal, compelling enough to coax any lass into doing his bidding.

Most telling of all, in his eyes, in the way he moved, she sensed a holding back, as if he could not allow the true essence of himself to show. Sabrina possessed great familiarity with such restraint. Those born to nobility, her mother often said, could not afford to reveal their inmost wants and needs to anyone. Those born to nobility were destined for loneliness, and learning to hide one's inner weaknesses was a lesson taught from birth.

She had learned. And so, it seemed, had he.

He murmured something in a voice so kingly that it resonated deep within her and roused an ache to hear more. The champion must be able to exhort people to his cause. Oh, if only he could be the champion—she had no doubt men would line up behind him to do battle.

She leaned closer to him, just a little, drawn by that rumbling timbre. He spoke louder, in the Anglish/English she had tried so hard to master, and she wanted to scream from frustration, for she could not understand him.

Until he said, "Hell."

Until he said, "Damn."

She held herself still as a newly set fence post, terrified as understanding flooded through her.

She knew not how she came to be in that black-dark cell where the king stored his glass, but she remembered well enough all that had transpired before awakening there. She had changed into her wedding dress. She had risked disaster by slipping on the Druid's Tear before her wedding day. She had prayed to the true Christian God—but she had also gripped the ancient talisman and called out to those long-dead priests of the ancient pagan gods, begging them for a miracle.

Somehow she had been overheard, and like any heretic, must die for her sacrilege.

She need only examine what had occurred since she'd regained her senses to confirm this fear. The king had called her *bad*, an English word she understood. He had taken the Druid's Tear from her with almost his first movement, and waved it at her in an angry manner, his fury no doubt inspired by her misuse of the object.

This man, whose arms had held her close, whose laugh had kindled a warm glow inside of her—this man, who despite such brief acquaintance had let her dare dream that all men need not be like those she had known in her life—he would be the one to destroy her.

He might, at that very moment, be trying to tell her how he planned to end her life, for he continued to speak. The dreaded *Hell*s and *damn*s seasoned his words, words that taunted her with their strangeness and yet an eerie familiarity, too, as though she was but a hairsbreadth away from understanding everything he said.

She concentrated.

"Rumble, murmur, naught farre, rumble, murmur manny peoplle, rumble, murmur, stoppe and change clothes . . ."

Excitement blossomed as she recognized a few of the words. She tried spelling them in her head, and comparing them against the English she'd labored so hard to learn. With time, with practice, she might speak this tongue. Perhaps she had wronged Robert in resenting his insistence that she learn the enemy's language.

Robert. What part did Robert of Allingham play in all this? He coveted Desmond Muir. He would not hand her over for execution unless he had somehow managed to wed her and gain all that belonged to her by right of blood.

The blank emptiness that separated her last memory of her chamber, and awakening within the king's prison, suddenly took on ominous import.

The Druid's Tear *had* burst into life, meaning she had indeed started upon the journey that would lead her to the champion. Perhaps Robert had found out, and knowing her intention to beg out of the marriage, had dosed her bedtime wine and carried out the wedding . . . and the consummation . . . while she was insensate. She might at this moment be wed, and bedded, and have no memory of it.

Her stomach roiled at the thought.

She had to know. Somehow she would have to convince this executioner king to return her to Desmond Muir so she could see what had happened. If she found Robert installed as champion . . . her heart quickened with hope. She would not mind in the least if Robert had set her aside, so long as she could assure herself that her duty had been done, that a champion had come to her lands. She could steal away again and leave Desmond Muir in the hands of the champion.

Never see her homeland again. She waited for pangs of regret, and none came. What did come was a tormenting twist of her conscience telling her she could not simply hope things had worked out well. She had to know.

To do so, she had to escape this man, or enlist his help. At the least she had to learn where she had been taken, so she would know how to make her way back.

He did not seem inclined to let her go.

Nor would he be easy to escape. She had fought him and done her worst. She'd kicked and screamed, to no avail.

There was also the matter of the Druid's Tear. Robert

had erred greatly in casting her out with the stone still gracing her neck. The sacred relic belonged to Desmond Muir. Somehow she would have to return the necklace. Which meant she must get it back from the king.

She rested a tentative hand along his forearm. She probed her memory for the right words, and prayed she would pronounce them correctly.

"My . . . my lord."

He dropped the reins and slammed his hand down over hers, as if swatting a bee. The horse stopped, and the wagon came to a halt while the king stared down at her hand in disbelief.

Sabrina realized her mistake at once. She should not have touched his royal person. He might not have been told that her blood was as noble as his.

Although she could have taken offense, Sabrina chose conciliation. She slid her hand away and smiled up at him, marveling that she could still take such pleasure in his aspect when she knew he would be her destruction.

"Sabrina," she said, giving him her name. She smiled at him again, putting into it all her hope that he might grant her a few days' grace before ending her life.

His eyes narrowed. His lips hardened into a thin line. He inched away as if afraid to expose his back to her and slid from the end of the wagon seat.

He left her there, alone.

Run.

She sat frozen by indecision. Her instinct screamed at her to make an escape; her ingrained sense of duty reminded her that she could not leave without the Druid's Tear. Her mind told her she knew not where she was, that one so flimsily clad and shod could never elude him.

His last look at her had not promised compassion.

Instinct eventually won out.

She edged one leg off the bench, and angled her body

toward the far end of the seat, ready to make some small effort . . . and he came up beside her, a wry smile twisting his lips, contempt lighting his eyes.

He said something, but she made not even the slightest effort to understand. There seemed no point. He had left her for the purpose of removing his kingly midnight-sky garments. He had bedecked himself now in cloth of black, grim and high-collared.

Men might wear such clothes to butcher a pig.

Neil had learned at great cost that some women found an army uniform darned near irresistible, but he'd never known a female to be so blatant about her preferences as this one he found himself stuck with.

Sabrina.

She'd taken one look at his new clothes and let out such a miserable moan that you'd think he'd struck a stake through her heart instead of simply changing out of his uniform and into his medicine-hawking suit.

She sat ramrod-stiff, shaking. She gripped her hands together in an attitude of prayer. Then she squeezed her eyes shut so tight that her whole face squinched up. She inched her chin toward the sky, one minute fraction at a time, until her throat lay open and vulnerable.

Damnedest thing he'd ever seen, almost as if she expected him to pull out a knife and slit her throat. What could have brought about such a change? Not three minutes earlier, she'd run her hand along his arm and smiled up at him with a look so provocative that he'd nearly burst his britches.

He didn't like it when women smiled at him. Usually.

At the moment, he'd prefer a smile instead of her sitting there with her neck bared, expecting the worst. She had her eyes closed so tight that she didn't even notice when he shook his head and walked back to his own side of the wagon.

He stood there for a moment, looking at her holding herself so straight and ready to meet her fate. He felt a stirring of admiration. She apparently thought he meant to kill her, and she didn't flinch, didn't cry, didn't beg.

He couldn't think of many men who would await death with such courage.

"Nothing more dangerous than horseflies around here at the moment," he said, swinging himself up onto the bench.

She clapped her hands over her neck and whirled around to face him. A surprised little squeak eked out of her.

"Let go before you choke yourself," he suggested.

She just sat there with her hands wrapped around her throat.

"Listen—you have to stop being so jumpy."

She let her hands drop down her front. He couldn't help watching the way she smoothed her gown against her breasts on the way to her lap. She was the quietest woman he'd ever met, barely saying a word and yet somehow managing to let him know that she didn't quite understand what he was talking about when he limited himself to his usual curt way of speaking.

"Nobody's going to hurt you." She cocked her head, and for some reason that made him realize he hadn't told her the whole truth. "Well, at least I can say for sure that I'm not going to hurt you. I can't swear to it that some Indian buck won't come running out of the woods and accept your invitation if you keep on sticking your neck out like you did before."

He didn't want to frighten her, but the Indian threat was very real. "Promise you won't do that again."

"Promise."

"Good. Real good. Now, we're no more than five miles out from that settlement I just told you about. Place called Bamper." He slapped the reins and started the horse in motion. "So why don't you just hand over the money you owe me. We can part company at the settlement."

She gave no indication that she'd heard him. She slumped into a frozen huddle in the farthest corner of the seat, with her head downcast and her beautiful hair hiding her face from him. He didn't like that. He much preferred her high-and-mighty posture, her chin tilted at just the right angle, even if her excellent posture did make him feel like a clumsy, slump-shouldered oaf who took up more than his fair share of the too-small space.

"Tell the truth now," he said. "You came from that settlement, right?" She admitted nothing. "Now, I can't quite figure how you ended up in my wagon, but I've been thinking that maybe you fell and hurt your head or something, and wandered on this road until I found you."

"Found," she whispered. She made a little hiccoughing sound, like someone swallowing a sob.

Neil sighed. "It's too late to pretend you don't understand. You seem to know enough to get by. I know you can understand me."

She sniffled a little.

He sighed again. "Why are you making me talk so much? I'm not the kind of fellow who likes jabbering on and on. Just tell me straight—did you wander away from Bamper?"

She didn't answer.

"Look at yourself," Neil said. "You look like a pampered woman. Your skin is . . . well, let's just say I don't think you've done much washing in lye soap. I've never seen wool woven quite like that dress you're wearing—almost feels like silk. Those shoes of yours aren't good for anything but bedroom wear. I'll bet someone's out here hunting for you right now. I'd be hunting for you, if I'd lost you."

He clamped his teeth together, but it was too late to call back that particular admission.

"Hunting," she said. She nodded as if he'd just confirmed something she'd suspected. "You. Hunting. For . . . you."

"For *me*," Neil corrected. "Hunting for *me*. I mean, yes—I did say 'hunting for you,' but from your point of view you'd say 'hunting for *me*.' I mean, I was not hunting for you; I didn't know you existed until you wrecked my stock, so how the hell could I have been hunting for you?"

But even though he ended his convoluted explanation with a spate of swallowed curses, he knew he'd spoken a lie. He'd once believed a special woman was out there, waiting to be found. He'd looked, too. What he'd ended up with, though, had permanently soured him on continuing the search.

He didn't want to think about the past. He wished she would start chattering, or singing, or squirming around—anything for a distraction. No such luck. She rationed her words even more sparingly than he did. Someone had to liven up things or he'd have no choice but sink back into his memories.

"We'll reach the settlement in an hour or two. That's why I changed my clothes—it wouldn't do for anyone to see me in my army duds. You don't have to know the reasons why. I wouldn't even mention this to you, if you hadn't happened to catch me before I'd changed into these medicine-hawking duds. Just keep that information to yourself, okay? About the army clothes, I mean."

Maybe there was something to be said for blathering away like an old woman. Sabrina seemed to perk up after he explained why he'd changed out of his uniform. Her spine stiffened some, and that proud chin of hers tilted up, which sent the heavy fall of her hair sliding back to reveal her fine profile.

"Mean." She shook her head. "Not so, my lord."

He wanted to curse; he wanted to smile. Curse, because it seemed to him that she understood only about one out of twenty words he said to her, which meant he'd have to talk twenty times more than he cared to talk. Smile, because the words she latched onto had a way of letting him know she had a good opinion of him. He'd been called plenty of names in his time, but *my lord* was a new one.

Not that he'd want to be addressed like that, not really. He wouldn't mind at all if she just used his name, if she maintained that same tone of voice.

Well, he wouldn't have much time to enjoy it, even if she did. She probably belonged to some man in Bamper. If nobody at the settlement was actively looking for her, he'd have to find someone to take her off his hands. Maybe even pay someone to board her for a while, until whoever she belonged to showed up to claim her.

That idea didn't sit well, though he couldn't say why it troubled him to think of some man coming along and crooking his finger at her, and her traipsing obediently along. Maybe it was the money. If he had to pay board for her, he'd be out even more money than he was already. But he had no choice. He couldn't saddle himself with a passenger at this stage of his mission, especially one who seemed able to distract him with the slightest movement of her little finger.

Somehow, though he'd been watching the road and thinking about what to do with her, he'd been aware that she had placed her hand on the small pouch she wore tied at her waist. She stroked the pouch as if it were a purring kitten, and Neil couldn't take his eyes away from the perfect oval of her nail, the slender shape of her hand.

He couldn't sit there all day staring at her finger. Well, maybe he could. But he shouldn't. Sweat broke out on his forehead. He sought refuge where he never had before—in conversation.

"You're probably wondering why I'm doing this. I can't tell you all the details. It's a matter between me and President Andrew Johnson and a certain Irishman who may or may not be the greatest hero this territory will ever know."

"Irish . . . hero?" Her lips parted. She leaned forward while excitement lit her eyes. "Champion?"

She certainly seemed determined to find someone she could call a champion. He'd told her too much already, but she seemed so eager to hear more that he couldn't disappoint her. Maybe talking out the problem with her would help him firm up his plans. No, that made no sense.

"It's better for all concerned if you don't know exactly what I'm up to. Remember—you can't tell about the army uniform. I need to ride into Fort Benton with everybody believing I'm a medicine hawker and not an army captain. I figure I need a little practice, since I never considered myself cut out to be a salesman. These stops I'm making along the way will help hone my performance. That's all I can tell you."

She made no comment. Good—she wasn't the prying type. So why did he seem unable to keep his lip buttoned?

"Well, okay, I can probably tell you that this stop in Bamper will be my first time to out-and-out do some medicine hawking. The quack who sold me this rig wrote down some patter for me to memorize, but I never bothered. Too many damned words."

She tilted her head a little to one side. An adorable frown creased her brow while she concentrated very hard on his lips. He wished he'd put on his hat, so he could take it off and fan himself with it.

"I know, I know, you're probably laughing to yourself about the 'too many words' part, but I swear it's so. I haven't talked so much since . . . well, since . . ."

He just let his jabbering trail away, because he couldn't really pinpoint the last time he'd spilled so much to anyone. Not even to the woman he'd married, the woman who'd gone to her grave accusing him of not caring about her enough to tell her what was in his heart.

She'd been right about that. But what she hadn't known was that there wasn't much of anything in his heart worth talking about.

Sabrina shifted her attention away from his lips. She smiled at him. "Aye, my lord."

A smile like that could warm a man's heart for a long time.

What was so special about Sabrina's smile? He studied the curve of her lips, the warmth shining in her eyes. Behind her, trees and sky and clouds created a constantly shifting backdrop. The smile held steady, burning its image into his mind.

He was the first to look away.

Silence didn't seem so unendurable with Sabrina's smile filling his thoughts. The wagon noises didn't annoy him so much, either, almost as if having another person on the seat with him absorbed some of the sounds. Maybe that was why folks tended to congregate in towns, to keep the sounds of silence at bay.

When he completed this mission and struck out on his own, he'd be alone. Nothing but his memories to keep him company. Nobody sitting at his side to deflect the silence.

He'd get himself a dog.

He'd always wanted a dog, but his military obligations had made that impossible. He closed his eyes, trying to imagine the kind of dog he'd choose. Damned if his mind didn't instead conjure up that image of Sabrina, smiling at him.

Seemed dumb to sit there with his eyes closed, thinking

of an old smile when the woman full of fresh smiles sat right next to him.

Seemed dumber to look at her.

She'd be gone soon. Might as well get used to being alone, without distractions. Without smiles.

Maybe someone in the settlement would have a spare pup for sale. A good dog would offer amusing company, take a man's mind off things he'd rather not ponder.

Sabrina shifted and twisted her shoulders. She leaned forward, stretching. Her gown gaped open, revealing a tantalizing glimpse of round curves, of shadowed valley. The wind caught her hair and blew a stray tendril his way. It brushed his cheek, soft, smelling of flowers, and it drove every thought straight out of his head.

No dog on this earth would manage that little feat. Maybe he'd better round up a half dozen.

Chapter Three

Neil recognized the outcropping of rock—it had been well marked on the surveillance map tucked into his shirt pocket. The small settlement of Bamper lay less than a mile away. He stopped the wagon close enough to the outcropping that shadows cast by it dappled the wagon.

"Does this look familiar to you?" he asked Sabrina.

He figured she'd have to say yes or no. Rock piles like this one weren't all that common in this area.

By her actions, it looked like her answer was no. She gripped the curving front board and studied the mass of stone that sprouted from the ground, concentrating with a thoroughness that told him she was intrigued.

Before he could give her a hand, she'd slid out of the wagon and picked her way across the rock-strewn soil to stand at the base of the outcropping.

The stones dwarfed her. The wind kicked up, pasting her gown against her as she poised there, straight and slim. The sun struck red-gold sparks from her hair as she cupped her hand over her forehead against the glare. She moved her head little by little, examining everything, and then suddenly stiffened and stared at one thing so long that he had to look for himself to see what it was she found so fascinating.

She seemed hypnotized by one particular grouping of rocks. It looked to Neil like a big slab of stone had sheared off the largest section of outcropping and tumbled to rest on top of two upward-jutting tongues of granite, forming a sort of squared-off, upside-down *U*. It reminded him a little of a picture he'd once seen, of a place in England where a whole bunch of these upside-down *U*s had been arranged in a circle.

"We have to get a move on," he called.

She started climbing.

"Sabrina!"

She ignored his summons. She showed an amazing aptitude for finding hand- and footholds as she scampered up the side of that outcropping, aiming straight for the formation that had captured her interest.

Neil had done his share of climbing, for tactical purposes usually. Rock face presented any number of hazards. Razor-sharp shards slit skin. Chunks that seemed solid broke loose and fell when you expected them to hold solid, breaking bones or affecting balance. Shifting stone slid out from under boots. Boots? Hell, Sabrina wore nothing but dainty little cloth slippers, completely unsuitable for walking on a smooth path, let alone climbing rock.

Cursing, he jumped out of the wagon and made it halfway to the rocks before he remembered his rifle, and he had to go back. Only an idiot would leave his rifle behind when the Indian threat hovered. He pulled the rifle from its sheath, wondering how he would manage to climb while holding on to the weapon.

Maybe that was why it took him what seemed an eternity

to pick his way up the side of the outcropping. With each careful step, his instincts urged him to hurry, taunting him with the image of Sabrina losing her balance and falling. Scraping that marvelously soft skin against a thousand razor-edged stones. Tumbling, breaking delicate bones . . .

"Sabrina!"

Nothing but wind whistling through gaps in the stone answered him.

And then with a faint slither, a slurry of crushed gravel and dirt trickled past him, telling him she still climbed.

"This is exactly why I don't want anything to do with women," he hollered as he forged ahead. "Females are always doing something crazy. They need to be taken care of all the time, and I don't have that kind of time. I ought to just go back down to my wagon and leave you here, if that's what you want. I never asked for your company, you know. I don't have any obligation to you. It's not my fault if you get yourself all banged up."

His griping echoed from the stone, bouncing back against his ears. Odd to hear the sentiments that usually swirled inside his head taking life so that he could actually hear them. Odder still to realize how crotchety and self-righteous he sounded.

A rock bounced past, missing him by inches. He ducked anyway, the way soldiers did when the crack of rifle fire announced they'd been turned into targets. They always ducked, even though every man knew it was sheer luck more than maneuvering skill that got them out of the way when bullets whizzed by their heads.

Something about that instinctive motion, something about chasing after a helpless person who had been thrust into his care, released images in Neil's mind that he'd fought for months to obliterate. Nothing but rock filled his vision, and yet he could see Johnny Fasler's wide-eyed disbelief as his legs buckled beneath him while red sprayed from his head. Nothing but wind and skittering stone made any sound, but somehow he heard his own voice, hoarse with the effort of screaming. *Down, down, down. Reb fire incoming, get down!*

Sweat trickled down his cheek, and it hadn't sprung up just from the exertion of climbing. He paused and rested his forehead against a rough boulder. He dug his fingers into crevices of unyielding stone. He knew from past experience that nothing but pain washed out old agony. He prayed that the pain of granite piercing his skin would draw his mind out of hell. Prayed it would work before he mangled his hands.

A rich, throaty humming overrode the sound of the wind.

Humming interspersed with strange words sung—no, *chanted*—in a language he didn't understand. Not Indian, or at least none of the Indian he'd picked up.

It wasn't only the wind being tamed by that music. Gradually the gunfire and screaming in his head quieted, soothed by the soft song.

Scarcely daring to believe he'd dodged the nightmares, he loosened his grip on the rock. His hands ached, but nothing more than indentations marred his palms.

The strange song pulled him. He started climbing again, seeking its source.

Sabrina.

She stood with her eyes closed right in the center of the upside-down *U*, her face tilted to the sky. Her hair streamed behind her in a shimmering banner. Her arms were spread wide. She appeared to be bathing in wind and sun. The strong breeze caught her chanting and swirled it high to touch the clouds, and down low again, sighing through the rocks.

The rebuke Neil had meant to shout died unborn in his throat. It seemed wrong somehow to interrupt her.

Her posture, her precise chanting, reminded him of ritual prayer. Something sacred. Something ancient and holy.

She clasped her hands and lifted them to her breast, precisely where her diamond would have been glittering if it hadn't been confiscated and hidden in his pocket.

Her hands closed over nothing. Her eyes opened, and even from where he stood he could see the profound sadness dimming their emerald fire as her singing faltered and stopped.

Guilt raced through him. Stupid, baseless guilt, he told himself. He had every right to hold on to that necklace until she paid him for the bottles she'd broken.

She's already paid you, whispered a tiny voice inside him. *You're standing here thinking about bottles and sacred rituals and how beautiful she looks lit by the sun, when you could be still lost in the past.*

Always before, when the memories leaked free, it had taken hours—sometimes days—to lock them away and escape their hold. Whiskey, women, crowded saloons, and raucous singing were never enough to crowd out the pain.

Something about Sabrina exerted such a pull on him that it had yanked him right out of his misery.

He didn't like being in debt. He would return the diamond, he decided. Just as soon as he got her down off this hunk of rock.

He could tell the minute she first realized he was there. A wariness stiffened her, and her agony over her missing pendant smoothed into blankness. He didn't like it that she could so easily hide herself away from him.

Nor did he like realizing how jumbled his thoughts had become. One minute he resented her. The next minute he wanted to rush to her and gather her in his arms, test her arms and legs to make sure she hadn't broken anything.

She'd barged in on him mere hours earlier, and since

then he'd been tossed and turned like a rowboat set adrift in the ocean. He hadn't devoted two minutes to planning his strategy for investigating Meagher, and he'd completely forgotten about practicing the medicine-hawking patter he had to master to complete his disguise.

"Champion?" she asked again, with a little hitch at the end, as if she already knew he would deny it.

The hell of it was, at the moment he wished he didn't have to deny it.

She spelled trouble. And he couldn't ignore the possibility that she'd been foisted on him deliberately. She'd seemed entirely too interested when he'd mentioned Meagher to her. Maybe someone in Meagher's camp had heard about Neil's mission and sent Sabrina to spy on him.

"Take a look out there," he said, indicating behind her, where from their vantage point on the outcropping they could see the small settlement crouched upon the prairie. "Look familiar to you? Look like home?"

"Home?" She didn't even bother turning around, or peeking over her shoulder toward where he'd pointed. "Nay."

Her whispered denial rang with truth and a sadness that bled with sincerity. Maybe she'd looked at the settlement before he climbed up this far, and felt brokenhearted at knowing she was far from home.

Or maybe she hadn't looked, didn't want to look, and had reasons of her own for tricking him into hauling her around with him.

Either way, he was entirely too susceptible to the distractions she presented. The sooner he rid himself of her, the better.

"Let's go," he said. "We have to make up some time."

* * *

Bamper's one street started out straight enough, but near the end of its five-hundred-yard run it curved to the side, as if the road builders had gotten a little too drunk to toe a level line. Home-brewed liquor, probably, considering there was no saloon among the half dozen or so rickety structures lining the street.

"Any of this look familiar to you?" he asked Sabrina. "Home?"

She shook her head.

He let the horse pick its own pace as they entered the settlement. Through one open door he spotted shelves stocked with a few canned goods. A couple of barrels on the front porch looked as if they might hold flour and pickles. He wouldn't have expected to find a general store in such a small community, but maybe it made sense. The map showed only one additional settlement between here and Fort Benton. Folks traveling the road had to stock up somewhere.

Wind-weathered cabins could never match the elegance of homes in settled areas. Nonetheless, Bamper appeared more prosperous than he'd expected. More careless, too, for he didn't notice any guards posted to watch for Indians, or to announce the arrival of a medicine wagon.

Laundry flapped from clotheslines at the backs of the buildings. Fields, most with knee-high foliage that looked like corn and wheat, stretched out across the valley. Men worked in the fields; a few women, too, wearing coal-scuttle bonnets that shielded their faces from the sun.

He tried to imagine Sabrina out there in the fields, her beautiful hair hidden in one of those ugly bonnets, the wind pasting her skirts against those long legs while she thunked a hoe into the ground, gouging weeds out by the roots.

Her hand rested on her knee, the palm facing up. No, that hand had never wielded a hoe.

A woman stepped from one of the buildings. She peered toward them, and with an excited cry, commenced clanging a bell hanging from her porch.

Neil stopped the wagon and leaned closer to Sabrina, speaking low so his voice wouldn't carry. He tapped the edge of his forefinger against his lips, the universal sign for keeping a secret. "Remember—you can't mention my army uniform."

She pressed a finger to her lips, too.

Several women joined the bell ringer. They stared at the wagon, at Neil and Sabrina, with the avidity of those who seldom see new faces. Their dresses hung loose on them, as if they'd lost too much flesh over a hard winter and summer had not yet provided enough bounty to fill them back up again. The colors of their dresses had faded, and they had the shapelessness that came from too many washings and too much wear.

Neil knew that if he'd been close enough to make out their features, he'd be hard-pressed to tell their ages. Frontier life exacted a harsh toll from women.

He was suddenly glad Sabrina didn't call this place home.

The bell had summoned the workers from the fields. Folks started drifting toward the wagon. Kids popped out from nowhere, yelling with excitement as they raced to be the first to touch the garishly painted sides.

"Hold on there, you don't want to spook the horse," Neil cautioned them as he slid from the bench.

He tugged at the high collar of his black coat. He wasn't used to wearing a coat that fell so far past his hips. It seemed to bind his legs as he walked. He debated shucking the coat altogether, but couldn't recall ever seeing a medicine hawker without a big black coat. He couldn't recall ever seeing one who didn't spout words in a nonstop stream, either. Too late now to wish he'd memorized that speech. There'd been plenty of time to practice it before Sabrina had come along—he'd just never considered it worth the trouble.

He looked out at the crowd gathering at the back of the wagon and felt his throat seize up so badly he'd have thought an Indian had him in a death throttle.

He took a few deep breaths and tried to sort out his thoughts. So far all he had was Sabrina's word that she didn't belong here. Maybe he ought to take her to the back of the wagon where the settlers had clustered and let them take a good look at her. If no one shouted "Here she is, home at last!" then he'd know she'd told him the truth.

The thought of her standing next to him cheered him considerably. Only because it might prove she hadn't lied to him. Yes, that was the only reason why he wanted her at his side.

"Hey, mister—you got a cure in that there wagon for my rheumatiz?"

"It's a medicine wagon, ain't it?" Neil countered as he stalked around to Sabrina's side of the wagon.

He raised his arms to lift her out of the wagon. She drew back, affronted.

"C'mon, princess, no time for that," he muttered, waggling his fingers at her.

She leaned over and very gingerly touched her fingers to his, and then scooted back as if afraid that he'd be angry she dared touch him. *Good Lord, you'd think the woman had never been lifted out of a wagon before.*

Neil dove into the gap between the seat and the front panel and grabbed her by both ankles. He dragged her to the edge of the seat, and then switched his grip to her waist before she could escape. He paused for a moment, stunned at how good it felt to have his hands holding that slim curve. He hoisted her and swung her and so thoroughly enjoyed the feel of her sliding through his arms that he wanted to do it all over again once her feet hit the ground.

She didn't give him a chance. She scooted around him to a point at least five feet away. She stood with one hand touching the wagon, as if it were her sole anchor of familiarity.

He supposed he couldn't blame her for hanging on to a wagon instead of him. He'd confiscated her diamond and confused her. Still, something inside craved that touch of hers. Something inside thought it might be a fine thing to have a woman like her turn to him in trust.

"Hey, mister, when's the show start?"

Dread curled in his gut.

He hadn't expected it to be difficult to stand in front of a few people and sell them his elixir. He couldn't count the times he'd paced back and forth in front of an entire platoon of soldiers, every one of whom had his attention fixed firmly upon him. His voice had never wavered. His composure never cracked. He'd never felt this jumpy inside.

"When's the show start?" someone called again.

They wanted a show. He patted his coat and heard the crackle of the paper where his speech had been written. Wouldn't do him a damned bit of good now. Sabrina stared at him, looking puzzled, as if she couldn't understand why he was so nervous about talking to these people. The heat of embarrassment added to his discomfort.

She was probably laughing inside, remembering how she'd asked him if he was a champion. Champion. A champion was brave and bold, doer of great deeds, winner of all battles. Not someone who'd lost the stomach for battle, who'd learned the hard way that no matter how hard you tried to protect someone, you often failed. A champion certainly didn't find himself all but stuttering for fear of addressing a small group of settlers.

"Hey, medicine man—we got better things to do than stand here all day."

Neil whirled to face the crowd. "Who said that?" he demanded. Nobody admitted to calling out.

This was nothing like the army.

He didn't know how to handle a pack of recalcitrant settlers, but he sure knew how to wring information from men under his command.

"All right, all of you—line up."

"Say, who the hell do you think you are to—"

"Line up! Now!"

They did, though it was one sorry line, with women's skirts belling out and kids' small feet not coming toe-to-toe with the adults' feet. They'd done their best, though, and he felt some of his nervousness drain away. Didn't seem to be much difference between ordering a band of raw recruits and holding the attention of a bunch of overworked homesteaders.

"Stand straight," Neil called. "Heads up! Shoulders back! So some of you have more important things to do than buy my medicine." He prowled the length of the line, looking for signs. "There you are." He gripped an old man by the shoulder and tugged him away from the others.

Ebenezer, who'd sold him the wagon, said that the first sale was always the hardest. Ebenezer claimed that if he could get one person to buy a bottle of elixir, he'd sell a dozen. The man struggling to free himself from Neil's iron grip looked like a likely candidate to start a buying rush.

"You were the one who called out for a rheumatiz cure, right?"

"How . . . how did you know?" the old man quavered.

"Well, hell, look at you, man. One shoulder lower than

the other, hips all lurchy. Fingers so swollen they look like overstuffed sausage casings. I've never known a man to need rheumatiz medicine as bad as you."

He grabbed the man's collar and hauled him closer to the wagon, and then opened the door and drew out a bottle of Ebenezer's Energizing Elixir. "That'll be one dollar. Uh, please."

The man pressed a silver dollar into Neil's hand, and then hobbled back to his place in line.

"Next!" Silence greeted his invitation. Sometimes the marks needed a little encouragement, Ebenezer had advised. "Come on, folks, you're one sick-looking lot."

A woman raised her hand.

"What's wrong with you?"

"Ain't me. It's Melrose. He's sickly."

"Who the hell is Melrose?"

"Uh, me, sir." Another old man stepped forward.

"And what's wrong with you, Melrose?"

"Well, sir, I, uh, I sorter lose my breath when I walk more'n five minutes, and—"

"Here." Neil pushed a bottle of elixir at the old man. "That'll be a dollar."

"Wait a minute." Melrose frowned down at his bottle. "You didn't even listen to all my symptoms. You don't know what my problems are, and you're giving me the same durned medicine you gave to Bob."

A few in the crowd called out in agreement. An angry murmur started low and began to swell. The line started to break up. Ebenezer had warned him against allowing that to happen. Once they drifted away, they were gone for good.

"Drink it," Neil said.

"Won't."

"Drink it!"

"You can't make me."

"Wanna bet?"

Melrose showed a lot of spunk for an oldster. "For all I know, it'll kill me!"

"It won't kill you. It's a damned miracle cure."

Miracle.

Sabrina felt almost dizzy with relief at her understanding of the word. Of course! She had prayed for a miracle, both to her beloved true God and the frightening ancient Druids, just before slipping the Druid's Tear over her head.

Miracles were not granted merely for the asking. One had to work for them.

One had to *earn* them.

She had been so confused, so overwhelmed with the strangeness of all that had happened to her that she'd let herself be pushed and prodded and ordered about. For all her life, she'd allowed others to tell her what to do, what to think. All Desmond women had behaved in such a way.

Could it be that the reason the true champion had not yet come to save them was because no Desmond woman had proved herself worthy of a champion?

Perhaps this upheaval had occurred in answer to her prayer. Perhaps she had been given this chance to prove her worth as the chosen Desmond woman.

If so, it was time to show herself to be the type of woman who would make a fit mate for the true Irish champion. The champion would not be content to saddle himself with a helpless, whimpering mouse of a girl.

She would begin by helping the king, who had somehow immersed himself in trouble. At first his subjects had seemed eager to show him obeisance and followed his every command. Now they had turned on him, even after he had pressed priceless glass gifts upon two of them, because he had shown his fallibility.

He had not recognized the illness of the old man called Melrose.

She could help him.

She ran to his side. He had every right to clout the contentious subject standing before him, but doing so would only fan the crowd's ire to higher levels.

"My lord," she whispered. She closed her hand over the fist he'd balled against his leg. "My lord."

The king's fist uncurled at her touch.

She went next to Melrose, who gazed at her with stupefied delight when she caught his face between her hands and smiled at him. She did not know the words. She opened her mouth, wide, and he copied her as she hoped he would, enabling her to look inside. She looked next into his eyes, noting with sadness the death signs deep within. To be sure, she pressed her hand against his heart and felt the faint afterflutter that heralded doom.

"At least someone in this outfit seems to know what she's doing," Melrose said with a defiant glare at the king. He pulled the stopper from the glass flacon and waved it beneath Sabrina's nose. "Get a load of what he forced me to buy, honey. What do you think?"

Fumes so potent that they made her eyes water rose from the flacon. Like wine, only stronger, much stronger— and perfect for her needs.

She rummaged quickly through the pouch of simples she wore at her waist. Nothing could cure Melrose, but a tisane would ease his discomfort. She found the small cloth bag that held her heart-soothing blend. She carefully poured some of the crumbled herbs into the liquid, and showed Melrose how he must drink it, just a little. Melrose seemed to understand.

"Hey, I'll buy me some of that grouch's nasty medicine if the little lady sweetens it for me," someone called.

Sabrina memorized his words, hoping that later she might understand the tongue well enough to know why the king's people laughed. The terrible tension that had gripped them all dissipated, and they crowded around the king, pleading for beneficence. He dispensed gifts to all, and accepted tribute from them in the form of coins and rectangular things that looked something like stiff cloth.

Everyone left, until she was alone once more with the king.

"Well," he said, staring with some amazement at the coins and odd cloths, "what do you know?"

Her heart swelled with pride in him. He seemed more pleased by the all-but-useless trinkets that had been pressed upon him by his people than he had been with his precious glass.

For the briefest moment he allowed his restraint to slip, and she caught a glimpse of the generous spirit he guarded so carefully.

"Champion," she said decisively, daring to take a poke at his chest.

He did not take offense. He smiled and shook his head. "You're going to have to set your sights a little higher for your champion, sweetheart."

She wished she could understand the full rush of his words. He spoke too quickly, and when she tried to watch his lips she found herself far too distracted by his face.

His face, his form, the way he moved, the strength that could not be hidden by his voluminous coat—she found all of him distracting. She had always assessed every man she met against one criteria—his suitability as a champion. Although that duty was still uppermost in her mind, she found that with this one, she would rather look at him as a man.

"Not champion," she said.

"That's right," he said, and some of his splendor dimmed.

Chapter Four

She practically shimmered, Neil thought, she was so pleased to have been of help to him. It wasn't her fault that he'd felt that odd little twist to his heart when she'd nodded and said *not champion* . . . that was what he'd been telling her all along.

She had every right to congratulate herself. If not for her intervention, his first attempt at medicine sales would have been a complete and total disaster.

Instead it was merely a three-quarters disaster.

He groaned and rubbed his hand over his face.

"My lord?" She touched his hand. She seemed to enjoy stealing little touches; she couldn't know how it affected him. He jerked away from her as though she'd pressed a red-hot branding iron against his skin, as though he was afraid she was marking him as belonging to her.

"None of that," he said. "Something happens to my brain when you get too close to me."

She backed away, distress written all over her. He knew

he ought to take back his words, considering they weren't exactly true. Something did happen to him when she got too close, but his brain wasn't the only part of him that was affected.

Her eyes brimmed with unshed tears.

"You didn't do anything wrong." He meant it as an apology, but it didn't wipe away her misery. She backed away even more. Guilt stabbed, pointing out that his apology left a lot to be desired, especially since she wasn't to blame.

"This is my fault. I made a royal mess of this first effort."

"Royal." She nodded, as if he'd confirmed her secret opinion.

He supposed he owed her more of an explanation.

"You probably couldn't tell, but my damned teeth were practically chattering, I got so nervous at the idea of trying to sell medicine to these folks. My insides shook, and my knees quaked. Something snapped inside, and I started barking out orders at these civilians as if they were soldiers under my command. I don't know how to act like a regular man. I only know how to act like an army captain."

He let out his breath with a little whoosh. He'd never articulated that particular weakness before.

She didn't laugh, didn't mock.

I don't know how to act like a regular man. I only know how to act like an army captain. The shakiness he thought he'd banished returned full force. He'd acted like a regular man only once, when he'd fallen prey to weakness and ended up married to a woman he didn't love. Since then he'd used his army rank and uniform like a shield. Maybe that was why facing this crowd as an ordinary medicine man had been so hard.

Revealing the truth about himself to an audience of one was just as nerve-racking as baring his ignorance of salesmanship to a crowd of strangers. Maybe more nerve-racking. He wished Sabrina would come closer and touch him again, even though he'd told her to stay away.

He must be losing his mind.

"Every man among them probably suspects by now that I'm military."

She hesitated, bit her lip, and nodded.

He closed his eyes, groaned, and flopped back against the side of the wagon. He'd blown his secret identity and hadn't managed to ask a single question about Thomas Francis Meagher, either. If he started doing so now, one of these settlers might piece one thing together with another, and figure out his mission.

He *really* wished Sabrina would ignore his directive and come to him.

He counted to five, and she didn't come. Counted to ten and she still didn't come. He opened one eye, and then jolted upright when he realized she wasn't standing where he'd seen her last.

No, she'd gone off and stood smack in the middle of the street, and the men of Bamper surrounded her like wasps buzzing a sun-ripe peach.

One of them said something to her, and she not only smiled, she laughed—a bright, trilling sound that would have cheered the sourest-natured man alive.

She'd never laughed like that the whole time she'd been alone with him.

He heaved himself away from the wagon and stalked toward her, eating the distance with long-legged strides. Her hair tumbled over her shoulders and down her back in a glorious auburn cascade, inviting a man to touch and stroke in a way no well-combed, prim, pinned-up bun could ever do. The mud red gown clung to her in just the right places, so that the little smudges of dust and dirt she'd collected on her rock-climbing expedition seemed set there on purpose. From the way the townsmen gaped at her, Neil knew it didn't matter a bit to them that she'd spent the best part of the day eating road dust, climbing rocks . . . beating up an army captain.

She noticed his approach. Her laughter faded, her posture stiffened. She spread her arms, as if she were symbolically herding the men into a group and offering them to him.

He realized that she'd presented him with an opportunity. He could charge into the midst of that group like an angry bull and chase the men away, or he could wander in friendly and smiling and hope to wipe out the wrong impression he'd made earlier.

He tugged at his collar. He cleared his throat. He straightened his shoulders. Pasting a wide smile on his face, he strode into the midst of the group with his hand extended. "Well, well, well," he said. "I see you're keeping Sabrina company."

They ignored him.

"Go on, miss," said one of them. "Tell us which one of us is the handsomest."

Sabrina giggled.

Anger began its slow burn in Neil's vitals. "Seems to me you men have more important things to do than stand around gawking at this gal."

"I can't think of anything more important," answered one of them.

"At least nothing that's as much fun," qualified another.

The slow burn kindled into a roiling boil. "I guess you don't think it's important to avoid getting scalped. I drove my wagon right into this place without a single one of you raising an alarm."

"You planning to scalp us?" asked one of the worst gawkers.

"No, man, I'm talking about Indians. You ought to have someone watching out for them."

"We did," said one of them. "For months."

They all nodded their heads. Another man spoke up. "Never saw so much as a bear claw or a feather. Come planting time, we needed every man in the fields. Can't see the sense in posting guards when nothing worse than a wolf prowls on by. Or a medicine wagon."

"You ought to post guards."

"Listen, Mr. Ebenezer, don't you go insinuatin' that we don't know what's best for our homes and our families. We won't stand for a stranger waltzing into town accusing us of not owning up to our responsibilities."

To a man, they turned their backs on him and returned their attention to Sabrina.

Look on the positive side, he told himself as the thorough dismissal of his warning sank in. They believed he was the Ebenezer named in Ebenezer's Energizing Elixir. Maybe his lapse into military tactics hadn't been as obvious as he'd feared, for they would surely have accorded his opinion more value if they believed him to be a military man.

But on the negative side, he couldn't shake his gut feeling that they underestimated the Indian threat. They might not have seen any, but he'd noticed signs here and there along the trail. If he hadn't been so distracted by Sabrina, he might've inspected some of the signs. If she hadn't delayed him and thrown him off schedule, he would have followed some of the suspicious trails, because the troops garrisoned at Fort Benton would appreciate the report. Maybe they were old, no longer used. Or maybe they weren't.

Sabrina laughed again at something. The men crowded a little closer, paying so much attention that he wouldn't be surprised if sweat broke out on their brows. If *she* asked them to post guards, they'd probably be fighting over the honor of being the first to stand watch.

A swell of loneliness took him by surprise. He wondered what it would be like to walk into the midst of a group of strangers and gain their trust and friendship with no effort. Just thinking about that sort of thing made him feel almost queasy. He'd always prided himself on maintaining an aloofness, on being so self-sufficient that he didn't need anybody's company.

They'd probably heed his warning if they'd warmed up to him a little. They might pay attention if they knew he was an army captain. But when good, solid advice came from the mouth of a medicine hawker whom they considered a grouch, they'd sooner risk their scalps.

And that was exactly why he was leaving the army after this mission. No matter how hard a man tried, no matter how noble his intentions, weaker people would do stupid things. They'd die, and with their last breath they'd be asking why you'd let them down.

"I'll bet Mr. Meagher will be disappointed to hear that you're ignoring his directive," Neil said with false casualness.

"Mr. Meagher?" The townsmen's attention snapped back to him.

"You mean General Meagher," said one.

Neil's interest quickened. President Johnson had specifically asked him to investigate whether Meagher continued to portray himself as an active military general.

"Last I heard, he'd mustered out of the army and entered politics," Neil said.

"Well, he'll always be General Meagher to us. The man's a bona fide hero." Murmurs of agreement greeted the announcement. "He's doing all he can to make Montana safe for us settlers. A pure-tee hero."

"Hero?" asked Sabrina. "Champion?"

"No!" Neil had shouted the denial before realizing the settlers might find his vehemence a little puzzling. He paused, regaining control, and then strove for an easy, conversational tone that didn't betray the annoyance that cropped up every time Sabrina showed so much interest in Thomas Meagher. "I heard he withdrew the army from the populated areas and took them up north to chase Indians that weren't there. Cost the United States government more than a million dollars."

"What of it? Maybe him chasing those Indians is the reason we haven't seen any around here."

"Champion?" Sabrina asked again.

"You'd like General Meagher." The youngest settler gripped Sabrina by the arm. Neil automatically reached for his gun, which wasn't there. He gritted his teeth while the settler pulled Sabrina closer to his side. "General Meagher is the bravest, most famous man in Montana."

"Bravest," said Sabrina.

"He's a hero. Nobody can lead a battle as good as him."

"Hero. Battle."

"Don't matter if he's using a sword, or a rifle, or a pistol. He'd lead a charge into the pits of hell, if it meant winning a fight for the Union. He led troops at some of the most famous battles during the War Between the States: Mechanicsburg. Antietam."

Sabrina listened with rapt attention. The settlers stood taller, as if subtly saluting the absent General Meagher. Disgust swamped Neil. This wasn't going well at all. He was supposed to be collecting damaging evidence about Meagher, not standing there listening to an endless list of accolades from folks who obviously idolized him.

"You know," said one of them, with a somewhat shame-faced glance in Neil's direction, "maybe if General Meagher thinks we ought to post guards, well, maybe we ought to post guards."

"I'll take the first watch."

The settler who had hold of Sabrina pulled her a little closer.

All at once Neil no longer cared whether these men warmed up to him. He didn't like their type, anyway. Didn't care for the man pawing Sabrina; didn't like the way their tales set her to glowing with admiration over a man she'd never met; didn't care at all to listen to these settlers list Meagher's accomplishments as though the man were the country's greatest patriot rather than a possible saboteur.

He forced himself through the crowd of men and with a quick, sharp jab dislodged the settler's grip on Sabrina's arm. "Let her go."

"I was just—"

"Get yer hands off her, Billy," said a townsman. He glared at Neil. "As the man pointed out, we got better things to do than stand around jawing with the likes of him." He turned to Sabrina and gave her a polite nod. "Pleased to make *your* acquaintance, ma'am."

They about-faced and aimed for various dwellings, with a few casting longing glances back at her before closing their doors with firm thumps.

Neil watched with mixed emotions as they closed themselves away. He'd accomplished something good if they did, indeed, begin to take the Indian threat more seriously. But he'd alienated them from the first, and he didn't understand what it was about him that made people take against him.

No . . . what he didn't understand was why it suddenly started bothering him. He'd never been affected that way before.

Up until now, the ability to repel closeness had seemed a valuable skill for a career military man who couldn't afford to get attached to his men. The knack had carried over into his personal life, though, affecting his brief marriage, and keeping him lonely ever since.

He'd thought he didn't mind. Until he realized that Sabrina never quite relaxed in his company, and that she laughed only with other people.

A woman darted from her small, weathered cabin, sneaking a glance at the tightly closed houses as if she didn't want to be seen seeking Neil's company.

"Hey, you—medicine man," she called. "You and the missus lookin' to rent a room for the night?"

"Missus?" Neil squawked out the word, stunned that someone would think he and Sabrina were married.

"Stewart," said the woman, a little breathless from her quick approach. "Mrs. Maisie Stewart. You can call me Maisie."

Neil hadn't been asking for an introduction, but welcomed the woman's misunderstanding to cover his lapse.

"Neil Kenyon," he said, still somewhat dazed by Maisie Stewart's assumption. He bit back a curse when he realized he should have used an alias.

Sabrina's head snapped up. "Neil?"

Something soft and warm expanded inside him at hearing her say his name. He hadn't told her, in all these hours, what to call him.

Something like awe lit her expression. Her lips moved silently, as if she tested words she was afraid to say out loud, and then he swore she whispered something that sounded a hell of a lot like her usual *champion*. Followed by her usual *my lord*.

"Seems your missus thinks right highly of you." Maisie cast him a reproving look that told him she didn't share Sabrina's opinion. "And you not even considerate enough to introduce us. Ain't no call to be standoffish. We don't hold formalities here, and we'll be packed right close and personal in my little house."

Maisie assumed they were man and wife. Maisie assumed they wanted to share a bed for the night. Either one of those assumptions was enough on its own to make the hairs on the back of Neil's neck stand on end. Both assumptions together paralyzed his throat into silence.

"Sabrina." She introduced herself, which did nothing to ease Neil's agony.

She had this way of speaking that played real nice against his ears, a musical richness in her voice that reminded him that people sometimes burst into song for no reason at all. Not that he'd ever done anything like that. But on those rare occasions when Sabrina spoke aloud, when he heard her lilt and that odd trilling of her *R*s, well, he had no trouble imagining that she might be the type of woman who would warble a chorus of tra-la-las while she washed the supper dishes.

Except that those hands of hers had never been plunged into wash water. He'd bet the rest of his inventory on it.

"Pleased to meet you, I'm sure," said Maisie. She tucked her arm through Sabrina's and started leading her toward the house. "That's a right pretty name you have, too. Irish, right?"

Sabrina smiled.

Irish! Of course. The auburn hair, the fair, glowing skin, the sea mist-green eyes.

An Irish*woman* had somehow come on board his wagon while he was engaged in a secret presidential mission to arrest an Irish*man*. His half-formed suspicions hardened, the way they should have earlier if he hadn't been moping around, wondering why she tended to flinch away from his touch. She had a knack for luring him into letting down his guard. Once again the hairs on his neck stood on end, and it wasn't because of Maisie Stewart's assumption that he and Sabrina were married.

"Where do you think you're taking her?" Neil caught up with them in two strides and hooked his arm around Sabrina's waist. She stiffened at once, the way she'd done

every time he'd touched her. Then, with a barely percepti-
ble tremor, she relaxed. He hadn't expected her to do
that, and so the pressure of his hold pulled her back against
him, until her shoulder blades rested against his chest and
the curve of her waist fit just right along his hips.

Damn, but it was difficult to remain properly suspicious
of her motives with her so warm and soft against him.

Maisie sent him a surprisingly lecherous grin. "Newly-
weds, huh?"

"No."

The old woman's sharp gaze studied Sabrina's skimpy
wool shift, her tumbled hair, and her ringless left hand.
"Humpf. Well, don't get so worked up, medicine man. I
ain't taking her far. Take a good look around you. No hotel.
No rooming house. The menfolk stomped off looking like
they was plenty steamed against you, and I wouldn't hold
my breath waiting for them to come back. There ain't
nobody but me waving you in to partake of Bamper hospi-
tality."

She spoke the truth. Every house had been shut against
them—doors closed, curtains drawn, shutters pulled tight.

Maisie's expression softened, as if she understood what
it meant to find oneself an outcast.

"The sun's fixing to set any minute. No sense in standing
out here when we can set inside with a nice, cool drink.
A good meal and all the sassafras you can drink comes
with the room. You can picket your horse out back. Good
grass back there, and a stream. Cheap at any price."

"I don't care what you charge. I don't . . ." Neil stopped
himself. He'd been about to decline the offer of Maisie's
sleeping room without considering the consequences.

The sun was indeed on the verge of setting. If he
extracted Sabrina from Maisie Stewart's clutches, he'd have
no choice but to drive them out of town and make a camp
somewhere along the trail. After all the warnings he'd

issued about Indians, it seemed doubly foolish to bed down in some isolated camp after dark. The next settlement lay a half day's ride ahead. There wouldn't be enough moonlight at this phase to allow him to attempt to travel at night.

He had only one bedroll. He hadn't expected company to show up in the back of his locked wagon.

He possessed one cup, one plate, one fork, one knife. He would have to share them with Sabrina if they traveled together tonight. From then on, anytime he used those simple utensils, he'd remember her tongue sliding against the tines of his fork, her lips closing over the edge of his cup, her fingers curled around the handle of his knife.

He'd be haunted forevermore by the memory of her lush curves snuggled in his bedroll.

His duty dictated he keep Sabrina with him until she proved she wasn't connected to Meagher in any way. Until that very moment, he hadn't considered that keeping Sabrina with him meant sleeping near her, sitting next to her, listening to her breathe, for virtually every minute of every day.

He ought to just leave her here, stranded, with no means of reaching Fort Benton. It wouldn't matter then if she'd been sent to spy on him. His mission would be completed before she found some way to notify her coconspirators.

But he couldn't abandon her now. He remembered the avid speculation on Mrs. Stewart's face as she'd studied Sabrina's disheveled appearance. The old woman might as well have shouted out loud that she thought Sabrina was some kind of soiled dove. If Neil left her behind, after everybody in the settlement knew they'd ridden in together, she'd be branded a whore. A whore with the bad sense to pair up with a grouch.

Take her with him and risk his mission. Leave her here and let her face the consequences on her own. The choice ought to be easy. He couldn't understand why it seemed impossible to decide what to do at the moment.

"I don't care what you charge," Neil repeated. "I don't want Sabrina to sleep outdoors tonight."

"Well, come on in, then." Mrs. Stewart beamed at him, and squeezed Sabrina's arm.

"No, you two go ahead. I have to tend to the horse."

"You'll be in for supper."

"Uh, no. No. If it's not too much trouble, you might bring me a plate. I'll eat and sleep in the wagon."

Mrs. Stewart frowned uncertainly. Sabrina had a serene smile upon her face. Neil couldn't tell whether she was pleased to be rid of him for a few hours, or whether she simply didn't understand what was going on. Despite his suspicions about her, it bothered him that she sometimes acted as if she didn't understand half of what was going on around her.

"All my stock's in this wagon," Neil said, landing a thump on the wagon wall. "I'm not saying there are thieves in Bamper, but a man can't be too careful."

"I guess not," Mrs. Stewart agreed. "C'mon, Mrs. Kenyon."

Mrs. Kenyon. A gnawing emptiness gripped Neil as the women walked away from him. Sabrina glanced over her shoulder. Trepidation darkened her glorious eyes. Neil made a movement toward her. He took a deep breath, ready to use his loudest captain's voice to order the old woman to stop.

Sabrina still stared at him. She pressed her lips together, the way people did when they were trying not to cry.

"Sabrina!" he roared.

Joy lit her whole being. She moved as if she meant to pull away from Mrs. Stewart, and Neil realized what a fool he'd been to call out to her.

For the sake of his mission, for the sake of his sanity, he

had to manage at least a few hours out of her company. She muddled his thinking. She wormed her way into his thoughts with her touches and her smiles and her *my lords*. She represented a complication he didn't need, in more ways than one. He couldn't afford to let her get too close, in case she'd been sent to undermine his mission. If she was innocent of such duplicity, he double-damn couldn't let her get close, because he had no place in his life for a woman who needed as much looking after as she did.

"Sleep well, Sabrina," he called. And then he swiveled on his heel and walked away from her.

He made it clear to the opposite side of the wagon. Though it had not been a particularly exhausting day, he was overcome by a profound need to flop back against the wagon wall for the second time in less than an hour. He leaned there, breathing harder than he had any reason to, and wondered why she'd seemed so sad to leave him.

The diamond.

His pocket dragged down from the weight of the stone— funny how he hadn't noticed the heaviness until that moment. He pulled out Sabrina's necklace and had to blink twice to make sure he'd fished the right jewel out of his pocket.

Something had happened to the diamond. The facets appeared dulled, as if someone had come along and dipped the stone into melted wax. He polished it against his britches, but nothing rubbed off. He held it up toward the setting sun, but the dizzying array of color that had sparkled from the diamond when Sabrina had been with him simply did not reappear. As if it missed her. The way he was missing her. As if without her near, all life had leaked from the stone.

That old diamond might as well be a hunk of worthless glass, something to add to his collection in the back of the wagon. An image filtered through his mind—a dull, colorless man driving all alone with a wagon full of dull, colorless glass.

He hoped Mrs. Stewart brought dinner soon, because hunger must have addled his head. He wasn't normally prone to such ridiculous fancies. There was a perfectly good reason why the diamond had seemingly lost its luster—evening encroached, dimming the sun. Diamonds no doubt sparkled best beneath full sun. Men felt perkier, too, when gold light bathed them from above, which explained why he found himself a little downhearted at the moment.

He shoved the diamond back into his pocket. He remembered that the stone had felt hot when he'd first touched it, when he was holding it in one hand and Sabrina in the other. Now, through the thin cloth of his pocket, the damned diamond felt like a chunk of ice threatening to numb him from head to toe.

For no good reason, he kicked the wagon axle where it poked through the center of the wheel. Hard. So hard that pain shafted from his toes to his knee, and he wondered if he'd busted a toe.

Chapter Five

The dwelling where Maisie Stewart led Sabrina appeared squat and small as any peasant cottage from the outside, but inside, a wealth of comforts filled its space.

Light flickered inside glass-chimneyed lamps. Sabrina scarcely had time to remark on such a wondrous device when she realized the elegance of the fine-legged chairs ringing a table. The gleaming wood tabletop lay free of the nicks and scrapes tables ever endured from banging mailed fists or carelessly flung tankards.

All manner of strange and beautiful things crowded the small space. Many objects struck her as so strange, she had no idea of their purpose. Portraits of startling reality, painted by an artist who favored browns and grays, covered an entire wall. A large settle sat across from a fireplace. The hearth lay mysteriously bare of wood and swept clean of ashes, with nothing cooking, although a cautious sniff brought to Sabrina the rich, moist scent of boiling stew, the mouthwatering odor of baking bread.

Wooden stairs pierced the center of the room, dividing it in two without the restriction of a wall. "Two bedrooms up there," Maisie said. "Your man could've had all the privacy he wanted. Maybe he's the noisy type. Or maybe you are?"

Sabrina shrugged her shoulders, not understanding, but sensing that a question had been asked of her.

"Well, no need to stand there looking out of place." Maisie tugged at Sabrina, drawing her farther into the chamber. "This is your home for as long as you want it to be. I know it ain't much, but plenty of folks endure worse out on those far-flung homesteads. Dig themselves a hole in the dirt to live in, some of them. Me, I like the comfort of knowing someone's within hollerin' range. Bamper suits me."

The woman's face creased with a friendly smile. Her eyes sparkled with kindness. Sabrina wished she could understand more than a few words of what Maisie Stewart said. Even more, she wished for a strong enough command of the tongue to ask the questions that demanded answering.

The beautiful surroundings, the good smell of food, the presence of another woman, seemed deliberately designed to counter every one of her torments. She should feel soothed. Instead her instincts warned her much was amiss, for none of this made sense. Vast wealth enclosed in a peasant's cottage. Villeins arguing with kings. Herself, sworn to one man but feeling a quickening of her woman's heart in the presence of another.

Neil. The man who denied being champion, when his very name meant champion in her tongue.

She wanted to fling herself into this sympathetic lady's arms and cry tears of confusion. But for all her life she had been told Desmond women did not cry.

And so she had not cried. Nor would she cry now.

She swallowed and straightened her shoulders, which always served to lend her strength.

"In this worlde ther be bore a myghty champion," she said. "He that men wolde laude and prayse, for his actys be grete. He wolde be my champion, ffor lif, and for deth from Desmond not departe."

"What're you saying, honey?" Maisie asked.

Maisie did not understand her! The realization shocked Sabrina to her core—*she* was the one being tested, not the very kind Maisie.

"Him I seeketh—he that wolde strugyle for oure redempcioun, oure owne champion. For my dutys leving bihynde unpayed, I prayeth Iesu excuseth my synne. I prayeth to be ioyned to this manly knyght to kepen and governe Desmond, in trouthe and honour, fredom and curteisye."

Maisie's brow creased. Her lips moved, as if she repeated some of Sabrina's words to herself. A huge smile brightened her face.

"Well, I'll be—if you don't talk just like my aunt Katherine. She married my uncle Richard, uncle on my father's side, way back in—oh, Lordy—had to be eighteen twenty-seven or thereabouts. They're both gone now, God rest their souls. C'mon over here—I'll show you her picture." She tugged Sabrina's hand and drew her closer to the portrait gallery.

She pointed with great pride and affection toward the likenesses of a stern-looking woman and man, painted in faded blacks and grays. The images were startlingly lifelike, particularly in the eyes. Sabrina fought the urge to cross herself, certain such awesome skill must have the hand of the Devil in it somewhere, else why would the painter have limited himself to the colors of death?

"Aunt Katherine came from an island off the coast of Maryland. Smith Island, I do believe it was called. She talked funny, just like you. It's not so different from normal talk, once you get the hang of it. She taught me, and I taught her. When I was a little girl I plumb loved talking secretlike with her in that language. She claimed it was old-timey English. Said her whole island was full of folks who kept on speaking English the way they did back in the olden days."

"English," Sabrina eagerly seized upon the familiar word.

"That Mr. Neil Kenyon of yours must've plucked you off that island and set you down here without teaching you a word of what you need to know."

"Neil." Weakness sapped her stiff-shouldered pride. She remembered with shame how eagerly she had spun about when he'd called her name, thinking he wanted her to return to him. Certes, she had failed that portion of the test.

Maisie made a mock spitting motion, which told Sabrina her failure had been profound. "Neil. I can tell by the way you shake every time you say his name that he has you completely under his thumb. Well, I've seen his type before. I don't admit this to everyone, but the late Mr. Stewart started out the same. Bossy and demanding and determined to keep a woman in her place. This is him right here."

She pointed to another painting, this one of a wide-faced, whiskered fellow who wore an expression of bewilderment. The same skilled painter had captured him, this time with tinges of brown seeping into the blacks and grays. Awed, Sabrina ran her finger over the portrait. She drew back with a little shriek, for the painting felt more like smooth metal than paint-daubed cloth.

"Daguerreotype," said Maisie. "Fool man considered himself so handsome he had three dozen made. Here, I'll give you one since you seem so taken with it." She opened the drawer of a small table that stood below the portraits, and to Sabrina's disbelieving eyes she fanned out an entire handful of portraits identical to the one upon the wall. She pushed them toward Sabrina. "Go on, pick one. I've been trying to get rid of these for a good ten years now."

Sabrina hesitated, uncertain what Maisie expected of her.

"This one's good as any." Maisie pushed one portrait forward with her finger. Sabrina accepted it and held it in her hands with the reverence she might accord a rosary, although that, too, might count against her if her sacrilegious intents were being marked.

She peeked at the portrait. Such finely beaten metal, thinner than any she'd ever seen—and not a hammer mark to mar its smoothness. The edges had been so finely honed that she felt certain she could cut cloth with this. She could not imagine what manner of paint had been used, for no clumps or thick areas rose above the metal. She scraped at the corner with her finger, and dislodged nothing.

Her breath threatened to desert her. Her heart thudded with alarm. There could be no doubt that this painting was a sign. She held within her hands proof that nothing she saw was as she expected it to be. Again, to her disgust, she felt tears brim. Never had she been the sort of woman to give way easily to tears, but since beginning this journey they stood ever at the ready. She swallowed and willed them away, telling herself yet again: *Desmond women do not cry.*

But Maisie had noticed her struggle to master the tears. "See, I was right. You're all flustered, worrying about what that man of yours will do if he catches you looking at another fellow, even if this one's been dead and gone for a good three years now. Lost him during the War Between the States—did I mention that? Don't think I did. Anyway, we had our good moments and our bad moments. Kind of miss him sometimes. Never thought I'd say that, but he did mellow after the first few years, and got to be downright enjoyable company near the end, before he went off to war.''

"War." Neil had mentioned something about a war. "Neil. My lord."

"Back to him again! I'll tell you, your fellow at his best beats mine at his worst. Making you call him 'my lord.' Humpf! Probably tells you he likes your hair down like that, but I'm telling you, honey, it's a secret plot to keep you tangled up, so you can't move too fast. Bet he makes you wear those slippers and that flimsy nightdress so you can't run off on him.''

Sabrina nodded, wanting to seem agreeable. Maisie grew agitated rather than pleased.

"I'll tell you what—men in general still have a debt to pay for the nonsense I took from Mr. Stewart. Oh, like I said, I straightened him out eventually, but you know, it still smarts when I think back on it. I know just how to help you call your man's bluff.''

"Help."

"Sure, honey. I can have you chattering like a magpie in two days flat. That ought to stick real good in his craw.''

She tucked her arm through Sabrina's and tapped her foot. "Hmmm. You know what else—we can get you something more suitable to wear, too, which ought to fry his beans but good. I got some clothes that don't quite make it around this old body anymore, but they'd do right fine for you with a little nip here and a tuck or two there. It'd make me right happy to see you wearing them, especially under these circumstances. C'mon over to the sewing machine.''

She tugged Sabrina across the floor. A trunk rested alongside an odd structure made of wood and intricately curved metal. Maisie threw open the trunk, revealing a wealth of clothing that surpassed Sabrina's bride wardrobe. Heedless of the worth of the clothes, she tossed one garment after another over her shoulder.

"Aha! This is what I had in mind."

She pulled forth what looked to be only the top half of a kirtle. She held it against Sabrina's shoulders and nodded with satisfaction. "You're big enough on top to fill this out right nice. You're like me—I had me a nice pair in my younger days, too. This blouse don't smell musty, and all these clothes was clean when I packed them away. I'll bet the skirt'll be fine, too, once we iron them up a little."

She dove back into the trunk and pulled free yet another half-formed garment, much larger and less well shaped than the first. She wrapped the edge of it halfway around Sabrina's waist and shook her head.

"What are you, a wasp? Lordy, you scarcely need a corset. I'll have to take in these seams a good two inches on either side. Won't take but five minutes. Let me put on my spectacles first. I almost always wear them in the house. Too vain to perch them on my nose when I go outside. Never thought I'd see the day."

She hooked her foot around a stool that rested beneath the wood-and-metal contrivance. She sat and began a pumping motion with one foot that summoned such a noise from the contrivance that Sabrina cried out and leaped back in alarm.

Maisie seemed unperturbed. She shook out the voluminous half-kirtle and found the seam running up one side. "Probably ought to pin it, but I have a pretty steady hand."

She placed the edge of the garment against a small row of teeth, and the contrivance proved itself to be a monster that chewed cloth. The teeth gnashed and rose up and down, swallowing the cloth into its metal maw . . . and yet letting it pass through unharmed on the other side.

Not quite unchanged, though, for alongside the first seam ran a second, perfectly stitched.

No seamstress had touched the garment. Sabrina would swear on it. The confusion within her shifted into something different, a kind of fog that threatened to smother her vitals and obliterate the clarity of her mind.

Maisie readied the other side of the garment for the monster's grinding teeth.

"Go give that stew pot a good stir, and set a couple of flatirons on the stove. We'll press these as soon as I finish this seam."

Sabrina knew she'd been given another test, one she was certain to fail, for she could not move her limbs, could not sort out any of the words Maisie had said.

Something was wrong, terribly wrong. She watched the cloth develop its new seam, and knew that she had been taken so far away from Desmond Muir that she might never find her way back home again.

A chill froze her to her core. She swayed, and feared that she might humiliate herself by fainting.

Maisie gathered the garments and turned away from the contrivance. She dropped them and caught Sabrina by the shoulders and gave her a hard shake.

"Don't you turn chicken on me. What on earth has that man done to you, to make you get so scared at the thought of changing your clothes? I pegged him for a bossy man, but he doesn't look like the sort who would actually take a hand to you. You don't look bruised up. He doesn't hit you, does he, honey? You say the word and I'll have the fellows run Mr. Neil Kenyon right out of town."

Sabrina grasped the familiar. "Neil. My lord."

Maisie sighed. "Well, look at that, just saying his name is bringing some of the color back to your face. Maybe he ain't so bad after all. Can you make yourself look sick like that on purpose?"

"Not . . . cry," Sabrina whispered.

"That's all right. Just acting sick ought to work out real nice. We'll just pretend you're feeling poorly for three or four days. Won't give him a chance to see you or talk to you until you've learned to speak up for yourself. How's that sound?"

Sabrina covertly studied Maisie, and decided a nod from her would best please the woman.

And so it seemed. Maisie nodded back.

"From the way he looks at you, I got no doubt he's been riding you hard. You might not mind that part so much, but I'm sure the rest of it must wear on your nerves. I'll let him think you're in the family way. That'll give him something to worry about. By the time he catches on, you'll have blossomed like a rose, and you'll have me to thank."

"Thank," Sabrina said. She remembered the lesson Neil had given her—*you* versus *me*. "Thank *you*."

"No need, no need." Maisie waved her hand. "You wouldn't believe how it tickles me to flummox a man again. There's nothing like getting a man so confused he can't think straight. Thought I'd have but one chance in my life. Besides, I won't mind the company."

Neil's fist pounded a staccato beat against the door. It cracked open so quickly that he knew someone had been waiting for him. His pulse quickened. He shifted his weight, ready to walk through the doorway, when he realized it had stopped moving after opening only an inch.

Within that narrow space he caught the glimmer of lamplight reflecting from spectacles. A curl of steel gray hair poked from beneath the gathered edge of a nightcap. And then the rough, no-nonsense drawl belonging to Maisie Stewart ordered him away. "She's sick. Go away."

With that the old harridan slammed the door in Neil's

face. He heard the slide of a metal bolt and the unmistakable thud of a wooden bar slammed into place.

He stood dumbstruck for a moment, wondering why the woman had felt it necessary to take such precautions against him. An officer! A gentleman! He thundered his fist against the door once more. This time she slid open the window a few feet away and popped her head through.

"If you break down that door, you're gonna pay for a new one."

"Where's Sabrina?"

"She's in bed, where all sensible people are at this time of night."

"It's morning."

"I don't see any sunlight."

"It's coming." As if on cue, a bird let loose with a string of chirps, the first to break the silence that had seemed to last an eternity. "Did you hear that bird?"

"All I hear is some damn-fool man doing his best to wake up the whole settlement."

"I want my . . ." Neil swallowed. He'd meant to say *wife*, just to keep the ruse going, but the word stuck in his throat. "I want Sabrina."

"I told you—she's sick."

"You told me she's asleep."

"No, I didn't. I said she's in bed, which is right where she belongs after upchucking for the past hour. You do know what that means, I assume?"

"I know, all right. You poisoned her with that swill you called dinner."

Neil glared at the woman he'd thought so kind. She narrowed her eyes, obviously affronted by his comment, and then smirked. That smirk raised his suspicions—maybe she really had dosed his dinner with poison.

He'd eaten the meal she'd provided the night before, every bite, because a man had to keep up his strength and eat what he was given, even when it seemed to be singularly lacking in flavor. He'd felt sick and dispirited the whole night long, so uneasy and restless that he hadn't managed a single minute of sleep. Not that he usually managed much, but the tossing and turning that had kept him awake had seemed different somehow.

He liked the idea of blaming his bad night on Mrs. Stewart's food. It beat admitting that he might have been sunk in misery because Sabrina wasn't with him.

He might not have managed any more sleep if Sabrina had slept on the other side of his campfire. But his restlessness would have had a more pleasurable edge than the incessant worry that gnawed away at him. He'd tried, at first, to tamp down that worry, because he had no reason to feel so responsible for her. After many long hours, though, he'd stumbled onto several good reasons for his uneasiness.

Maybe Maisie Stewart was Sabrina's secret cohort, and together the two women were plotting ways to undermine his mission.

Or . . . Sabrina was such an innocent, she might accidentally divulge information he'd asked her to keep secret, such as his army uniform, even though she'd never managed in his hearing to string together more than two or three words at a time.

Or . . . or . . .

He couldn't at the moment remember the third reason. He'd thought up a third reason, he knew he had, but it had somehow slipped his mind because . . . because . . .

Because it was probably even dumber and stupider than the reasons he'd managed to remember. If one of his men had come to him with those kinds of suspicions, he would laugh him right out of the tent.

Only two people in the world knew of his mission: himself, and President Andrew Johnson. Neil had made his preparations in secret, not even telling the president about his scheme of traveling as a medicine man. If by some bizarre stroke of good fortune Meagher had learned of Neil's plans, there had been no time to recruit a beautiful young spy, or set up an intricate network of elderly females and cantankerous settlers to work against him.

He, Neil Kenyon, was a career soldier, honed by experience and training to recognize the mettle of a man. He'd sensed nothing suspicious about Sabrina, except for the fact that she was an Irishwoman and he was bound for Fort Benton to collect information on an Irishman.

And she'd seemed to perk right up when Thomas Meagher's name entered into a conversation.

Well, that and the fact that she'd pretty much popped in on him out of nowhere. A couple of coincidences. A few. He didn't believe in coincidences. Life had taught him that everything happened for a purpose.

Maybe that could be the third reason. He'd go plumb crazy if he didn't figure out the purpose behind Sabrina's sudden appearance in his wagon. Since her arrival his whole life had been turned upside down. He wasn't thinking the same. He wasn't acting the same. Hell, he sure wasn't talking the same.

"I want her." Neil injected every ounce of menace he could summon into his voice. "I want her right now."

"Too bad, champ," said Mrs. Stewart. "Tell you what— I might let you see her this afternoon, providing you show up looking nice and acting polite. We'll be at home between three and four o'clock."

She lunged outward and grabbed the edges of the shutters he hadn't noticed, and pulled them closed. He stalked the perimeter, but he could tell by the slamming sounds preceding him that she'd anticipated his move. Every window presented a blank, shuttered face to him. She'd shut the first floor of her house tight as a Chinese puzzle box.

He pounded on the door until his hand turned numb, but despite Mrs. Stewart's feigned fear for its safety, the door withstood the worst he could do. He called Sabrina's name a dozen times, a hundred times, until his throat turned raw and he realized that she'd certainly heard him—and failed to appear. Maybe she really was sick, as Mrs. Stewart claimed. He renewed his attack on the door.

Maybe she just didn't want to see him.

The distinctive ping of a rifle shot split the silence, and dirt spattered over Neil's boot. "I missed on purpose," hollered the shooter. "I won't miss the next time, so shut the hell up and let us get some sleep."

Damned slugabeds. A decent camp would be stirring by now, breakfast fires lit, latrine troops hurrying to get their tour of duty over and done with. Neil cleared his throat. He swiveled his neck and touched his hand to his breast where his army identification usually rested. It felt empty there, as empty as the rest of him.

That emptiness probably meant he was hungry again. He'd rather starve to death than ask Mrs. Hag Stewart for another bite of her bilious fare.

So she thought she *might* let him see Sabrina at three o'clock. *Ha.* She'd soon learn that nothing stood between a U.S. Army captain and his goal. Except for about ten hours. It was still too dark to read his pocket watch, but it had to be nearly five in the morning. Had to be.

Ten hours and counting.

But even as he congratulated himself for narrowing down the time, he realized one little fact that made his blood run cold.

He could be halfway to Fort Benton in ten hours.

Reaching Fort Benton and investigating Thomas Francis Meagher ought to be his goals. Seeing Sabrina again ought to be the last thing he wanted to do. If she was as sweet and innocent as she seemed, well, she'd be better off if he simply disappeared. If she was somehow trying to sabotage his investigation, leaving right now would seriously damage her plans. She'd be sitting in Maisie Stewart's house, twiddling her thumbs until three o'clock, expecting him to show up with hat in hand. By the time she realized he wasn't coming, he'd have an insurmountable head start.

No army captain worth his salt would pass on taking advantage of such a miscalculation in the enemy's thinking. The trouble was, he couldn't quite place Sabrina in the role of enemy, when every time he conjured up the image of her face he remembered her smiling at him, calling him *my lord*.

At the mere thought of leaving, his legs started shaking, as if he'd already run too far and they refused to take him one step farther.

He couldn't leave. He groped for reasons why he had to stay. To investigate Sabrina? His conscience wouldn't accept that. To simply luxuriate in the sight of her once more, to feel her warmth like a balm against a heart that been cold for far too long? His mind refused to consider that possibility. There had to be another reason for his lingering. He started pacing in the hopes that movement might clear his head, and he felt something hard and heavy thump against his thigh.

Her diamond, still stuffed into his pocket. He didn't know why he kept forgetting about the damned thing.

He smiled. That was why he couldn't leave. He had to return the diamond. And receive payment from her for the damage to his inventory.

Yes, that was the reason why he whistled a few bars of music on the way back to the wagon. She owed him money.

Chapter Six

Sabrina squirmed, but the cursed punishment garment did not relent at all. Darting a quick sidelong glance that told her Maisie's head was bent close to her sewing, she stole a hand toward her side and tried to insert her thumb between the tightly laced stays and her skin.

Maisie never raised her eyes, and yet she'd somehow noticed Sabrina's lapse.

"Stop fooling with your corset, Sabrina."

"I do not like it."

"I know you don't. None of us women like them."

"I like . . . my former dress."

"I told you—that skimpy shift ain't a dress, honey; it's underwear. It ain't proper for ladies to go about in their underwear, especially without a corset. You'll get used to dressing right."

Maisie had been promising her the same thing for three days now. Dragging, tedious days that ultimately passed, with no lessening of Sabrina's hatred of the corset. The wretched device exacted a horrid toll upon a woman's breathing, especially when Neil made his daily appearance on Maisie's doorstep. All air seemed to deflate from Sabrina's chest during the one brief glimpse of Neil she was permitted before Maisie slammed the door closed on him. Afterward, she always felt unaccountably weepy, which made it even more difficult to regain the calm, even breathing that was the mark of a true lady.

Her mother had taught her that maintaining an outward calm served to guard her weaknesses from her enemies. Maisie agreed in a way, saying that getting all flustered and breathless while a fellow was around led that fellow to believe he'd won the war without a fight.

Despite their wisdom, they differed greatly when it came to the deference a woman must show a man. Sabrina's mother had taught her always to bow her head in acceptance, to bite her tongue against anger, to close her eyes and think pleasant thoughts when the man to whom she was given exercised his bed rights upon her.

Maisie believed women had been placed upon the earth for the sole purpose of tormenting men into confusion.

Maisie believed men secretly enjoyed this sort of disrespect. That they found playful teasing to be . . . fun.

Maisie, despite her great age, blushed with remembered passions when whispering that wondrous pleasure awaited in bed for two people who had learned how to tease and torment each other into laughter.

Men and women enjoying each other . . . the concept would have struck Sabrina as impossible a week earlier. Now she had had the experience of working side by side with Neil for a mutual purpose. She had felt his hands, strong and commanding and yet gentle upon her, a touch that had roused a stirring in her middle that told her the pleasure she'd taken in his casual touches was but a hint of what could explode between them.

Save that she belonged to another man. The Irish champion. And Neil swore he was not that champion.

Save also that Maisie refused to allow Neil into the house, and Sabrina could not see how she might tease and torment him if he was ever on the outside while she was held trapped within, bound up in a corset.

"Will you permit Neil to visit today, Maisie?"

"Depends on him."

"He knocks promptly at three each day."

"Promptness don't count. I'm looking for signs that he's developed the proper respect for you."

Sabrina sighed inwardly. Maisie often mentioned this proper respect, as if she had somehow divined that Sabrina was royal by birth. She seemed singularly blinded toward Neil's royal qualities.

"If you allowed him to enter, he might make a formal bow, or some other sign of courtesy."

"I ain't talking about bowing and scraping, honey. I expect him to show up with his hair all neat and proper and his clothes brushed. He can approach the door like a gentleman instead of stomping up onto the stoop like a wild man. I expect him to greet me like I'm his long-lost grandma instead of his worst enemy. I expect him to spout pretty phrases to you and promise to treat you right. Someone has to teach that man a lesson, and it looks like I'm the one for the job."

"Oh, yes, you are, Maisie. You are an excellent teacher. But—" She bit her lip, hesitant to challenge her mentor.

"But what?"

"Could he not learn his lesson while I learn mine? Can you not teach both of us together, Maisie?"

Maisie chuckled. "Honey, there's a world of difference between what you need to know and what Mr. Neil Kenyon needs to learn. I don't know how he managed to get as far as he has in this world without getting himself killed. That man's hard to understand."

Sabrina knew that to be true. She had understood very little of the things Neil had said to her. Her degree of understanding would be much greater now.

"I have made great strides in English," she said.

"Indeed you have. I told you I'd have you chattering like a magpie in a couple of days. Boy, won't he be surprised."

"I can discourse at length with Neil." Sabrina gripped her hands together while pleasure flashed through her at the idea. Between Maisie's ceaseless chatter and truly inspired instruction, Sabrina felt comfortable with the English language. Her comprehension of the tongue, though it fell short of mastery, filled her with a sense of accomplishment unlike any she'd known before. English had brought her a friend in Maisie. English would allow her to discourse with Neil.

Or so she hoped.

She missed him with an intensity she found perplexing. She'd known him for less than the space of one day. She'd been apart from him for three times as long. It made no sense that she should yearn for him so.

The small mantel clock commenced the whirring sound that always preceded the chiming of the new hour. Maisie glanced toward the door. The clock tolled at precisely the moment a hard thump sounded against the door: a single, authoritative thump, not at all like the manic pounding that had occurred on previous days at exactly three o'clock.

"Well, what do you know about that."

With a broad smile creasing her face, Maisie set aside her sewing and went to the door. She opened it the merest crack, took one quick peek, and slammed it shut again. She gave forth a most unladylike whoop and spun about to face Sabrina.

"I think Mr. Neil Kenyon finally got the rules through

his thick head." Pure, gloating delight radiated from her. "Get ready to visit with your gentleman caller."

Sabrina's breath deserted her once again as Maisie swung open the door far, far wider than she'd ever done before.

"Well, looky who's here." Maisie feigned surprise. She stepped aside, permitting Neil to step into the room. He entered, seeming to draw with him the freshness and sunshine that Sabrina had missed so sorely.

He swept off his black hat.

Sabrina pressed her fist to her mouth, but not quickly enough to stifle a cry of dismay.

His hair, his glorious warm honey brown hair, no longer brushed against his shoulders in a wild tangle that manifested his virility. Someone had poured oil over his head and worked it through each strand until his hair clung to his skull like a helm.

And his mustache—oh, how she had secretly admired its lush fullness! It had been scraped away.

There was, however, something rather compelling about the firm, finely shaped lip now bared for her regard.

"My lo—" she began, but gulped and bit off the greeting when Maisie glared at her. Sabrina sent her a quick nod, grateful for the reminder.

"I must remember that you are not to be addressed as 'my lord,' " she explained.

"Why not?"

Even as something warm coursed through her at hearing his voice again, she fancied disappointment weighed his remark.

" 'Tis but one of many useful things I have learned. Maisie warned that calling you such could bring about a terrible, debilitating indisposition."

"Do tell." He glowered at Maisie. "And what awful thing might happen to me?"

"I scarcely dare speak of it. 'Tis too horrible to contemplate."

"I insist."

"Very well." She drew a deep breath. "If I persist in calling you 'my lord,' you might experience a swelling of the head so profound that you would find it difficult to walk through doorways."

Maisie let forth with an unrefined snort and a hiccoughing giggle. Her ill-placed humor startled Sabrina, considering how adamant the woman had been when warning her of the danger.

Neil stiffened, and his jaw dropped agape, proving that he, at least, respected the danger. She longed to run to him, to touch him, to reassure herself that he had not been harmed by having his head dipped in oil. But her friend and mentor had instructed her to remain seated, explaining that doing so was what Neil would expect.

And so it seemed. He cast a furious glare at Maisie. "You've certainly taught her well. What else do I have to look forward to?"

"Why don't you show your respects to the lady, and then we'll see."

He stalked across the room and came to stand right before Sabrina.

He wore his black executioner's garb, but the sight of it did not frighten Sabrina as it had at first—she was far too anxious to study each inch of him. She'd known he stood tall and broad of shoulder, but here in this small room he seemed larger than she'd remembered. More perfectly made. More noble and strong than any man. The very image of a champion, save for his stout denials.

She lifted her hand as she had been taught, and he caught it in his. His long fingers closed around hers. He bent from the waist, treated her to an enigmatic smile, and brushed his lips against her skin, exactly as Maisie had foretold he would do.

But Maisie had not prepared her for the sensations that would accompany the gesture. Soft, yet firm. Hot. A hint of roughness when the newly shaven place rasped over her knuckles. A tingling shot through her from the place touched by his lips, striking deep within.

Her breathing, already restricted by the corset and the excitement at seeing him again, grew even more labored. She struggled to make the quick, shallow gasps that Maisie swore ladies survived upon.

"What the hell? You're not going to cry, are you?"

Better he mistake her agitation for tears than for what it was—an unseemly weakness springing from his touch. And yet her pride would not permit him to think her a sobber.

"A Desmond woman does not cry."

"Desmond woman?"

His hold upon her tightened and he pulled her to her feet. The sudden motion, the proximity to him, made her sway on her feet, and he placed a steadying hand at her back. And then he let go of her, as if he'd touched iron still red-hot from the smith's forge rather than her own tightly bound self. Deprived of his strength, she flopped back down into her seat.

"You trussed her up in one of those damned corsets," he accused Maisie. "No wonder she turned sick. Look at her—she's about ready to keel over."

The old woman rose to her toes in agitation. "I'm thinking there's plenty of good reasons why she clams up and shakes like a leaf when you're around. Don't you have something nice to say to her instead of yelling your fool head off like you do all the time?"

"I don't yell all the time."

"Humpf."

Neil slanted a glance toward Sabrina. "I don't yell all the time, do I?"

Sabrina sent a prayer of thanksgiving to the Lord. Neil had presented her with the perfect opportunity to show him how well she'd improved in her understanding of his speech.

"Yes, you do."

His mouth dropped open, accompanied by a quick motion of his head, as if unable to credit her words. Perhaps she'd failed to show the proper appreciation of his kingly shouting. Men placed great store in such things.

"You are most . . . vehement in all your words and deeds, my lord." Maisie clucked her tongue in disapproval. Sabrina knew a moment's panic, but Neil's head remained the same size. She would guard her tongue more carefully in the future. "You . . . you could rival a bull in the fierceness of your aspect. Wolves would slink away in fear at the way the earth quivers beneath your angry stride. Your enemies must fear the narrowing of your eyes, the focusing of your regard, more than any rabbit fears the attention of a hawk. You are a terrible, frightening man, and . . . and you yell all the time."

She gazed modestly down at her clasped hands, knowing that, except for the single *my lord,* she'd done exceptionally well. Especially there at the end. Maisie had schooled her in the social arts, explaining that in the presence of others, a lady always said things to reflect well upon the gentleman, and that she should always return the conversation to the topic raised by the gentleman.

"So that's it," Neil said, a dreadful calm replacing his usual bluster. "That's what you think of me."

An odd fluttering began within Sabrina. She'd made a mistake in some way, and did not know what it was or how to rectify it.

Neil stared at her, pain and disbelief darkening his eyes.

She smiled at him. She nodded. She did not know what else to do.

"I told you," said Maisie. "I told you to come prepared to spout some sweet words and pretty phrases."

"Well, I've never been a man who found much use for words."

"Maybe it's time you tried." Maisie gave him a little push. "Go on, say something nice to her."

He scowled down at his boots for a moment, and then brought his head up with a quick snap. "That dress doesn't look too bad on you. I liked your other one better, though."

"As did I," Sabrina agreed.

His shoulders straightened, and the hint of a smile played around his lips.

"I like your hair loose, but wearing it piled up on your head like that sort of shows off your face a little better. I didn't realize you had such a long, skinny neck."

Some women might be dismayed at hearing a man garbed as an executioner discuss the merits of one's neck, but Sabrina felt a small blossoming of warmth. He seemed pleased by her physical attributes, especially those he had not seen. Now, encased as she was in the cursed corset, there was even less of her available for his regard.

Maisie had taught her that a smart woman always gave a man some hints to let him know what he was missing. Trying not to appear too obvious, she angled her shoulders and thrust out her chest.

"Is that damned corset hurting you?"

Perhaps her hint had been too subtle.

"I have breasts," she offered.

"Uh, so you do." His gaze did not linger upon them, though. Perhaps he thought them unworthy of his regard. Maisie had assured her that her breasts were among her greatest assets, and there could be only one reason why he failed to notice.

"They are not so small or flattened as this corset makes them appear."

His face reddened. "They're just about the right size and shape, I'd say."

"Okay, that's enough for one visit." Maisie wedged herself between Sabrina and Neil, and pushed at Neil's chest. "Lordy, but you two are pitiful. Just pitiful. You get on out of here and come back tomorrow."

"No." He ignored Maisie's poking. He set his feet apart, the width of his shoulders, planting himself firmly in place. "I'm not leaving unless she comes with me."

"Well, why don't you shut up for a minute and recall the topic of your recent conversation."

He paled.

"This little gal doesn't exactly understand the significance of what she's saying. Unless you plan to stand guard over her every minute of every day, there's no telling what sort of trouble she'll get herself into."

"Some men could mistake her innocence for . . . for an invitation."

"Uh-huh." Maisie seemed pleased by his dismay.

Not so Sabrina. She decided she hated this new, quiet Neil; she much preferred the loud, yelling tyrant. She wished he would grasp her with the fierceness of a hawk. She wished he would confront Maisie with the determination of a starving wolf intent upon bearing her into his den.

Anything, anything but the suddenly faraway cast in his expression, as if he'd already taken his leave of her and would see her no more.

Her heart thudded an alarm, making it even more difficult to breathe. If he left her, she might never find the answer to the mystery of why she had been sent to this world gone impossibly strange. She might be held prisoner forever in this house with Maisie, when she must needs be proving her worth as the chosen Desmond woman.

Neil and Maisie were whispering, their heads together, plotting her fate without her consent.

Everything was going wrong. And she had tried so hard to make it right.

Desmond women did not cry. But, at times, maintaining a tearless state demanded a great deal of willpower.

She stood, and even that was wrong. The corset bound tighter about her ribs. The room seemed to dim, as if a mist had seeped through the walls. It affected the colors, turning everything dull and dark. It affected the sound, muffling even the ticking clock in silence so that naught but the overwrought pounding of her heart drummed against her ears.

She took one step toward Neil, and then another, but her feet seemed mired in bog, for no matter how she struggled, she could not get close enough to touch him.

She could not breathe. She could not see. She could not hear. She had failed in her duty. And Neil was leaving her behind.

Her knees buckled.

She swayed, proud and elegant, like a lily lifting its head above a bed of dandelions, and then she started to go down.

Neil moved faster than ever before in his life, and caught her before she hit the floor. His sudden lunge threw him off balance, though, and he ended up flat on his back on the floor, with Sabrina a light burden on top of him.

His hand went immediately to the side of her neck and found a reassuring pulse. Her breath came in quick, shallow pants. She'd fainted, pure and simple. His own heart rate slowed while relief flooded through him, and then it picked up again when he realized his position.

Flat on his back again, because of Sabrina. Too bad pleasure wasn't involved. Couldn't be involved. Would never be involved.

"She all right?" Maisie blinked down at him, her eyes owlish behind her spectacles. "You didn't hurt her, did you?"

"Yes, I'm fine, too. Thank you for your concern," said Neil. He angled himself up, carefully balancing Sabrina in his arms. "Back of my head doesn't hurt at all from cracking against your table."

"Your head hit my table? Goodness, I'd better check to see whether you broke it. New furniture ain't so easy to come by out here on the frontier."

"Get some cool water and a cloth for her forehead while you're at it."

He carried her to the sofa. He ought to lay her there and fan her with a handkerchief or something until she revived. The hell with that. He'd taken a tumble himself and his legs still weren't all that steady. Imagining what might have happened if her head had hit the table during a dead faint sapped his strength even more.

He settled onto the sofa himself and held her across his lap, her head nestled in the crook of his arm. He thumbed open the line of buttons running from her neck to her waist. He worked his way around her back, trying to ignore the way her breasts pushed against the corset, trying to forget what she'd said about them being larger and fuller than they appeared.

He found a cord and tugged, and then wrenched apart the crossed strings until he loosened the wretched garment. Her lungs expanded. So did her breasts.

It didn't seem right to be staring so blatantly at her charms while she lay unconscious. So he pulled her closer.

Pressed her tight against his chest and then had to bite back a gasp when her soft flesh yielded against his. He rested his chin against the top of her head, and somehow dislodged one of the pins that held her hair in place. The burnished tresses slipped free, silky strand by silky strand, until the fragrant cloud of her hair wrapped around them both.

She stirred, and he reluctantly opened his embrace to let her free.

"Neil?" She blinked up at him. Confusion clouded her eyes.

"Sshhh. Don't worry."

"You must think me weak. I am not. Never in my life have I done something so embarrassing."

"It's okay. Everything will be okay."

"Everything?"

"I'll make sure of it."

"You will?" A brilliant smile curved her lips. "Have you changed your mind? Are you the champion?"

"I'm no champion, sweetheart. You have to believe me on that."

Her joy faded. She turned her head, and her hand went to her temple when her hair slid across her face. She took a deep breath, and then another.

"I can now breathe."

"You don't need a corset."

"That is what I have told Maisie. She insists ladies must bind themselves in such a fashion."

"You're wrong about some things. Like when you keep trying to make me into a champion. But you're not wrong about the corset."

"Oh. Am I wrong to think you mean to leave me here in this new prison?"

He'd never looked at this arrangement from her point of view. He'd handed her over to Maisie without her consent. He couldn't blame her for thinking herself in prison, considering the corset.

"This isn't a prison, Sabrina."

She shook her head. "I prefer to be with you."

Something within him gloried at knowing she'd choose riding in a comfortless medicine wagon with him over the simple but abundant luxuries offered by Mrs. Stewart's home. Only for a moment, though, before his instincts whispered that she might have another reason for wanting to stay with him.

He should stand, he knew, because it wasn't proper to sit there and hold her with her blouse gaping open. He ought to let her regain her bearings while he gathered together whatever remnants of common sense he had left. She didn't seem to be aware of the pounding in his loins, the hard stab of desire that had risen in response to the feel of her, the weight of her, the way her voice resonated inside him.

He ought to move away from her, but if he did then for sure that old witch Maisie Stewart would take one look at him and see the evidence of how Sabrina affected him.

There was only one way to cool his ardor—to explore his suspicions about any ties she might have to Meagher. This was the time to do it, while her head was a little awhirl, while she'd lowered the usual caution she showed around him.

"Speaking of prisons—did you ever hear the story about how Thomas Francis Meagher escaped from a Tasmanian prison?" He watched carefully, judging her reaction. A Meagher supporter would know all the details of the man's life. But he could tell by the quick spark of interest that flared through her that she was hearing this information for the first time.

"No. Is it such a difficult feat?"

"Mmm-hmm. You see, Tasmania is way over in Australia.

The English queen had sentenced our dear Thomas to death because of his crimes against the English Crown."

"He fought English rule?" She straightened with interest. He missed her weight against his arm. It wouldn't do to allow himself to grow accustomed to feeling her next to him, so he just moved farther away from her.

"The Irish kicked up such a fuss that she changed the sentence to deportation to Australia, instead."

"The Irish admire him."

Excitement glittered like wildfire in her eyes, and Neil began wishing he'd never brought up the subject of Meagher. He decided he didn't need to tell her any more—it was apparent she didn't know these little tidbits about Meagher's heroics, and he couldn't imagine a single reason in the world why he should be holding her in his arms while regaling her with the exploits of another man.

"Thomas Meagher is the champion," she declared.

"No."

"He must be."

"No."

She closed her eyes and trembled. "Then my worst fear has come true. Robert is the true champion."

Robert? Who the hell was Robert? Someone she despised, judging by her expression. Since she seemed so all-fired determined to call *someone* a champion, it might as well be this mysterious Robert. Better someone she hated than Meagher.

Better anyone than himself.

"Maybe it's Robert," he said.

"Oh." She bit her lip and seemed to deflate.

"Well, who cares about Robert?" interrupted Maisie. "Tell her the rest about Governor Meagher."

"Nothing left to tell. And he was only acting governor for a while. The real governor's back in the territory now."

"Humpf. Then I'll tell her. The Irish ain't the only ones who admire General Meagher—"

"Mr. Meagher," Neil interrupted, annoyed that she'd given the man yet another title he didn't deserve. "He's not in the army anymore."

"He's not this anymore, he's not that anymore. He'll always be a governor and a general to me. Us Montana folks are right fond of him. Proud to have such a hero in our midst. I hear tell he had to swim two thousand miles in an ice-cold ocean after breaking out of that Tasmanian prison."

"No man could survive a two-thousand-mile swim. He didn't swim more than a couple hundred."

"That's about a hundred ninety-nine and three-quarters more miles than I care to swim. How about you, Mr. Kenyon? You ever swum that far?"

"No call to."

"More likely you ain't that good of a swimmer."

All this talk of swimming served the purpose of dousing his passions just as well as if he'd taken a dip in an ice-cold pond. He slid Sabrina off his lap and stood. She lay back on the sofa, her blouse gaping open, the curves of her breasts peeking over the edge of her corset, her hair a tangled invitation trailing to her waist. Her spirits seemed to have perked up considerably while listening to Maisie extoll Meagher's swimming stamina, as if that meant anything at all in Montana.

"You are sure Thomas Meagher is not the champion?" she asked, her question filled with wistful hope.

"Not a chance."

"Robert." She slumped.

"You can ask him the next time you see him," he said.

"I think you were on your way out of here," Maisie reminded him. "Alone."

A soft whimper of denial from Sabrina drew his attention

back to the sofa. The desire he'd thought he'd squelched roared back into insistent life.

And just as he'd feared, Maisie noticed.

She looked pointedly at his crotch and then rolled her eyes skyward.

"Now, I wasn't born yesterday, mister. I know you two aren't married. She seems to think she needs to stay with you to bring about some higher purpose. Don't know how you managed to convince her of that. Have you asked yourself what's going to happen to her when you get tired of slippin' twixt her sheets? Let me have a few more days to drum some sense into her head; then she'll be able to fend for herself when you decide to abandon her."

Neil rubbed one large hand over his face, and then raked his fingers through his hair, raising spikes amid the slicked-down strands. "You're right," he muttered. "I don't know what I was thinking. I never think straight around her. I can't take her with me."

Maisie nudged him toward the door. "You can leave her with me right now, if you want, and ride right out of here," she said, very quietly. "Folks here'll just think you deserted her. I won't breathe a word about her never being married to you. I'll see to it that she can shift for herself."

"Maybe that would be the best thing."

Maisie gave Neil an approving pat on his arm, as if he'd done something that increased his estimation in her eyes.

"You'd better be sure about this. Once you walk through that door, you're settin' her loose to get on with her life. If I catch you sniffing around her again, well, let me just say that I'm a pretty fair shot, and I tend to aim low."

"I'll roll out of town before dawn."

He figured he'd better aim straight for the outdoors without a backward glance. Otherwise, he didn't know how he'd walk away from her. If he didn't look back, nothing could stop him.

"My lord!"

That stopped him.

He kept his body facing front and allowed himself only a partial glance over his shoulder. She'd sat bolt upright. her hands gripped in her lap, her face white with terror.

"Strange things abound in this place." Her voice trembled. "Cookstoves. Daguerreotypes. Kerosene lamps. Glass everywhere."

"See what I mean?" Maisie tugged at his sleeve. "Say something to ease her mind."

"Now, Sabrina, none of those things are strange. It's just that . . . well, you haven't been here for long. You aren't settled in yet. This is a real nice place."

Her lip trembled. Her pallor faded even more, and something wild and frightened skittered through her, telling him that she might understand very well the confusion and uncertainty that came over him in her presence. And then her chin tilted up. He remembered how she'd claimed to be strong, and in that moment he realized the full extent of her strength.

"I . . . I prefer my other dress."

He couldn't answer her.

"Maisie is a very good teacher, Neil. Mayhap . . . perhaps she can teach you a lesson."

"She already has, sweetheart. She already has."

Maisie thumped him on the arm. "Here's your lesson again, in case you're tempted to forget—I aim low, and always hit what I'm after."

He clapped his hat onto his head.

"Neil." Sabrina swallowed hard. "Corsets."

He stepped out onto the stoop, and then sent one arm snaking back into the room. But only to grasp the edge of the door and pull it closed behind him, before he could give in to the urge to grab her and bring her with him.

Chapter Seven

Maisie's threats didn't scare him.

Neil studied the terrain between his hiding place and the tree that sat closest to the old woman's house. In fact, her warning about deliberately aiming low bothered him so little that he would walk right up to her door bold as you please, knock, and demand entry—except he didn't want Maisie to get into any trouble.

She didn't know he was an army officer. She didn't know that taking potshots at any of his parts, high or low, could land her in jail.

He had to see Sabrina for one minute, maybe less. He could be in and out of her room, mission accomplished, faster than he could explain to Maisie why he had to break his word about seeing Sabrina again.

The diamond. He'd forgotten all about the damned stone again. There was something weird about that diamond. The whole necklace weighed no more than a few ounces, no heavier than a couple of silver dollars. Maybe that was why he so often forgot about it.

He wasn't the type of man who forgot his obligations. He'd had ample opportunity to return the necklace to Sabrina. He would have thought that when he was with her, he'd remember how beautiful the diamond had looked glittering against her breasts. Instead, when he was with her, he didn't just forget that her diamond was in his pocket; he totally forgot the danged thing even existed. He might as well be carrying a single feather in his pocket for all that it troubled him.

But as soon as he left her, his thoughts centered on returning it to her, to the exclusion of all else.

He almost shook with the need to see her and personally slip the necklace over her head, as if some mysterious force had zoomed out of the sky like a lightning bolt and seared the idea onto his brain.

During those times, he'd swear the necklace weighed at least ten pounds. His pocket bulged. His pants hung so low on his hip that he feared they might drop.

Made no sense at all.

Just like his still being here in Bamper made no sense. He'd promised Maisie he'd clear out of the settlement. He didn't relish confronting the old woman. Doing so would only result in a long and frustrating admission that he'd confiscated such a valuable gem because Sabrina owed him a few dollars.

Getting past Maisie would take far too long, especially now, since it was well after midnight. Maisie'd probably get so annoyed that she *would* start shooting, which would wake half the town, including the person who'd threatened to shoot him the other morning if he didn't stop making a ruckus in the dark.

The weather seemed to favor his taking the indirect approach. The weak sliver of moonlight provided next to no illumination, and slow-moving clouds dimmed that scant light from time to time. No doubt about it, it made perfect sense to sneak across these few feet of open ground and up into that nice, spreading oak, and then shimmy across the branch that almost touched the window of Sabrina's room.

The old bat hadn't thought about shuttering the second-floor windows.

He noted an approaching cluster of scudding clouds that would darken the night even more. But before the clouds blotted the faint silver sliver of moon, he spotted a movement from inside the window. Maisie must have realized her lapse in security.

He hunkered back, disappointed, and then bolted upright when the figure dove through the window and landed on the very branch he'd marked for himself.

Whoever had done such a stupid thing gave a small cry of distress: purely female, purely terrified. And no wonder—her grip was none too steady. She'd landed amid the leafy, fragile new growth rather than on the sturdy main branch. The branch dipped, groaning ominously, while the limb leaper thrashed to gain a more secure hold, making things even worse. Her slim torso twisted, and he recognized the silhouette.

Just as he'd feared. Sabrina.

He surged from his hiding place. The limb hung twelve feet above the ground—not all that high, if she were only paying attention to the danger. A well-planned drop would land her on her feet, no worse for the wear. But a panicked, out-of-balance fall could result in a broken neck. Something inside him clenched, hurting, at the thought of Sabrina lying in a lifeless heap beneath that tree.

He'd run across the fields of Gettysburg while bullets whizzed past his head and plowed into the earth at his feet. The sprint from shadows to Sabrina seemed to take longer than his most hellish charge.

She maintained the barest hold on the branch by the time he skidded to a halt right under her.

"Don't panic, sweetheart," he called. "Hold on tight as you can, and swing your legs down. I'll grab on to you, and you can let go."

She always drew away when he touched her, holding herself aloof as if she were some kind of queen and he an uppity peasant. She grew still, which was probably the best thing that she could do in this circumstance, and he prayed it wasn't because she intended to cringe away from him now.

"Will you catch me, Neil? Will you hold me safe?"

"I will," he vowed, even though he'd sworn he'd never make such promises to a woman ever again.

She didn't pay the least bit of attention to what he'd told her to do. She simply gave him a quick nod and let go, trusting him completely.

He caught her in his arms, along with a shower of leaves and broken twigs. She was soft and smooth in her reddish brown shift, uncorseted, her feet encased in her ridiculous delicate slippers. Her hair, freed from its upswept style, drifted over him in a weightless embrace.

"What in the hell did you think you were doing?"

Now that she was safe in his arms, anger at the risk she'd taken surged through him.

"Shh." She pressed her fingers to his lips. She smelled of crushed green leaves, of tree sap, of woman. "Maisie will hear."

"I don't care. Don't you know how stupid—"

"Neil!" She pinched his lips together. "She has made the most dire threats against your person."

"I heard," he mumbled.

"Not the whole of her plans. She said she gave you 'the

polite society version.' To me she explained the gelding process in great detail." Sabrina closed her eyes and shuddered. "You would not enjoy it."

"I guess not," he admitted, although with the way his body reacted to holding her, gelding might be the only solution that offered any peace. "Listen, we have to talk. Just for a minute or two. I'm going to carry you to the wagon so we're not overheard."

"I can walk. I did not injure myself."

"Those shoes of yours aren't worth a damn outside the house. I'll carry you."

"All right." She sighed, and settled back in the crook of his arm. "But move quickly. I cannot spare much time to talk with you."

He wondered where she'd been headed in the middle of the night that had her in such an all-fired hurry to get there. To the mysterious Robert, probably. He decided it was none of his business. That didn't stop the slow burn of envy.

"I don't have time to talk, either. And besides, I don't have much to say."

With each step her bottom bounced against his belly, making him wish he'd ignored the flimsiness of her shoes. He couldn't very well put her down without a good reason, and he couldn't think straight enough to manufacture a good reason. Seemed as if there was nothing to do to distract himself from the way she felt except to talk.

The only subject that came to mind was his curiosity about what brought her out.

"There's not a whole lot to do after midnight in Bamper unless you came out looking for me."

"I did not know you would be here. Maisie told me you had left without me."

"I should have left hours ago."

"But you did not." He couldn't tell for sure, but he thought she might be smiling a little.

"I was just getting ready to leave."

"So was I."

"Now we're back to where we started. Where did you think you were going? Were you going to try catching up to me?" The notion pleased him, even if he would've had to waste time by bringing her back.

"Oh, no, I had no intention of looking for you. I had to make my escape while Maisie sleeps. She is very kind, but I can no longer postpone my duty. I must find Robert."

His suspicion had been right.

"Robert? Who the hell is Robert?" He came to a halt and his arms closed around her a little more tightly. She reached up and placed her finger against his lips again.

"You are yelling again, my lord."

He swallowed a curse, firmed up his grip on her, and forged once more toward the wagon. She settled back in his arms.

"Robert is the champion. You told me so yourself."

He remembered halfheartedly going along with that theory in the interest of drawing her attention away from Meagher and his own lack of championship qualities.

"I assume you know somebody named Robert and how to find him."

"I do know him." She offered no additional information, and Neil decided he wasn't interested enough to ask.

He had to set her down so she could climb up onto the seat. Watching her from such close proximity was a bad idea, giving him as it did such an eyeful of the way her waist curved, her hips flared, as the thin shift molded itself to long legs while she climbed.

He cursed to himself a little more as he stalked around the wagon to his own side. He would give her the diamond, wish her well, and send her on her search for this mysterious Robert, that was what he would do.

Diamond, good luck, good-bye. That sounded right.

Diamond, good luck, good-bye.

He levered himself up onto his seat while he ran over his plan once more in his mind. *Diamond, good luck, good-bye.* No need to waste a single word on any other topic.

"Who the hell is Robert?" he asked as soon as his butt hit the bench.

"My husband."

"You're married?" His voice rasped a little from the effort of holding it back to a mild roar.

"I . . . I am not certain." But before Neil could comprehend why her statement filled him with relief, she baffled him again. "The last thing I remember before waking in your prison chamber was my grievous error in clasping the Druid's Tear round my neck. Robert must have heard my sacrilegious prayer begging to be freed of my betrothal to him. He must have given me over to you for punishment. My parents do not hold me in much esteem, but I know they would not give me over to Robert without benefit of vows. So I assume I am married, although I do not remember the vow making . . . or the aftermath."

His head swam. She spoke in perfectly intelligible English, but he couldn't seem to comprehend the meaning of what she said any better than if she had reverted to that ancient-sounding chanting she'd favored before.

"The aftermath?"

She slid an embarrassed glance at him, and though it was difficult to tell beneath moonlight, he thought she blushed.

"Robert made no secret of his lusts. First, he coveted my lands. Second, he coveted my body. To gain the lands, he must needs wed me. Once I belonged to him, he could do as he pleased with my body. I know Robert of Allingham well enough to be certain he would not have wed me and discarded me without first claiming what was his by right of law. Only after his lusts were slaked would he hand me over to you for punishment."

"You're not making any sense," Neil said, while he seethed with hatred and envy for Robert. "You were not handed over to me for punishment."

"Then why was I given to you?"

"You weren't *given* to me for anything. You showed up all on your own, without any help from anyone."

"No, my lord, I did not. I awoke in the dark black of your cell, and knew not where I was until you set me free. Though, truth to tell, I still do not know where I am."

He didn't like being reminded of how frightened she'd been during that first day.

"Sabrina, my wagon is not a prison. It's a simple patent medicine vehicle. I spent every last cent I possess to buy it as a cover for my assignment, and once I'm finished, I'm going to sell it to regain my nest egg. So don't go calling it a prison wagon—someone's bound to overhear and it could affect the value."

"I was right," she said. "So much glass—an entire kingdom's wealth. Which country do you rule, Neil? I have never heard of a king traveling about the way you do."

"I'm not a king; I'm an army captain. Or at least I'm an army captain for the next few weeks." He was straying onto dangerous ground here in telling her more than she needed to know. As usual, she was making his head spin with confusion. What was unusual was his maddening tendency to talk nonstop to her. Always before, when confronted with a predicament, he'd shut up tighter than a bank vault.

"Listen to me. I'm not a champion. I'm not a king. This wagon is not a prison. Nobody gave you to me. This Robert you're talking about sounds like a world-class idiot who doesn't deserve to touch the hem of your gown, let alone be married to you."

"You agreed he was the champion."

"I lied."

"Oh, no. You would not lie to me."

Total trust shone from her. It did something strange to his heart.

"I just said he was the champion to make you feel better. You seemed so determined to pin the title on someone. I figured, better him than . . . than your other choices."

Her mouth dropped in dismay. "You mean . . . you mean you really do not know the identity of the champion?"

"Not only do I not know the champion's identity—I also have no idea why in the hell you're so set on finding one."

"To fulfill the legend."

"What legend?"

"The legend of the Druid's Tear."

Her diamond. He'd forgotten all about it again. He resolved to remember to give it to her the minute he got to the bottom of this little mystery. He patted his pocket, making sure it was still there.

"I don't know the legend."

"A Desmond woman who wears the Druid's Tear will bring the true Irish champion home to her people. He will rally their spirit, strengthen their might, so they might hold steady against the English."

Her voice rang with sincerity. Her whole body thrummed with purpose.

"That's one hell of a delusion," he said. "You have an extraordinary imagination."

"I merely tell you the truth."

"You have to be crazy to think one woman and one man can save a whole country."

"Not any woman and man. The chosen Desmond woman, and her champion."

"Sweetheart, you don't really believe that. Somehow you have real life mixed up with one of those ancient myths."

"Not a myth. A legend. And it says—"

"I don't care what the legend says," he cut in while anger and agony surged through him. "It doesn't matter how much a man loves his country, or how he dedicates his life to serving it—when brother fights against brother, both sides lose. Nobody wins when the defeated continue to hate the winners, or when the winners laugh down their noses at the losers. War doesn't end when the generals sign a surrender—it drags on for years and years, while people starve and can't find work. The soldiers who fought, believing they were right, start to question themselves when they have to look people in the eye and know they're responsible for killing the ones they loved."

"You speak with great familiarity of such matters, Neil."

He'd never spoken of these things to anyone. Never revealed the raw hurt that still ached inside; never admitted out loud that he held it a personal failure that the country he loved had been whacked by bloody war. He knew, at some level, that his belief made no sense. Nor did it make sense that he couldn't seem to stop blurting out his agony, now that she'd gotten him started.

"I understand well enough that I can ask you this: Do you realize what you expect of this champion? You want him to urge men into battle, men who will look up to him and place all their trust and faith in him. He will know this, and it will tear him apart inside because he knows a certain number of them will die, a certain number will be crippled for life, a certain number will emerge apparently whole, but lost in a strange world of nightmares. You want him to stand for a concept that might not be able to survive, no matter how hard he fights to hold it together. You want him to tear his heart in two, and trample his spirit into the dust, and end his days knowing that his best wasn't good enough."

"Whatever he gives of himself will come back a hundred-fold."

"Won't matter much to him if there's nothing of himself left to accept it."

Her eyes, wide and stricken, brimmed with the tears she said she never shed. "No woman could ask so much of the man she loves."

He laughed, short and bitter. "Oh, she could ask. A man in love will do just about anything his woman asks."

"I asked you. Many times. You always say you cannot be my champion."

His heart did an odd flop. "We're not in love."

"Aye." She subsided against him, her head resting against his shoulder.

Since she seemed kind of depressed, he put his arm around her waist and tucked her close.

"Then it is fortunate indeed that I am married to Robert. I will not be so very distressed if he destroys himself in the fight to salvage the Irish spirit."

"Maybe you are really married to the man, then, considering your opinion of him."

" 'Twould be a simple matter to determine. You could examine me."

Apprehension curled within him. Those old feelings he'd stirred up ought to have haunted him for hours. Instead, with four words, *you could examine me*, she'd banished the melancholy, filling him instead with dread.

"What do you mean, examine you?"

"I have been told that learned men can determine whether or not a woman is a virgin. Would you perchance be trained in such a skill, Neil?"

Now it was his turn to blush beneath the cover of moonlight. His conversations with her had the tendency to throw his brain into a tailspin, until he couldn't stop himself from blurting out the most ridiculous things, but she had him beat. Maisie hadn't exaggerated when she'd claimed Sabrina's words would get her in trouble someday.

"Well, I don't know that *trained* is exactly the word I'd use, but yes, I know how to tell the difference between a virgin and a . . . not-virgin."

She moved away from him and started wiggling.

"Sabrina, what are you doing?"

"Removing my shift, my lord. 'Twill be easier for you to conduct the examination if I disrobe."

The hem of her dress had inched past midthigh when Neil's hand shot out to stop her.

"I am not going to examine your virginity!"

Her hand was small beneath his, and curled even smaller to grip her hem, and so the tips of his fingers brushed the exquisitely tender skin of her thigh.

"Why not?" She lifted her chin in challenge.

"Because I know only one way to, uh, make that kind of examination. Even if you're a virgin when I start, you won't be one when I finish, so that's why I won't do it."

Her lip trembled. "And so you deny me the right to prove all I say is true."

"Determining whether or not you're a virgin won't prove a thing, Sabrina. There are other men besides Robert in this world. You could've lost your virginity to anyone."

Her mouth opened into a startled *O.* One tear leaked free, making a lie of her claim that a Desmond woman never cried.

His heart seemed to twist; he'd wronged her, and now, when he ought to be babbling apologies left and right, his throat seized on him and he couldn't utter a word.

She drew a great, shuddering breath. She stiffened her shoulders. Her chin tipped.

"Sabrina," he muttered, and she slanted him such a disdainful glare that he drew away from it.

But not far enough. His movement seemed to snap her unnatural control. With an outraged cry, she pushed at his chest, but since he was heavier than she, he didn't go anywhere, while she skidded backward to the far end of the bench. She sniffled, and impatiently dashed away the tear that trickled down her cheek, and then she slipped off the edge of the bench and ran off into the night.

Chapter Eight

Sabrina raced for the trees.

She always found blessed solitude when a leafy green canopy sheltered her from prying eyes. When duty threatened to overwhelm her, it helped to sit with her back pressed against the rough bark, her toes digging into the earth, lifting her face for the cool rush of Irish air against her skin, secure on Irish soil, in communion with the land that was her heritage and her responsibility.

She gained the woods and darted deep into the trees before she felt it was safe to stop to catch her breath. She braced herself against a trunk, waiting for the old, familiar sense of belonging to soothe her. Her hands traced the ridges and whorls of the bark once, and then again when she realized she could not recognize the type of tree.

Impossible.

She knew by touch the species of every tree that plunged roots into Irish soil. She clawed at a low-growing clump and ripped away a leaf to study. Moonlight filtered through the branches, faint, but enough to illuminate the shape she held. She had never seen its like.

She crushed the leaf when she made a fist, and used the fist to smother the sob that welled from her soul.

Nothing was as it should be.

She threw back her head and called to the sky, "I am Sabrina, lady of Desmond Muir."

The breeze caught her words as she spoke them, and dissipated them into the night.

Neil thought her insane. He told her that she did not understand the difference between real life and a myth.

If it were so . . . all her life until this day had been a dream; she had been schooled every minute to accept a duty that did not exist.

No. It was the work of the Devil, to lead her thoughts in such a direction. To banish his evil presence, she cried out again.

"I am Sabrina, lady of Desmond Muir."

Nobody answered her yea.

Instead, the wind seemed to whisper what Neil had said to her: *You have to be crazy to think one woman and one man can save a whole country.* He had so clearly echoed the fears that had haunted her for so long. His words and her thoughts spoke together with one voice.

She had so often wished she might be freed of her obligations. But now she saw a danger in freedom that she had never suspected. Without her duty, what was the purpose in her life?

She had been born to draw a champion to Ireland's soil. No matter that the chosen champion made her skin crawl and her knees quake with fear. Pray God he roused the same sensations in the hated English king. She had to find Robert and beg him to return them both to her lands, where they could bolster her people's spirit, rouse them to the patriotic fervor they would need to withstand Edward of England's unceasing attacks. If she failed in her duty, the spirit of Ireland could be dimmed forever.

How could she find Robert when she could not even find herself?

The inner weakness she always tried so hard to quell reared its head in the form of another helpless sob. This time she fisted both hands against her mouth.

Her blood pounded the incessant message: *You have failed. You have failed. You have failed. . . .*

Something brushed her arm, and she shrieked.

"I swear, you are the jumpiest woman I've ever met when it comes to touching."

Neil. Her pulse settled. She forced her hands down to her side, grateful for the darkness, for she could still feel the imprint of her fists against her lips and feared she might have bruised herself. He would be distressed, she knew, to see signs of misuse, even if caused by her own hand.

"You found me."

"Wasn't hard. You kept yelling out your name every couple of minutes."

"Not for the purpose of drawing you to me."

"No?"

She could tell he did not believe her in this matter, either. She sought a quelling retort. None came to mind, no doubt because he was right to disbelieve her denial. Now that he was here, joy so thoroughly eclipsed her despair that she knew, in her heart, she'd been hoping all along that he would come after her.

This, too, was wrong. Her very soul was in danger of eternal damnation. If he held her close, told her again that no woman could achieve what she sought . . . if he asked her to turn her back on her responsibilities . . . she would do it.

"Why did you come after me?" She wondered if he could sense how important his answer would be to her.

He caught her hand. Her blood quickened its pace. He traced her fingers, urging her to open her palm to him. Her heart thundered. Would he kiss her upon that soft, impossibly sensitive flesh? Would he declare himself to be her personal champion?

He placed something cold and heavy in her hand, and closed her fingers over it.

"Here. This is yours."

Scarcely able to focus for the disappointment washing through her, she glanced down at her closed fist. So profound was her despondency that she imagined that a crystal white glow seeped through the spaces between her fingers.

"Your necklace," he said. He cleared his throat. "I've been meaning to give it back to you for a while. I fixed that link I broke. You can wear it again."

"You came after me to return the Druid's Tear?"

"I couldn't keep it. I know you owe me some money, but, well, I don't really care about the money anymore."

"Nor do you care about me." She bit her lip, but too late to avoid revealing her bitter disappointment. Her soul was safe. Her heart might not survive.

He was silent for a moment. She heard the soft creak of leather and imagined he must have forced his hands deep into his pockets, straining his belt.

"I came after you."

"Only to return my property."

"That's a good reason, wouldn't you say?"

"It is not the reason a woman wants to hear at a time like this."

She did not understand why she persisted in baiting him—unless it was Maisie's training coming to the fore. Maisie would have approved of how thoroughly she'd perplexed Neil with her comments.

He rubbed his hand over his face. She braced herself, for surely he would begin to yell.

"You're right," he said, so quietly that at first she thought she had imagined his statement. "I've never been able to tell if it's the right time to go after a woman, and I sure never learned the right time to stay away."

"Perhaps you might improve with practice."

"If that were true, I'd still be married."

"Married?" Her throat ached, as if she'd yelled as loudly as he was prone to do. As he had done when she announced herself to be married to Robert of Allingham. "You are married, Neil?"

"Now, see, there I go again. Why did I have to blurt that out?" He moved away from her, not far, making quick, choppy, scuffling sounds that led her to think he might be kicking at stones. "I'm not married anymore. She's dead."

"And you do not like to speak of your loss."

He grew still. "I don't like to speak of her at all."

"You . . . you miss her so terribly?"

"No—that's just it. I don't miss her at all."

Certes, it must be a sin of some kind to feel one's heart leaping with joy at hearing that a man did not mourn his dead spouse. A double sin, for she had no right to care where this man's heart dwelled.

"It's that matter of timing I mentioned," he said. "I knew I didn't have any business going after her. We'd received our orders and everyone knew it would be a long war with no guarantee of coming home. A man has no business fooling with a woman when he can't be sure he'll ever return. I knew that. She knew that. The whole town got together to send us off to war in style. Music, food, a regular party, as if war ought to be celebrated. She wanted to dance and I didn't see any harm in it. Looking back, that dancing was the first mistake ... aw, hell, I can't believe I'm telling you this stuff.''

She rested her hand against his chest. She could feel his breath, somewhat labored, in accord with his mood. She sensed, too, a subtle leaning toward her, as if despite his professed anger at himself, he *wanted* to tell her the story of his wife. Here, in the dark, with just the two of them and the trees to hear.

"I would like to know what happened," she said.

"I think you can guess what happened. A little too much whiskey for me and too much sherry for her. Dancing too close, touching too much. Me suddenly realizing that I could be exiting this earth without leaving any kind of mark on it. She somehow excited in a way I'd never knew women could get at the thought of sending me off with her scent on my skin."

"It is ever so before battle," she said. "I have seen it, time and again when the ladies make their farewells to their knights."

"I didn't show her an ounce of chivalry, Sabrina. I took what she offered. Two months later I got a letter telling me she was with child. I managed to get leave and I married her. I tried to do the right thing. It wasn't enough. I made it back to visit a couple of times, and all that did was prove we weren't suited. I should've left her be, left her untouched and free to find someone she could love. She died, along with the baby, while I was off fighting Rebs."

"I am so sorry." She leaned into him. His arms went around her. "How difficult it must have been for you to be away from them when they needed you."

"No, that's the hell of it. I welcomed my duty. I knew while we were standing in front of the preacher that we weren't suited. The few days we spent together after the wedding proved it to us both. I ran back to the front, happy to get away from her. I led men to fight against their kin, their friends, and never once regretted I was shedding blood instead of sitting by the fire sipping tea with the woman I'd married. Sometimes I think that damned war wouldn't have dragged on half so long if I hadn't been praying so hard that I wouldn't have to go home."

"Now 'tis you who holds delusions. One man cannot win a war, and one man cannot prolong it by merely wishing, any more than he can end it with prayers."

"Then what's all this nonsense you keep bringing up about a champion? You're looking for someone to end a war, right?"

"My champion will win wars, but he will also be content with small victories. He can save us all beginning with one person, one square of land at a time."

The notion seemed to stun him, as if he found it impossible to believe that tiny successes fostered hope in men's hearts and souls.

"Wars do not begin or end on wishes or prayers," she said. "If they did, this war would be ended by now, for I have prayed for little else."

"The war ended more than a year ago, Sabrina."

" 'Tis true we won one small skirmish last year. Not enough to discourage the English for much longer. It will not be long before they realize the west is our weakest point, and attack on that front."

"You have the enemies really mixed up, sweetheart. Only Americans fought this war—no English. You got the directions wrong, too. This war was pure north against south."

"It is true that the English occasionally raid to the north, but the Scots are most fierce, and—"

"The English haven't tried any funny business on American soil since eighteen hundred and twelve."

"Eighteen hundred and twelve?" Sorrow welled within, threatening to choke her. "So many dead."

"Now you're getting your wars mixed up. I don't know

if they'll ever have an accurate figure for the number of casualties we suffered during the War Between the States. I was trying to tell you that the English haven't fought here, on American soil, since the War of Eighteen-twelve. The year eighteen-twelve, not the number of casualties."

His hand had strayed to her back, and worked its way up until his fingers stroked from her neck to her scalp. His caress was so light, so in accord with her heartbeat, that she felt certain he was not aware of how intimately he touched her.

She sighed and closed her eyes with the pleasure of it. She smiled, bemused by his miscalling of the date.

"Oh, Neil, now 'tis you who are confused. I mind the calendar myself. I assure you, this is the year of our Lord twelve ninety-eight."

His hand stilled. And then he raked through her hair in a suddenly firm and determined manner, probing her skull.

"I never thought of it," he said. "I'll bet you took a knock on the head before you hid yourself in my wagon."

"You will find no lump upon my head." She shook his hand away and stepped back, angry that he seemed ever determined to doubt the truth of what she told him. "I did not hide in your wagon. I was placed there against my will."

He paid no heed to her denial.

"That explains everything. Here, let me look into your eyes." To her consternation, he thumbed at her eyelid and peered intently into her inner soul. "Damn, it's too dark to see anything."

"Stop doing that." She stepped away from him again.

He accepted her demand, if not her truth, for he made no more moves to examine her.

"Probably wouldn't tell me much, seeing as I'm not a doctor. But the medicos always did that to the boys on the front when they got concussed. I didn't feel any lumps on your head. Anybody fire a rifle real close to your ears lately?"

"I have never seen a rifle until yours."

"A concussion can cause amnesia as well as confusion. The docs had a bunch of questions for situations like years. They always asked them what year it is."

"I have told you. It is the year of our Lord twelve ninety-eight."

He smiled! She could see the flash of moonlight against his teeth.

"So you've told me. Tell me where you are."

Now, there was a question she could not answer. She felt a flutter of panic begin in her belly.

"I pray I am within walking distance of my castle at Desmond Muir."

"Sabrina, sweetheart, we're deep in the heart of Montana Territory. No castles here that I know of, and nothing is within walking distance. Not even safe to walk on account of the Indians. Just one more question—who's the president?"

She pretended indifference to cover her ignorance. "It matters naught to me."

"You'd better answer, or you'll fail the test. He's the most important man in the country. C'mon—the president. Everyone knows his name."

She could not fail. Far too much depended upon her being proven worthy of her role. A tremor seized her.

"My wedding was six years in the planning." She spoke carefully, certain she could convince him of her sensibility even if she did not know the answer to his question. "For every day of those six years I understood I would be wed on the twenty-fifth day of June, twelve ninety-eight. I myself dispatched the runners months ahead of time. Important personages traveled vast distances to be on hand to witness the vow making. From the farthest reaches of Ireland. From the wild hills of Scotland. From Wales, and France— a few secret supporters even stole across the border from England. The most important men from many countries are known to me. Nobody who calls himself the president. There is no land in my world called Montana.''

Neil stood quiet, and the moon no longer caught him reveling in unseemly humor at her expense.

"We'll find a doctor. We'll take care of whatever's gone wrong."

"There is naught wrong with me!"

Her hand throbbed, and she realized she'd been clutching the Druid's Tear with such desperation that the stone dug into her skin. She shook her fist at him. "This will prove it to you. The Druid's Tear lay cold and dead for centuries. It burst into life only when I began this journey to find the champion. Look at it."

She opened her hand. The stone lay amid tangled gold chain. But something was wrong. Though not completely dormant, it glowed a dull white, no fire at all, almost as if she held a miniature moon in her palm.

"I meant to tell you about that." Neil cleared his throat again. "Doesn't look like the same stone, but I swear that's your Druid's Tear. Must've picked up some lint from sitting in my pocket so long. I tried rubbing it clean, but that's the best I could do."

"No." She closed her hand around the stone again while waves of despair churned through her. "Too much has gone awry. I will not allow this to fail me as well."

She shuddered inwardly at the thought of what she must do, but she lifted the chain and settled it around her neck.

"This is how it is done. The chosen Desmond woman

dons the Druid's Tear and wishes with all her heart that she will find the true champion as she takes the first steps of her journey."

Wheeling blindly, she walked away from him.

"Where do you think you're going? Sabrina, stop."

She put one foot in front of the other. And another. The path before her seemed a bit easier to see—perhaps the moon had escaped from behind a cloud, for something brightened her way.

"Sabrina." He spoke at her ear, jolting her with his nearness. "Stop. Please stop."

She obeyed.

He touched her shoulders and gently guided her around until she faced him. She did not think she could bear looking at his face at that moment, and so she stared straight ahead at the broad expanse of his chest.

Light danced against his dark shirt.

"I'll be damned," he whispered. "Look at your diamond."

She could not manage more than the briefest glance, for dazzling brilliance burst from the stone, shooting beacons of light into the darkened sky. This was what had made the path easier to follow. The stone had returned to life the moment she'd turned her back on Neil.

She wanted to weep.

"I must go. The stone spoke when I turned away from you. It tells me I must find Robert."

"Robert." Neil's jaw snapped shut. Through gritted teeth, he said, "Your precious Druid's Tear doesn't seem to know what it's doing. If Robert was your champion, it should have taken you straight to him. Instead, it brought you to me."

"But why? You are not the champion."

"I know I'm not the champion! I don't know why it brought you to me." He threw his head back and heaved an exasperated sigh. "Jesus, listen to me. I'm talking as if I believe that a necklace carried you through time. Well, hell, if I'm going to believe a delusion I might as well jump right into it. Maybe the necklace sent you here to get you away from Robert."

She pressed her hand to her forehead, dizzied by the comprehension that dawned.

"Of course. That is exactly what has happened. I have traveled nigh until six hundred years into the future! Oh, Neil, do you realize what this means?" She did not bother trying to hide her delight.

"It means you need some rest."

"No, no, no! I am too filled with excitement to require rest. Everything is so clear to me now. The Druid's Tear started me on a journey through time because Robert is not the champion—nor is any other man of my time fit to be champion. And so the stone sent me to you."

"Sabrina, I don't like the way this conversation is going, not at all. I told you—I'm no champion."

"I know that. But . . . you have a wagon."

"A wagon. The Druid's Tear sent you to me because I bought a medicine wagon."

"Aye. Since nothing is within walking distance, I must needs have transportation. You are not the champion, but you have the heart and soul of a warrior. You will keep me safe while I seek the champion."

He said nothing.

"Neil? Can you not appreciate the glory of what has happened?"

"Let me get this straight—the Druid's Tear has decided that of all the men who ever lived, I'm the perfect chauffeur for you. I'm supposed to haul you around while you call every man you meet 'my lord.' Spring you loose if you happen to accidentally lock yourself in someone else's wagon. Step in and make sure there aren't any misunderstandings if a fellow gets all excited after you ask him to examine your virginity.''

''You have already proven yourself able to handle those tasks,'' she said. '' 'Tis my opinion that the Druid's Tear has chosen well.''

His shoulders heaved. He choked. Worried, she stepped closer to him and caught his face between her hands.

He wasn't ailing. He was laughing.

When she tried to draw away, affronted, he wrapped one arm so tight around her waist that she was pressed full against him. She could feel his heartbeat thudding into hers, the quake of his humor vibrating against her skin. His warmth penetrated her shift.

''Will you help me?'' she whispered, staring up at him.

''Ah, hell,'' he said. His breath stirred her hair. She let her hands drift over his arm, let her fingers curl around the corded strength that held her so tight.

''It's not that I don't appreciate being singled out for glory by the Druid's Tear. I'm just a little too busy at the moment to haul you everywhere you might want to go. I'll take you as far as the next settlement along the road.'' His head bent close over hers, his words low and rumbling against her ear. ''After that, you're on your own. After we find you some decent shoes. And maybe a cape or something to wear over your dress. Deal?''

She shifted her head to look up at him, which brought her lips disconcertingly close to his. ''Deal,'' she whispered, wishing he would never let her go.

But he did. He bundled her onto the wagon seat with great efficiency, and with a slap of the reins prompted the horse into motion.

''Maisie will be disappointed to find you gone,'' he said. ''But at least you got away with your nice dress.''

He seemed completely unaffected by the sensations that

coursed through her. She would do well to emulate his manner of speaking and his detachment.

"She will not be disappointed to find you gone, but at least you got away with your manly attributes intact."

He made a strange, wheezing sound, but must have been pleased with her response, for he did not correct her.

Chapter Nine

They had covered two miles, maybe less, when Neil realized he'd been worrying about the wrong thing.

With every squeal of wheel, each thud of hoof against hard-packed dirt, he'd been berating himself for changing his mind about keeping Sabrina with him.

Not that she was bad company; quite the opposite. She traveled better than most soldiers he'd known. She kept to her side of the wagon. She didn't chatter, and didn't squirm around complaining about the lack of comfort. Didn't scratch, didn't spit, didn't fall asleep and snore. If not for the diamond gleaming at her breast, she'd be almost invisible in the dark.

An invisible woman ought to be no distraction at all. Especially on a night with so little moonlight, and deep darkness surrounding them. Even if he wanted to look at her, which he didn't, he wouldn't be able to see her expression. Even if he wanted to touch her, which he didn't, he'd have to grope around to find her. Dangerous.

Not the touching, but the hunting. While groping, a splinter might pierce his flesh, or he might get his fingers caught between a couple of boards.

Then again, good, honest pain might bring about the return of his common sense.

He didn't quite know where his common sense had gone, but it had fled the moment Sabrina made him laugh. He couldn't remember the last time he'd laughed out loud. She'd brought him smiles and chuckles and now full-blown laughter. Laughing had never before seemed important to him, and now for some reason he didn't want to lose it again.

At least not right away.

And so he sat next to her, not all that close, traveling in the dark, knowing it was wrong to have her with him and even more wrong to like having her there. Truly worrisome. Worrisome enough that he didn't feel like laughing anymore, and so troubling he couldn't think about anything else—until the right wagon wheel dipped and almost capsized the wagon.

Instinct took over. He lunged to grab the back of Sabrina's gown before she slid off the edge of the seat. Once he had hold of her, he used his free hand to haul on the off rein, guiding the horse back onto the road.

The horse sidled to a halt and stood there snorting and shaking its head. Neil heard the shifting and clinking of his inventory as the bottles of elixir bounced around a little. Awareness of how narrowly they'd escaped disaster caused his pulse to skitter. He'd reached for Sabrina before tending to business, which violated every tactic he'd learned in the army. That split-second lapse in judgment could have killed them both, and destroyed the wagon as well, if it had capsized on top of them.

He felt Sabrina's slight tremor because somehow she'd gotten mashed up against his chest. He couldn't imagine how she'd managed to land there. He'd been dumb enough to grab her and dig in like an anchor, intending to just hang onto her so she didn't take a nasty tumble out of the wagon.

He surely hadn't been so dumb that he'd pulled her that close. The only logical way she could have ended up tucked under his chin was if she'd inched her way up the precariously sloping seat, fighting gravity.

Right. Then why did his shoulder and upper arm ache, as if he'd held on—and drawn her close—with all his strength?

He'd almost killed them, driving blind, forgetting his training, sunk in thought when he should have been paying attention to the road. He should have been watching and listening for Indians. Things a man who possessed an ounce of common sense would do.

"We'd better make camp here for the night," he said. "It's not safe to push for the next settlement. There's not enough moonlight."

She nodded and said something, which he couldn't make out on account of her face pressing against his shirt. Or maybe he couldn't hear because he felt the movement of her lips straight through his well-worn cotton, and his pulse got to beating so hard that it drowned out every other sound.

"I'm going to get down and walk." He knew he shouldn't revel so much in holding her close, so he set her away from him. "I'll lead the horse until I find a likely spot to camp for the night."

"Take care, Neil—'tis dangerous," she said, a soft blessing.

Take care. Common courtesy, as ordinary as the jingling of the harness, the muffled thump of the horse's hooves. *Take care—'tis dangerous* didn't sound so ordinary spoken in her enchantingly accented voice.

The sentiment curled warm around his heart while he caught the horse's bridle near the bit and started walking in the dark. He'd have thought he'd never been sent off to do something without good wishes before. He'd had good wishes aplenty, especially when going off to the war.

Give them Johnny Rebs hell, Neil, with a clap on the shoulder.

Make them wish they'd never bucked the Union, Neil, with a punch to the shoulder.

Bring our boys home, Captain, with a patriotic salute.

We don't have to pretend it hurts to say good-bye, while his men waited outside, thinking he might need a moment of privacy while his wife bade him farewell.

He walked, blind again, while his thoughts swirled. There wasn't an honest-to-God *Take care* in the bunch. Never had been. His folks had died of fever without having the chance to say "So long." President Johnson had sent him to Montana, concerned only that he make haste and return quickly with evidence damaging to Meagher.

Nobody, until a muddleheaded woman who fancied herself belonging six hundred years in the past got herself locked inside his wagon, had ever urged him to take care of himself.

"Are you all right back there?" he called.

"Certes. What harm could possibly come to me?"

"I don't know. Maybe your head hurts."

She answered with an exasperated sigh.

He couldn't help smiling, even though he reserved his opinion that she'd taken a blow to the head.

"I see a stream."

"How can you see anything on such a dark night?"

"Look, where those woods thin out to the left. You can see the moonlight reflecting off the water."

"Warriors possess sharp eyes, but know when to seek shelter."

He shook his head, smiling again. He didn't know how she'd learned to talk that way, but he was getting used to it. Liked it, in fact. And if he wasn't mistaken there was another *Take care* buried in there somewhere.

"Looks like we're not the first to call this a good place to stop," he said once they reached the shelter of the trees. A circle of stones surrounded the remnants of an earlier campfire. "We're in luck. There's still enough wood here to throw a little light and heat while I forage for more."

"What should I do?" asked Sabrina.

"There's a sack under the seat. I keep my matches and coffee supplies in there." He began undoing the harness. "I'll water the horse and pick up some wood on my way back. Coffee would be nice. There's enough water in the canteen for a pot. You can light the fire and get things started."

"How can I light the fire?"

"Like I said, matches are in the sack. You ought to be able to find everything else you need for the night in the back of the wagon."

As soon as he issued the advice, a trickle of his common sense seeped back home. Smiles no longer tugged his lips; the warmth dissipated around his heart. He was about to spend the night in the middle of the wilderness alone with a woman he dared not touch, and he had only one bedroll.

That should be easy enough to resolve. He seldom slept. The passage of time had taught him that dreams couldn't catch hold if he took his rest in ten-minute snatches here and there and kept his mind carefully blank while staring out into the dark night.

No reason why he couldn't just prop himself up against a tree and watch out for Indians while she slept in the bedroll. Problem solved.

The trouble was, he couldn't see himself explaining this plan to her. He knew in his gut that she would object to using the bedroll for herself. Where that discussion would lead, he couldn't even begin to imagine. She seemed uncommonly . . . unembarrassed about the human body. She talked about breasts and virginity and male attributes with a frankness he found refreshing and, well, somehow stimulating.

He could just imagine her directing that glorious sea green gaze at him and pointing out how much sense it would make to share the bedroll. They could keep each other warm. He could examine her virginity at his leisure. He didn't know what he would do if she made suggestions along those lines.

No, that wasn't true—he was only lying to himself if he tried pretending he didn't know what would happen. The brain paralysis that gripped him anytime he spent more than five minutes in her company would wipe out his common sense once more. The two of them would be rolling around in that bedroll all night long. Maybe for the next two or three days as well. Heat flooded his loins at just daring to dream of claiming Sabrina as his own.

Whoosh, there went his common sense again. His plans for the future didn't include a woman.

He led the horse to the stream, wondering how long he could stay out of camp without causing her to worry. Maybe if he stayed for an hour or two, she'd grow tired, seek the bedroll, and resolve the problem without requiring him to make any explanations.

Maybe if he stayed here watering the horse for twenty or thirty years, he'd be too old for his body to react to her.

Or maybe the ache of wanting her would grow stronger, the way it had been growing ever since he'd found her. He couldn't count the times he'd touched her hair, or pulled her close, or inhaled her scent, hoping that he might eventually sate those cravings. So far he'd done nothing but whet an appetite that wouldn't subside.

The horse lifted its head. Water dripped from its muzzle, the droplets sparkling like individual diamonds as they cascaded to the ground. The glittering made him wonder how the Druid's Tear might look if Sabrina wore it—and nothing else.

He didn't know what it meant to learn that everything, even a horse drinking water, brought his thoughts back to Sabrina.

"Maybe I'm the one who got knocked in the head," he said to the horse.

Well, lurking in the dark, waiting for the smell of coffee to percolate through the woods, wasn't doing a bit of good to clear his head. And he didn't smell any coffee.

That was because she hadn't made any coffee, he discovered as he led the horse back to the small clearing. She hadn't readied the pot, nor had she lit the fire. She sat ramrod straight on the wagon seat with the sack of things on her lap, staring straight ahead at nothing, reminding him of the way he had spent tortured hours through the night.

Concern ate at him. That, too, was an emotion he hadn't allowed himself to feel for a long time. He'd had no defense against laughter, because he hadn't thought he'd ever find much to laugh about again.

Concern was another matter. He knew how to pinch it down before he started to care too much.

"What's the matter, princess? Need help climbing out of the wagon?"

He tethered the horse as he spoke, knowing he sounded like the grouch that old man in Bamper had accused him of being, and sarcastic to boot. He told himself his rudeness stemmed from seeing that his plan hadn't worked. He'd still have to confront her over the bedroll.

She turned her head toward him. The brilliant glimmer of her eyes seemed to rival the diamond.

"You're not crying." He stated it, didn't ask. Asking implied concern.

"Desmond women do not cry."

"So you've told me. It appears Desmond women don't help set up camp, either."

"That is true."

"Any particular reason?"

" 'Tis the job of squires and camp wenches."

"Hmm. Well, what do you suppose we ought to do? I'm no squire, and you're no camp wench."

"I . . . I thought you might understand."

Such agony quavered in her voice that it tore straight through Neil's black mood. So what if she hadn't lit the damned fire and set the damned coffeepot on a rock? And it wouldn't kill him to show a little concern this one time. Just this once. He just needed a minute to figure out what to say.

She broke the silence before he found his words.

"You are so woefully inept yourself that I hoped—"

"Woefully inept?" he broke in on her. "I'll have you know I'm one of the most able men in the entire United States Army, which is the main reason why I'm here right now arguing about my, um, eptness. Woefully inept, my ass," he added in a muffled mutter.

He kicked the dirt near the unlit campfire, and then stopped because his numb brain stirred enough to realize it didn't make sense to bury that handful of half-charred sticks. His defense of his abilities rang a little hollow as he realized he'd clean forgotten to gather the wood they needed.

"You did not seem so greatly skilled when trying to cure that sick old man in Bamper," she said. "You offered him naught but strong spirits, untempered by healing balms, when 'twas evident he ailed from his heart."

"Who are you talking about—oh, that old coot Melrose.

I thought I did a good job there. In case you haven't noticed, I'm driving a patent medicine wagon, and selling that medicine goes along with . . . with the wagon."

"Why do you not sell effective medicines from your wagon?"

He snorted. "If I did that, I'd probably end up killing more customers than I'd save. They'd die of shock. Nobody really expects patent medicine to do any good."

"Then why do you engage in such a nefarious scheme?"

"Well, because . . . because . . ." He was beginning to feel as inept as she'd accused him of being. Worse, her reproachful gaze made him remember the threadbare state of Melrose's shirt, the overall sense of poverty most residents of Bamper exuded. He'd sold his elixir to all of them. "I've already told you more than I should about my mission."

"I have been thinking about what you've told me. I do not believe you."

"What?"

"*You* have somehow become mixed up." She sent him a sly smile. "Perhaps after knocking yourself in the head."

He narrowed his eyes. "You're just saying that because I don't believe your crazy story."

"Aha! So you admit that you disbelieve me."

"Sabrina, what you said about traveling from the past to find the Irish champion makes no sense."

"Nor does it make sense for someone who knows naught of the healing arts, and naught of a gentle manner with people, to be engaged in the selling of medicine."

"Well, then, I picked the perfect fake profession, because *nothing* logical has taken place since you've come along."

"I, sirrah, might say the same."

She sat impossibly straight, her chin tilted high, looking

the very image of an Irish princess who'd been maltreated by one of her subjects.

"I don't believe this. You sit there daring me to prove that everything I say is true."

"Is that not what you dare of me?"

"Well, the difference is I can prove I'm an army captain. I have a uniform."

"I can prove I am the chosen Desmond woman. I have the Druid's Tear."

"If I was the sort of man who made threats against women, I could remind you that I took that diamond away from you once, and I can take it away again. And if I did, I might just throw the damned thing into the creek."

"Then 'tis fortunate you are not that sort of man, for if you were, I might discover myself to be the sort of woman who would rend your army uniform to shreds. Tiny shreds, suitable for nesting material, so that when I cast it out the crows would carry away every last thread. And then neither of us would possess proof of anything."

He could just imagine her doing that, too. Damned if the notion of Sabrina standing in a cornfield flinging out army-issue blue threads didn't put another smile on his face. He put his hands on his hips and shook his head, acknowledging her as the winner of their little verbal battle.

For a brief, heart-stopping moment, she smiled in return. Her whole being lit with an inner joy. But then puzzlement overcame her and she put her hand to the Druid's Tear.

He recalled how the necklace had drawn his attention from time to time in just that way, seeming to grow heavier, demanding to be acknowledged.

Always it led him back to Sabrina.

She held the stone, and her glory dimmed while the diamond burned brighter. The diamond always led him to her, but he couldn't shake the sensation that the damned stone was trying to lead her away from him.

He shook his head again. He was thinking crazy again, attributing motive to a hunk of jewelry.

"There is a way for me to prove the truth of what I say. If you will help me." She spoke little above a whisper, so he had to move close to the wagon to hear. "Will you help me?"

"Depends." She'd said nothing to cause the wild pounding of his heart, the clenching of his stomach. He never felt those sensations unless engaged in a fight, when he knew he might take a staggering blow.

"Will you take me to find Thomas Francis Meagher?"

He had to reach for the wagon; he needed support. All his old suspicions about her stormed through his mind, taunting him.

"Why?" he managed to croak.

"From all I have heard, I think . . . I think he might be the champion I seek. Will you deny this to me now, the way you have before?"

He wished he could. From the way her lip trembled, and the soft tremor that shook her into sadness, he knew she wished he could deny it, too.

He had to do something far, far worse.

"Sabrina, I can't tell you whether or not he's the man you're looking to find. All I can tell you is that I *hope* he's not your champion."

She gripped her hands together. Her eyes seemed to plead with him to name another in Meagher's place.

Himself, for instance.

For one insane moment, he thought he might be able to do it. Offer to become her champion. Plunge himself back into the hell of fighting battles he could never win. With Sabrina to come home to at the end of the day, it might not be so hard, especially if small successes came one person, one scrap of land at a time.

For one insane moment, his throat ached with the need to pledge himself.

Old voices, old doubts and fears, resurrected themselves to mock him with haunting laughter.

Who did he think he was kidding? He was no champion.

She knew it, too. She'd stopped asking him. She wanted to be taken to Meagher.

Once again he'd proven his susceptibility to her. He'd actually begun believing her crazy story for a minute, almost dared turn his back on the one thing he knew for certain—he couldn't save himself, let alone anything else.

He pounded his fist against the wagon, both to clear his head and to lend emphasis to what he said.

She jumped, taken by surprise. And he told himself that the trepidation with which she looked at him was a good thing, because she had to understand the full import of what he meant to say.

"You want Tom Meagher, I'll take you to Tom Meagher. But for both our sakes, I hope he's not your man. I might very well have to destroy him."

Chapter Ten

The brew called coffee bubbled in its special pot, sending forth an exotic, earthy aroma. Sabrina inhaled, savoring the scent of the drink, the scent of the man next to her. The man who moved with uncharacteristic stiffness, as if his spirit had been shattered and he was afraid one wrong movement would cause him to break into a thousand pieces.

She had done this to him.

Neil's inner fires had dimmed the moment she declared her belief that Thomas Meagher might be her champion.

She yearned to touch him, hold his face between her hands and tell him she had no choice. Her duty as the chosen Desmond woman decreed she must furnish a champion. He had refused the duty. He had assured her Robert was not the one.

Her heart, as a woman who had fallen in love with Neil Kenyon, had recognized that single, wondrous moment when he'd shown, in his eyes, that he would sacrifice everything to be her champion, if she asked.

She loved him. She could not ask him to pledge his torn and tattered spirit to her cause.

Neil had spoken right. The champion was destined to fail. Oh, there might be small successes she'd mentioned, enough to bolster the Irish spirit so her people might endure. But there would be no decisive victory, and she sensed that for him, anything less would loom as failure in his mind.

The champion would go to his grave knowing he had given all he had to give, and it still was not enough. Neil had already done this. To ask it of him again would be to destroy him.

He settled a shallow, empty cookpot atop the fire next to the coffee. "Hungry?"

"No."

"You're just saying that because you don't want to cook." He spoke teasingly, the way Maisie had encouraged her to do. She could not summon the spirit for it.

"I do not know how to cook."

"Now, I wonder why that doesn't surprise me." He winked at her, and cast her a lopsided grin.

He smiled so seldom. Such a minor shifting of his lips lent him a playfulness that made her want to smile despite the sore wounding of her pride in realizing she must have been wrong in believing she'd broken his heart.

This inner turmoil was new to her. Up until now, life had seemed so simple. Somewhat empty, but simple. Live for the land and the people, die for the land and the people.

Her mother had said she had done her best to guard Sabrina from the uselessness of love, and Sabrina now had a glimmer of understanding that showed how wise her mother had been. This Neil Kenyon, who used his outward bluster to hide a heart as lonely and wounded as her own, was all too easy to love.

She loved him. She loved a man who did not believe her when she spoke the truth. She shivered.

"You can pitch in anytime and help," he said. "It'll help keep you warm to work around the fire."

She felt the heat of shame upon her skin, and was thankful that he would not be able to see.

"What would you like me to do?"

"Take turns, for starters. We'll have to share the eating and drinking utensils. When I'm on duty I drink my coffee black, but I'll admit here and now that for relaxation there's nothing like a good, hot cup of coffee with a spoon of sugar and a good dollop of milk. How about you?"

"I do not know. I have never had coffee."

"Maisie didn't drink coffee?"

"Maisie believed hot drinks wreak havoc upon a woman's digestion. She held a very strong opinion that coffee and tea bring about belches and other embarrassing sounds. I am not certain I believe her in this matter."

"And why is that?"

"The men of Desmond Muir drink little besides ale and wine, and I daresay no woman could match them for belching and . . . other embarrassing sounds."

His faint smile flashed again. "Sounds like the men of Desmond Muir have a lot in common with American soldiers. Corsets are what's bad for a woman's digestion. But Maisie's right—some folks can't drink coffee. I always hold that it depends more on who's doing the brewing than who's doing the drinking. We'll see how it affects you. Fetch me the sugar and a can of milk out of that bag. I'll fix us a good cup."

She bit her lip to keep from telling him that she did not know these new things he'd requested, either.

She was not a stupid woman. She could fake competency.

She delved into the bag he'd indicated and withdrew a small pouch. A peek inside revealed pale brown, dry chunks. She poked at it, and small grains clung to her finger. She dared not taste it lest it be poison. She rubbed her finger clean against her shift.

Next she pulled forth a cylindrical metal object. It was not as heavy as an iron ingot of similar size, and it made a strange sloshing sound, as if the metal had not solidified in the center. It looked to be good for little besides throwing at an enemy's head.

The bag was full of useless things.

Milk she knew well, but there were no cows about. Sugar? Cans? Maisie had mentioned sugar, and called it a vile substance that caused a lady's form to expand in horrid billows of fat. She had remarked that pioneer women worth their salt knew how to can, and had promised to teach Sabrina, but Sabrina's illicit departure had ended the lessons before she'd had the chance to learn the purpose and appearance of a can.

She had traveled into the future. Merely acknowledging the fact did not make it easy to endure.

"I like to put the sugar in the cup before I pour in the coffee," Neil said. "Get a move on, Sabrina. Doing familiar things might help jog your memory."

"None of this is familiar to me!" she blurted out.

"So you just happen to be holding the milk and sugar by complete accident."

It would serve him right if she *did* heave the strange metal cylinder at his head. His stubborn refusal to believe her would make it easier to forgive herself for causing him pain. "Take them, then," she said, pushing them at him.

She sat on top of the cursed supply bag and vowed not to laugh too heartily when he realized he had accepted poison and poorly wrought metal in place of sugar and milk.

But he seemed not to notice. He pulled a walnut-size chunk of the brown poison from the bag and crumbled it into his tin mug. He fished a knife from his pocket and thumbed it open, revealing a blade with a curious hook at the end, shaped rather like a miniature pike. He plunged this hook into the metal cylinder and made some quick up-and-down motions with his wrist. Within a few heart-beats, he pried a thin, jagged circle of metal from the top of the cylinder.

"I sure hate to disturb you, princess, but this skillet's hot. Fish a can of beans out from under your little bottom."

"I do not know what is—"

He waved the cylinder at her. "These little cans hold milk. The beans are in the bigger cans."

"Oh, *this* is a can." She reached for the cylinder. Neil caught her hand before she grabbed the circle he'd cut. Her traitorous body thrilled at his strong grip.

He was not affected. He placed her hand upon her thigh and gave her an absent pat.

"Watch you don't cut yourself. That metal's sharp. I need those beans."

She rummaged through the sack for one of the larger cans, and while he busied himself with knifing it, she peered into the opening he had made in the first can. He'd claimed it held milk. Pale liquid did indeed fill the can he'd opened. It was difficult to tell the color for certain because the firelight flickered golden against it.

"I'll wait to see how strong the coffee turns out before we add the milk," Neil said. He spilled the contents of the second can into the empty cookpot. It sizzled.

"Milk." She touched a tentative finger to the liquid. It felt like milk. She licked her fingertip and made a face. It did not taste like milk.

"Canned can't stand up against fresh," Neil agreed.

"But having this Borden's on the trail sure expands the menu, if you know what I mean."

She wasn't sure she knew what he meant, but the taste of the milk on her tongue told her that she ought to become accustomed to not understanding. She had much to learn.

She reached for the small pouch and withdrew a small lump of the brown substance. She placed it on her tongue, and almost at once found herself closing her eyes with delight while sweetness exploded in her mouth.

"Better than honey," she declared.

"Well, I hope you enjoy that sugar because we don't have much to look forward to when it comes to dinner. What would you prefer—beans, or beans?"

"I am hungry. Is there not something we could cook more quickly than beans?"

"Won't find much quicker than beans. I'd say these are about done. Here, taste and see if they're hot enough for you." He spooned a portion of something from the flat cookpot into her mouth.

Cooking beans was a tiresome business, involving much soaking and a half day's boiling. But Neil had simply spilled some from his can into the cookpot, and now they filled her mouth, so well cooked they barely required chewing.

The lingering taste of sugar and milk . . . the strange but intoxicating scent of the coffee . . . beans that required less cooking time than it took to boil water . . . how strange that it should be her sense of taste that brought to her full force the enormity of the change that had been thrust upon her.

Everything she had known was gone. The people she sought to save were gone, vanished into bones and dust. Her home had no doubt been eroded by winds and rain and the ceaselessly questing roots that ever sought to crumble stone.

Today, in the year 1867, all that was true.

Tomorrow, if she found the champion, she would return to her rightful time and place. All would be familiar to her. But in her heart she would know how quickly it would pass, how brief her triumph, how eternal her separation from the man she loved. Premonition struck, promising her endless years of a very unique hell on earth.

For the champion, it would be different. But he, too, must leave behind all he had come to love in this world, knowing he would never see beloved faces, favorite treasures, ever again.

She had only imagined the glory in store for the champion. She had never thought about its cost. Neil had warned her of some of the effects. Now she understood a fuller measure of sacrifice.

She stood, somewhat shakily. Doing something familiar might help her, Neil had said. And since naught here was familiar save her own body, she walked. In slow, almost staggering steps, for her mind was too consumed with the enormity of what had happened to her to devote attention to the proper movement of her feet.

"Sabrina? Don't go off too far. Remember what I told you about the Indians."

She shook her head. He did not understand.

"Sabrina!"

She plowed right into him. Somehow he had stepped in front of her and caught her in his arms. She blinked and realized he'd done so to prevent her from crashing headlong into the huge tree that stood at his back.

His arms around her felt real and solid. The warmth emanating from him penetrated the icy premonition that held her in its grip. She leaned forward, craving this connection with reality. She needed to hear breathing other than her own, needed to feel flesh and muscle press against hers to prove she existed. His arms tightened, drawing her closer still, and she melted against him. Here, in his arms, with his heart beating sure and steady against her breast, she felt as if she were truly in the right place, the only possible place she belonged.

"Hold me. Touch me."

"Sabrina." He sighed her name with hungry despair. He kept one arm anchored around her while he lifted a shaking hand to her hair. He twined his fingers through the tumbled strands and drew her head back. His lips brushed her forehead and then trailed down, kissing her closed eyelids, tracing hot over her cheeks, burning firm and sure against the tender skin of her throat. His pulse pounded into hers, making her blood sing with the glory of being alive.

She let out a small gasp of pleasure, and it seemed he, too, required intimate contact. His mouth closed over hers, absorbing her very breath into his body; his tongue quested against hers, which seemed to be rooted in a place deep within her center, judging by the jolt of pleasure that crackled through her. He tasted rich and dark, tempered with a faint sweetness. She guessed this shocking kiss might be her first taste of coffee, and remembered the sugar she'd sampled and hoped he found the taste of her equally intoxicating.

But he held her in that embrace for all too brief a time. With a subtle shifting of his body, he set her away from him.

"No," she whispered, and moved close to him again.

"I have one bedroll, Sabrina. And holding you like this makes me imagine all sorts of things I want to do with you in that bedroll. One bedroll."

Desolation swept through her. She loved him. She would always love him, through centuries, through eternity, but never would she have more than these few hours, perhaps a few days, to claim his body with a lover's embrace.

He wanted her as well. She was not ignorant of the workings of a man's body, and she knew what caused the iron-hard heat she felt pressing into her belly. He wanted her, but would not join with her . . . because of a bedroll.

Fury unlike any she had ever known before raged through her. She had accepted her lot as a Desmond woman. She had subjugated desires to the demands of being designated the chosen one, the Desmond woman who might bring the Irish champion to her people. She had girded herself to marry Robert. She had not succumbed to tears and fits when she found herself transported into the future. She stood ready to do her duty when she came face-to-face with the champion.

She wanted but one thing to savor in this reality, one thing to remember for all the endless days to come.

Hearing that an insignificant bundle of bedding was the sole reason why she could not yield herself to Neil's possession was impossible to accept.

She swallowed hard against the howling anger that threatened to explode from her throat while she ran to the wagon and wrenched the cursed bedroll from its place. She threw it to the ground and jumped upon it. Twice. How she wished she wore a knight's mailed boots, possessed a warrior's bulk! Her footwear, her weight, did naught but grind a bit of dust into the coarsely woven bedding. She curled her fingers around the cloth strap binding the roll and took off at a dead run toward the flowing creek.

"Sabrina!"

She did not spare him a glance. She ran faster than she had ever had cause to run and skidded to a stop at the edge of the water. With a mighty heave she tossed the bedroll into the center of the creek. It bobbed and tumbled end over end as a current caught it within its grasp and sent it swiftly floating downstream.

Neil pounded to a halt next to her. He did not touch her.

Knowledge pierced through the red fog clouding her mind. Perhaps he did not want her as she wanted him. If so, that was one more thing she must accept. She closed her eyes and shuddered.

"Feel better now?" he asked.

She nodded, even though turmoil gripped her still. The bedroll bumped up against a rock, and then emerged from the water just in time to disappear from sight around a curve in the creek. All at once she realized the enormity of what she'd done. She moaned.

"Feel a little silly?"

She nodded again, turmoil displaced with regret. "Your bedding had the weight of fine tapestry."

"They were just a couple of old, worn-out army blankets, Sabrina. No great loss." He laughed a little and shook his head as if unable to believe his own words.

Nor could she believe them. "There is no bedroll at all now. And still you do not touch me."

"It's not a good idea to touch, Sabrina. It's not . . . well, it's not right."

"Because I belong to the champion?"

He tensed. "You belong to no one but yourself. No man owns you. You have the right to choose."

What a strange concept. Quiet strength stole into her bones, allowing her to stand taller, lending her the courage to risk revealing her inner turmoil. "And if I choose you?"

He drew in breath with a sharp gasp. His hand clenched into a fist, as if only sheer force of will stopped him from using it to pull her close.

"You're not exactly in the right state of mind to be making those kinds of choices. Any man who would take advantage of you while you're so mixed-up doesn't deserve to be called a man."

"If I could prove to you that I am not . . . mixed-up—then you would . . . take advantage of me?"

He ran his finger down the bridge of her nose, and then through the valley between her breasts to her navel. She caught her breath, feeling his heat even through her gown. "In a heartbeat," he murmured. "But when you make comments like that, all you do is prove you're not ready. Maisie was right. You can't walk around saying such things to men, not these days."

Honesty would not permit her to claim she had full control of her senses. Her body issued urgent, silent demands for warmth and touch and pressures she did not understand.

"I cannot stay here with you like this. Not for very long."

"Probably not. Those stupid shoes of yours are almost in tatters, and your dress isn't holding up so good. Maybe we shouldn't have been so hasty in taking our leave of Maisie."

She wondered if he had deliberately misunderstood her. "I have always worn garments like these, even when venturing outside the castle walls. My maid keeps my garments in good repair, so my appearance does not usually suffer so much."

He lifted a strand of her hair. "You're a little bedraggled, sweetheart, but your appearance is fine."

The water reflected moonlight over his face, darkening the hollows of his cheeks but not hiding the blaze of desire in his eyes. She had witnessed lust directed her way many times. The casual, cheerful desires of a knight flushed with the success of battle. The hopeless, yearning glances of young men who knew she was destined for one of nobler blood. Robert's confident leer, promising to subdue her and bend her to his will no matter the cost to her pride.

Neil's passion burned with a different glow. She felt bathed by his desire as if it were warm, scented oil. Something within her thrilled at sensing the tenuous hold he held upon his control, while yet another something inside her honored and respected his determination to refrain from claiming her. He wanted her. His need, his desire, was evident in every inch of his tautly held body. But he would not take her while he believed she felt confused and uncertain.

This she could accept with good heart.

She wanted to reach for him, to lose her doubts and fears, if only for a little while, in the magic of his kisses and his strength. But when their lovemaking ended, she would be alone while all those terrors descended upon her once again.

Robert, the man her parents had chosen for her, wanted only to destroy her spirit and make her one of his less important possessions.

Neil, the man to whom she'd been sent by a most capricious fate, urged her to stand on her own and nurture the strength buried within her.

"It is the mark of a champion," she said softly, "to foster strength within those who hold him in esteem."

He grew very still, and then caught her by the arm. His hand trembled against her, and her heart soared. But it was at once apparent that he meant only to steer her back to the waning fire. "I have to round up some firewood to keep this blaze going. We're going to need the warmth."

She blushed, remembering the bedding she had thrown into the creek. "I will come with you."

"No, you stay right here. You can sit on that sack, or maybe spread out my spare clothes. I won't be gone long."

"Do not go alone. I promise I will not probe your wounds again."

She shouldn't have said that. She knew as she watched his expression close that he believed he hid his vulnerabilities from her.

"You're talking crazy again."

"No. You retreat when matters strike too close to your heart."

He did not deny what she said, but continued on as if she hadn't spoken at all. "I'm going just a little ways into the woods. No need to panic. I'll keep an eye on you."

"But will I be able to see you?"

"Probably not. You'll be sitting near the fire. It's sometimes hard to see into the dark when you have light at your back."

She shivered. She could not shake the dread certainty that he meant to lick his wounds alone in the dark. "Do not go."

He swore. "I shouldn't have tried so hard to convince you about the Indians."

"Indians." He seemed determined to pin her fears upon other matters. She knew so little about men and how they nursed their inner hurts. Perhaps his pride demanded solitary healing. If so, she must send him off with good heart, and not let him know how well she understood.

"Two times now you have gone into the woods and left me behind." He tensed, and she hurried to finish her explanation in a way that might ease his apprehension. "I have never before been completely alone in the dark."

"Never?"

"Never."

"Didn't you have your own room?"

"My handmaid always slept in an alcove off my room, so close we could listen to each other's breathing, and a guard always upon a pallet outside my door."

"Wasn't there some little nook or cranny in that big old castle where you could have a little privacy?"

She could not contain a peal of laughter. "Oh, Neil, 'tis evident you do not understand castle life. Such a swarm of humanity fills the walls. There were times when so many bodies slept upon the floor in the great hall that you could not pick your way across the chamber without stepping on someone's fingers or toes."

"Then I guess you never found yourself lonely."

"Never alone," she corrected.

"And why you never had to light your own fires or cook your own dinner. You didn't have to worry about a thing."

"Not so. There were many days when I prayed I would wake to find myself a lowly kitchen wench with nothing more to worry over than keeping the soup hot. Perhaps you cannot understand, Neil. For whatever reason, God placed my family in charge of so many. He made us responsible for their well-being, and yet in many ways left us helpless to protect them. When they chose to behave in stupid ways, we could not save them. When famine struck, we could not feed them. When the English attacked, we could not shield them from harm."

She must have imagined the sudden flare of recognition that made it seem he was about to tell her he did indeed understand. She wished he would stay. Together they might explore these ancient failures that held them both in far too strong a grip.

"I'll be back," was all he said before melting away into the dark.

He gained the woods, and then pressed back against a tree. He shook like a raw recruit facing his first cavalry charge. His mind taunted him with images he'd tried so hard to forget. The soldiers under his command. The wife he'd never loved. The baby who'd never drawn breath.

We could not save them . . .

We could not feed them . . .

We could not shield them from harm . . .

All he had to do was change the word *we* to *I* and he'd have a perfect duplication of the refrain that had been echoing through his head for the past five years.

He'd railed against the fate that had given him so much responsibility but so little real power. All the officer stripes and medals in the world couldn't stop a Rebel bullet from plowing into the belly of a sixteen-year-old farm boy who wore the Yankee blue. Sending home his pay hadn't magically conjured food for his pregnant wife when the local grocer's shelves had been stripped bare by starving soldiers.

He'd spent these past years believing he'd failed as a leader of men. As a husband. As a father.

For all these years he'd kept those wounds buried deep, too ashamed to reveal them to others, too certain that nobody would understand. But now someone did. An addle-brained, funny-talking, beautiful temptation of a woman whose clothes were falling apart around her, whose shoes were in such tatters that she couldn't run very fast if he decided to chase after her.

A woman who had trembled with desire in his arms, who had asked, *And if I choose you?*

She was right. He retreated when matters struck too close to the heart. His instincts urged him to run, to put as much distance as possible between them, before she realized he did not measure up to her impression of him.

He'd been running for a long time, though, without making his escape.

Sabrina urged him to stay put and consider that maybe, just maybe, no man alive could have managed any better than he'd done. The concept just about paralyzed him. But that, he realized with slow wonder, was better than running.

The scent of smoke swirled through the trees, reminding

him that their tiny campfire would be guttering out within moments unless he returned with an armload of wood. His body had learned long ago to perform what was demanded of it even while his mind retreated to another place. He bent for deadfall; he wrenched a good chunk free from a maple whose leafless state proved it to be dead where it stood. His long stride carried him unerringly back to the camp.

The empty camp. She was gone.

His arms dropped, and the wood clattered to his feet.

"No," he whispered. Despair raced through him. She'd left him.

But hard on the heels of that thought came one even worse: Indians. She was afraid to be alone in the dark, and he'd been so desperate to run off and hide for a while that he'd left her sitting there, defenseless against a threat she didn't seem to understand. Agony and self-recrimination ripped through him, twisting and tormenting, but he couldn't afford to indulge in it. He had to go after her, save her.

A wolf howled, eerily echoing the wildness inside him.

"I love the sound of wolves," said Sabrina.

Neil whirled at the voice and found her sitting on the bench of the wagon.

"What the hell are you doing sitting there?" he choked, while anger and relief threatened to close up his throat altogether. Relief rushed through him so hard that he didn't know how he managed to stay upright against its force.

"It seemed the best place. I did not want to spread your spare garments in the dirt. I have taken far too great a toll on your possessions as it is."

He bent and snatched up the wood he'd dropped, but the chunks didn't cooperate, wouldn't stay stacked in his arm. Maybe because he was still shaking so hard.

"You'll get cold sitting up there, so far from the fire."

"I am not accustomed to so much heat. My sleeping chamber lay far from the great hall's hearth. My bed was heaped with well-cured wolf pelts to guard against the cold."

"So that's why you like wolves so much," he guessed.

"Oh, no. I always wept inside when the huntsmen killed one. I love their song. It so perfectly echoes the feelings inside me."

The wolf howled again. Lonely, yearning, solitary, and maybe just a little crazed at the way humankind kept pushing it in directions a wolf was never meant to go.

Neil tended the fire far more diligently than it required. When he could no longer stop himself from looking at Sabrina, he saw she'd slumped against the wagon's sidewall. Her breast rose and fell, soft, sweet, oh, so tempting with the rhythm of sleep.

He rummaged through his sack and drew out his medicine-man jacket. He shook it free to release the folds. And then, careful not to wake her, he tucked the coat all around her.

Time to find a good tree to lean against. He certainly had plenty from which to choose.

Not one of them looked half as inviting as the empty half of the wagon seat next to Sabrina.

No law said he *had* to sleep under a tree. And it wasn't as though he hadn't spent hours already on a wagon seat next to her. Their traveling arrangement was so unconventional that he doubted folks would make much of a distinction between him keeping watch from the ground or from here on the seat, where he had a much better vantage point. Shelter from rain, too, if some decided to fall.

He'd be close at hand, too, if she woke during the night. She wasn't used to being alone. She might take comfort in having him within hand's reach.

It might be easier on him, too, to be able to take a quick glance to the side to make sure she was all right.

He couldn't prevent his weight from shifting the wagon as he climbed in. But he did move with extra care, making not a single sound as he settled down to keep his nightlong vigil.

Chapter Eleven

She woke to blissful comfort.

Odd. She blinked to clear the sleep from her eyes, wondering how it could be that the wagon seat chilled her bottom while the wall she leaned upon exuded heat of a kind that invited snuggling.

Odd, too, that this wall warmed her from her left when she always leaned upon the wall toward her right. No matter.

She smiled and turned her head to burrow into the heat and realized it was no wall that warmed her bones, but a living, breathing man. Neil.

He sprawled over an entire half of the seat. She was held snug in the curve of one arm. His other hand rested upon his rifle, which lay alongside his leg.

He'd declared his intention to sleep apart from her. He'd harangued her over the matter of a bedroll.

He'd stolen into the wagon without waking her, and

silently went about the business of guarding her against harm.

A delicious melting within her made her wonder how long he had sat there, keeping watch over her, before succumbing to exhaustion.

Sometime during the night, need had drawn the two of them together without either being aware of the pull. She did not know when she had sought and found his embrace. She doubted he did, either, this man who withdrew, retreated, whenever he felt his heart being touched.

She held her breath for a moment so she might hear the steady thump of that heart beneath her ear.

He slept soundly despite his claim that sleep always eluded him. She reveled in the rise and fall of his chest, in the even rhythm of his breathing. She tilted her head back by slow, careful degrees so she could see his face.

His mouth, which had claimed hers with such mastery the night before, had softened with slumber. A kind of awe pounded within her, to think he might have found healing sleep because he held her in his arms.

She might have lain thus with him for hours, letting him sleep, but in moving her head she had changed her field of vision. The sky had shifted from black night to the dark pewter that heralded dawn. That was as it should be. Soft fingers of color stole from the horizon to the east, also as it should be. The rest of the sky was wrong, though. On the western horizon, where no light should show, an obscene orange glow flickered and roiled.

"Neil?"

She called him at barely above a whisper, she so hated waking him, and because anguish over what she knew that glow meant constricted her throat. She reached up and touched his face. "Neil?"

Her touch sent him surging upright. She tumbled from his hold while with a swift motion he hoisted his rifle against his shoulder, his cheek pressed against the hilt. His finger curved around the trigger. He swung the weapon in a wide arc, and then lowered it.

"What the hell?" he muttered.

She touched his forearm. With reflexive speed, he turned the gun upon her. "Neil, 'tis only me!"

The rifle wavered. When he set it down to rest upon his thighs, his face had gone white with horror.

"I could have shot you."

"You did not."

"Jesus, Sabrina, I—"

She interrupted him, knowing he had no cause to feel remorse. "I thought you would want to know about the glow."

"The glow?" He scowled down at her.

She had to bite her lip to keep from smiling at the way his tousled hair lent him a boyish look that subtracted all threat from his glower.

"I might've shot you," he repeated. "Don't you know better than to sneak up on a man who's keeping watch?"

"I did not sneak. You were not keeping watch. You were asleep."

"I never sleep."

"Then you must have seen the glow," she said, knowing he had not.

He rubbed his hands over his eyes, swiveled his shoulders, and made a mighty yawn. She couldn't help smiling; he noticed, and snapped his mouth shut. "Maybe I drifted off for a few minutes. What's this about a glow?"

"An ominous orange lit the sky with the coming of dawn, along the horizon."

"Hell, that's just the sunrise, Sabrina."

She shook her head. "This glow came from the west. I have seen that same shade of orange, that same flickering light, once before, when the English sacked a small grouping of cottages that lay just beyond our castle lookout's sight. That glow heralds fire, Neil. A terrible fire."

"To the west, you say?" She pointed, directing him where to look. Dawn had brightened, making the orange glow more difficult to see. But Neil's eyes were keen. He cursed. "That's Mauser, the next settlement on the trail. Appears the Indians got to it before we did."

"We must hurry to see if we can help them."

"We must take a roundabout route and avoid that place altogether."

"You mean slink around them as if *we* were responsible for hurting them?" Disbelief led her to shout.

He shifted, looking uncomfortable. "Well, no, we didn't cause their suffering. But we can't make it all better for them, either."

"Nor would they expect so much of us! 'Tis God's role to make everything right, not ours. We can only do what we are able."

"You don't know what you're asking."

She suspected she knew exactly why his lips had gone thin with tension, his shoulders rigid as if they expected crushing weight to fall upon them.

Because of war, because of a union forced without love, Neil Kenyon had come face-to-face with his limitations. Some men accepted limitations. Others did not. Those who did not locked themselves into an eternal struggle, on the one hand recognizing their frailties, and on the other cursing the fate that had not granted them godlike power.

"We can soothe the wounded," she said. "We can dry an orphan's tears. We can bury the dead. 'Tis wrong to expect we might do more. All else is up to God."

He tightened his jaw until a tic pulsed along his jawline. She merely stared at him with all the confidence in him she could muster, knowing in her heart that a champion such as he could not turn away from those who needed him.

He blew an exasperated puff of air up into the disheveled hair clinging to his forehead.

"Aw, *hell*. Make sure we don't leave anything behind."

She smelled the devastation wrought by fire before they came in view of the village.

Warming fires, cooking fires, washing fires—all the fires that bent to man's will produced an abundance of friendly white smoke along with the characteristic and comforting scent of burning wood.

Fire that destroyed smelled of fear and lost hope.

Smoke hung in a gray, heavy pall over what must have been a thriving village. Heaps of smoldering ash marked where dwellings had once stood.

Shadowy forms moved through the blackened desolation, moving with such care that it seemed they feared to disturb rubble that was already beyond saving. A low, moaning sound swirled and eddied. It might have been the wind; or it might have been the collective sound of grief from the people who walked with no apparent purpose through the ruins, whose eyes stared disbelieving, uncomprehending, from ash-grimed faces.

Incongruously, a paddock holding a half-dozen horses remained whole and undamaged, as did several carts resting near the paddock fence. Children had flocked to this place of relative normalcy. The oldest stood watching while the younger ones laughed and chased each other around the heaps of clothing and goods that must have been tossed from burning buildings. They played among the pitiful remnants, oblivious to the depth of the losses their families had sustained.

"There are wounded." Sabrina pointed toward a stone

wall against which two men had been propped. Blood streaked in obscene trails down the soot-coated arm of one.

The other, with his teeth visibly gritted against pain, held what looked to be huge lumps of charred meat a few inches above his lap. His hands, she realized with sympathy. His arms quivered from the effort of holding his hands aloft, but Sabrina understood he could not set his ruined flesh against anything without adding to his excruciating agony. His hair had been all but singed away, and his clothes hung in blackened tatters, marking him as one who had tried to fight the fires with more courage than sense.

Neil's hands tightened around the reins. She could tell he warred within himself, his wounded heart urging retreat, his warrior's soul urging him to help.

"Their need is great," she murmured.

He let loose his breath. He slowly wound the reins around the wagon brake and slid from his seat. Sabrina, all but consumed with pride for him, scrambled to follow.

"Indians?" Neil asked when they neared the milling villagers.

A woman nodded. Her eyes were reddened from smoke and crying. Soot coated her face save for where she had tried to dash away her tears, leaving small circles of skin looking pale and extraordinarily fragile.

She waved a hand, encompassing the wreckage of the village. She blinked, and tears welled anew.

"It's all gone. Everything we worked for."

"How many dead?"

"None." She shook her head. "I don't understand. All these months I worried about some slinking savage cutting off my scalp and stealing my children—but they never came close. They just sat a hundred yards out on their horses and shot flaming arrows at us until every building caught fire. Everything's gone. Four years of hard work and sacrifice, and we're worse off than when we came here. I'd almost . . . almost rather it had been the other way."

Despair radiated from the woman, a despair Sabrina understood all too well. People could not keep trying and fighting, only to be defeated at every turn. That was why she had been sent to find a champion to bolster her people. It seemed these people required a champion of their own.

"You do not mean that," Sabrina said. "You're alive. You've lost things, that's all."

"We've lost *everything*."

"There are horses," Sabrina said, desperate to cheer this defeated woman. "And carts."

"They left those so we can get out of here," said the woman. "And I aim to please them. If you have any sense, you'll get out of Montana, too."

She left them and joined those who wandered, pausing first at one blackened heap and then another, the way mourners might visit the graves of their loved ones.

Neil watched her go, his expression bleak. His whole bearing revealed an outrage that seemed very much at odds with a man who had declared he would never again feel responsible for anyone but himself.

"Come, Neil," she said, resting a hand against his arm. "Let us try to help them."

He shook his head. "We can't do anything. They need too much."

"We do not need to solve all of their problems. One person at a time. One small success."

His head angled sharply toward hers.

"Your elixir," she said. "In combination with my remedies. Between us we might ease some of their suffering and offer a little hope."

"You make it sound as if trying will be enough."

"Trying is the best anyone can ever do, providing they try with all their hearts."

She thought he might argue with her. His jaw tightened as if with pain, and then softened the slightest bit. "Can you help that man with the burned hands?"

She touched the pouch at her waist. Oh, how she wished she had her full complement of cures. "I have a small amount of my very best *unguentum Amarium*," she said. "It will help, but I have so little."

"Can you make more?"

"No doubt 'twould have been a simple task before this fire destroyed all. I fear that many of the necessary ingredients will have been lost to flame."

"What do you need?"

She knew the recipe for this sovereign cure by heart. "Do you think you might hunt game, Neil? I will need equal amounts of grease from both a wild and a tame boar. And yet another equal amount of bear grease. It must be a male bear. While you are hunting, I will myself dig for the earthworms."

"You need boar grease?"

"Equal measures, about as much as I can cup within my two hands, from boars both wild and tame."

"And bear grease."

"From a male bear," she reminded him.

For some reason, being charged with such difficult tasks seemed to ease his despair. "Anything else you'd like me to fetch while you're digging for earthworms?"

"It is not so simple as you think to catch a wild boar, and bears do not yield as much grease at this time of year as they do nearer to winter," she warned. "It could take you many hours to find and kill and clean the game. And from the looks of things, the tamed boars will have all run off, so you will have that hunting to do as well."

"You'll be digging earthworms while I'm out catching grease on the hoof."

Bears had no hooves, but he seemed so captivated by the task that she could not correct him.

"It could take a long time to find worms, with the ground burned. They will seek the moist, cool depths. And then I must needs char the worms and grind them to a fine powder. It takes a fearsome long time to char earthworms. Just when you think they are finished, you find leathery spots, or plump areas that still seem full of water. I have often wondered how such wet creatures live beneath the earth."

The light had returned to Neil's eyes, and the smile that curved his lips was real. "And I've often wondered why they drown when you dangle them in a fishing pond. Tell me, Sabrina—exactly what did you stir into that elixir I sold to old Melrose?"

Men ordinarily showed no interest in the healing arts. "Zedoary root," Sabrina said. "Lovage seeds, with roots of peony, mistletoe, and myrrh—"

"That doesn't sound so bad. It didn't look like seeds and roots, though. It looked like powder."

"Of course. You must crush the herbs very fine to match the texture of the powdered millipedes. Millipedes are not so difficult to char as earthworms, and they are easier to grind, as well."

He suddenly took to coughing so hard that she feared he might need a cure himself, and then he shook his head. She wanted to touch his lips and bring back his smile. Instead she stroked her pouch.

" 'Tis good fortune I replenished my store of skull moss before . . . before coming here."

Neil did not seem to notice her hesitation. "Don't even mention skull moss to me. I've lived thirty years without knowing about skull moss, and I don't see any need to learn about it now.''

'' 'Tis just as well. I have no time to school you in the matter, for these people need my help.''

He cupped her elbow with his hand.

She waited for him to choose the direction.

The wagon waited behind them. The people waited ahead. He made no move to indicate which way he wanted to go. She took one small step forward. He did not loosen his hold; nor did he take a step to keep pace. She took another and paused, her pulse racing, wondering if he would prove himself coward or champion.

He came up behind her. His chest bumped against her shoulder. "Looks like we have some work to do."

"What's your name?" Neil asked as he settled himself into position behind the burned man. He gripped the man's shoulders and ignored his shrieks of pain as he shifted him to allow Sabrina easier access to his hands.

"Your name?" he repeated louder, loud enough to cover the thin gurgle of agony the man made. "Your name!"

The bullying worked. "H-Henry."

"Henry what?"

"Henry Pat . . . Pat . . . Patterson!" He shrieked the name when Sabrina's fingers fluttered over his hands.

She worked with a touch as light as a butterfly's, coating Henry's damaged hands with a razor-thin layer of her precious ointment.

"Talk to me, Henry," Neil ordered.

He tightened his hold, as much to support Henry as himself. The sweat on Henry's brow sprang from pain; the wetness Neil felt trickling along his own skin came from memories he'd sworn never to revisit. Memories of holding his soldiers in just this way while the sawbones hacked off mangled limbs. Saying their names seemed to settle them, as if reminding them they were men and not cattle being butchered alive.

Talking sometimes helped a little. Not much. But enough for the most stoic of the men to pretend they didn't feel the agony ripping through them while the doctors worked.

"Henry, talk to me!"

"What the hell am I supposed to talk about at a time like this?"

"That's good, real good." Neil gave Henry's shoulders an approving squeeze. "There's lots of interesting things we can talk about. Uh, let's see . . . you have any bear grease? Or wild boar grease?"

"I did." Henry gasped. "A little of both. I expect it's all burned up now."

Sabrina lifted a brow but said nothing. A smug smile curved her lips.

"Talk about something else," said Neil.

Sabrina pressed her lips together, smothering a giggle. He answered with a smile. These ministrations they were performing for poor Henry weren't at all funny, but he couldn't help smiling at finding himself in such complete accord with Sabrina. He knew exactly what she was thinking—that he wanted to change the subject so he wouldn't have to admit she'd been right about the settlers having animal grease. Which meant she knew exactly what he was thinking.

Thinking each other's thoughts made it easier, somehow, to hold down a man who wanted to writhe away in pain. With only his own thoughts to work with, he would've been convinced they were engaged in a futile effort. With Sabrina showing him her unique perspective, with Sabrina helping one person at a time, he dared to hope they might be making a difference.

"I sure could use a good slug of whiskey." Henry's comment ended with a yelp.

The settlers had gathered in a ragged semicircle, watching Sabrina's ministrations. There were at least half a dozen able-bodied adults standing there, doing nothing, while he and Sabrina helped their neighbor.

One particularly healthy-looking fellow shifted his feet uncomfortably, as if he'd just come to the same realization. "Ain't got no whiskey," he said. "Didn't have none even before the Indians burned us out."

"Who are you?"

"Eddie."

Neil motioned with his head toward the medicine wagon. "Go to the back of my wagon, Eddie, and fetch a bottle of my elixir." He mentally subtracted the cost of one bottle from the amount he'd hoped to gain from sales. Henry moaned. "Make that two," Neil amended. The settler nodded and took off at a run. Henry let out a thready shriek when Sabrina did something to his fingers. "Three bottles," Neil called. He could make up the three dollars somehow.

"Do you have some wool or soft cloth?" Sabrina asked those who'd gathered to watch.

"We managed to throw some things out of the houses before they burned," said a woman. "I could look."

Sabrina glanced at Neil. "There should be something we can use that won't demand a greater sacrifice from these people. We must find something clean for him to place his hands upon, else the soot will mingle with the unguent."

"Grass," Neil suggested, a little halfheartedly. He felt pretty sure he knew Sabrina had hoped he might offer some of his spare garments.

Eddie pounded back from the wagon, his arms filled

with bottles that clinked together when he stopped. "I brung six," he said.

Six dollars gone. Neil had a hard time working up much regret over the loss in light of the devastation surrounding them. Henry stared avidly at the elixir and licked his lips with such anticipation that Neil had to wonder whether more than pain drove his thirst.

"Start pouring them into him," Neil said.

Henry made sucking and swallowing noises as he glugged down Ebenezer's Energizing Elixir. Eddie tossed the empty bottle aside. Sabrina's eyes widened when the bottle shattered against a stone, and then she fixed Neil with an unfathomable stare.

"Perhaps I might tear off the edge of my gown." She reached toward her hem. Neil stopped her.

"Your gown isn't much cleaner than anybody else's clothes."

"I have no other clothes."

But he did. And she knew it.

He'd never considered himself a stingy man. He'd jump up and fetch something if she would just ask, flat out, "Neil, will you give me your spare shirt?" But she didn't ask. She simply stared at him, waiting for him to offer, and somehow offering was harder. Almost as if in his gut he knew that offering on his own would be like chiseling a hole in the wall he'd built around his heart.

He wondered if she knew that, too.

"We would've had some nice, soft bedding to tear up if a certain person hadn't tossed it all into the creek," he said.

Her regard held steady, never wavering.

"Aw, hell. Get over here, Eddie, and keep his head up off the ground." Neil carefully maneuvered Henry into Eddie's care. Eddie kept the second bottle of elixir pressed to Henry's lips. Henry never missed a beat.

Neil stalked to the wagon and rummaged in his pack. He couldn't give up his medicine-man suit, or the work clothes he was wearing, which left his army uniform. He supposed he didn't really need the uniform, considering he was traveling incognito. No, that wasn't exactly true—he might need to prove his captain's status, and the easiest way was with the insignia on his shirt. He tugged his uniform trousers free.

He felt a funny little lurch in his gut as he ripped his army pants right down the middle. Almost as if he'd torn a dividing line between past and future.

"There's an army stripe running down the sides of them britches," whispered someone in the crowd.

"Aw, *hell*." The words all but exploded from Neil.

He glared at the settlers. They inched closer to each other, instinctively bunching against him. "You did *not* see an army stripe," he lied at the top of his voice. He shook the trousers at them. "These are ordinary blue britches with some fancy sewing decorations."

"Yes, sir, fancy sewing decorations, sir," answered one of the men. Which would have suited Neil just fine if the man hadn't ended his comment with a somewhat shaky, but perfectly formed salute.

Neil rubbed his forehead and then, with a sigh, wadded one of his pant legs into a ball.

"Will this do?" he asked Sabrina.

" 'Tis perfect." She smiled at him as she accepted the blue bundle. Such satisfaction lit her that he'd have thought he'd handed her a brick of solid gold instead of half a pair of britches torn apart at the crotch. Tearing them in half sat a little easier on his mind. "Will you help me again?"

He almost started to say *You don't have to ask*.

Almost. He found himself so shaken by wanting to say it that he couldn't say anything at all.

He'd made the walk from his wagon to these wounded men two times. The first time all he'd wanted to do was turn around and run, and he would have if Sabrina hadn't been there to urge him to take that first step. This time he'd hurried, with nothing more on his mind than knowing Sabrina would need his help.

A man didn't undergo that sort of transformation just for the hell of it.

"I'll do whatever needs doing," he said, looking down at her, wondering how he'd been so blind that he hadn't noticed himself falling in love.

He knelt next to her and lifted Henry's hands as gently as he could, while she arranged the tough old woolen britches atop his stomach with as much care as if she handled the finest silk. Neil lowered Henry's hands into the nest she'd made. Henry didn't let loose with so much as a squeak. "How many bottles you got into him?" Neil asked Eddie.

"This is the third."

"That's enough. Give me the rest." He tucked one bottle in each of his back pockets, and wedged the last one into his waistband.

"What about me?" called the man whose arm was bleeding.

Sabrina brushed her hand against Henry's face and smiled at him, though he'd grown so bleary-eyed from downing all that elixir that Neil doubted Henry even noticed. She rose in a graceful motion and walked toward the other injured man. The whole group of settlers followed her like ducklings chasing after their mother.

Neil couldn't blame them. He figured he'd follow her wherever she wanted to go.

Sabrina bent over the wounded man and peered intently at his shoulder. "We must find the weapon that did this to you."

"An arrow."

"The wound no longer bleeds. It appears your flesh has been seared."

"My fault. I stepped between my cabin and a fire arrow. My wife pushed it through."

"Where is this brave woman?" Sabrina asked.

"I'm right here, ma'am." A woman stepped forward. If she hadn't been so covered in soot, she might've blushed, judging by the way she dimpled and smiled at Sabrina's compliment.

"We must have the arrow."

"I threw it yonder. Might take a minute to find it."

"Please."

They stood in silence while Sabrina studied the wound. She made no move to touch the man.

"Do you want me to tear the rest of these pants into strips?" Neil whispered into her ear.

"Why?"

"Well, to wrap around the wound."

"Why would I do such a thing?"

"You'll need something to dress the wound after you clean it."

She stared at him with blank incomprehension.

The settler's wife returned with the arrow. "I got so mad at this durned thing that I wanted to break it in two." She handed the arrow to Sabrina.

"Praise God you did not do so," Sabrina said. She frowned at Neil, and then turned her attention to the arrow. She seemed more interested in the arrow than the wounded man. "The blood is darkest in the first quarter of this weapon. That must mark the initial penetration. I will concentrate my attentions there. But since the arrow was pushed completely through the body, I believe we must treat the entire length."

She had been so quick to jump in and try to help folks

that Neil had never considered she might be squeamish about blood. But something was making her turn away from the wounded man.

"Uh—hold on there, folks. Sabrina, I'd like to talk to you for a minute." He gripped her arm and propelled her out of earshot.

"If you can't stand the sight of blood, just tell me. It's nothing to be ashamed of. I'll take care of his wound. I picked up a little medical knowledge myself along the way."

She made a little snort of disbelief.

"All right, Madam Doctor—how about pulling some laudanum out of that bag?"

"I have never heard of such."

"Quinine?"

"You speak words I do not understand."

He racked his mind for other medicinals. "Calomel?" She shook her head. "Mercury?"

She brightened. "A Greek god."

Someday he'd have to ask her how she managed to so thoroughly involve herself in her fantasy that she could make it seem real. But for now they had work to do.

"You must have something in your bag that I can use on this man."

"Very well—if you insist on tending his hurt directly." She rummaged through her pouch and drew out a small square of cloth. "Press this against the place where the arrow entered his flesh."

Neil regarded the cloth with grave suspicion. "What exactly is it?"

"Fair linen, which has been soaked in frog spawn, of course."

"Frog spawn?"

"Nine days' worth," she said with quiet satisfaction. "A most sovereign remedy. And now I must tend to the arrow." She plucked the torn pant leg from him and gave him a little push toward the injured settler.

Neil somehow managed to avoid tripping over the prostrate townsman. He watched, smiling, as Sabrina arranged the trouser leg like a shrine and, with great reverence, placed the arrow upon it. "What's she doing?" asked the wounded man, craning his head to watch.

"Beats hell out of me."

"What about my shoulder?"

Neil glanced down at the square of linen. Frog spawn. Nine days' worth. Most likely it was just an old hunk of cloth. Well, compared to some of the so-called cures he'd seen administered to soldiers, even if there was a little dried frog spawn on that cloth it might not hurt the fellow, considering that his wound had been burned clean by the flaming arrow.

He dropped to a knee and fished a bottle of elixir from his back pocket. He thumbed the cork free. "Drink this," he ordered, holding the bottle out. The wounded man snatched it in his good hand, and while he was blissfully guzzling another dollar's worth of Neil's profit, Neil pressed the cloth against the open wound. The man choked, but the pain wasn't enough, apparently, to turn him off drinking, for he kept on swallowing the elixir.

Sabrina delved into her pouch for another of her strange concoctions. Murmuring words that sounded like a witch's spell, she began polishing the arrow with some sort of compound. Something about the way she held herself, the way her voice spoke those ancient words with reverence and respect, made him think she took this playacting a hell of a lot more seriously than he did. As if she believed it. As if deep down in her heart she knew it was true.

His amusement at her antics shifted into dread. He loved her. He figured she might be halfway toward loving him. From now on, it would be the two of them, together.

Except she was convinced she had to go back to the year 1298 and wage war against the English. With a champion.

There had been healing women who'd come to the army camps after the worst battles. Some had seemed more learned than the doctors. Most had known little more than how to clean and dress a wound. But there had been one old hag who'd acted crazy like Sabrina, claiming that treating a weapon that caused a wound was more effective than treating the wound itself. Neil had physically tossed the old bat out of the camp when she'd insisted a soldier's cramped leg could be cured if he carried a mole's hind foot in his pocket. She had shrieked curses at him, warning that ungodly medicines like laudanum and calomel were cursed by the Devil, while her own cures using God's own creatures—things like moles and newts and frogs—had been devised hundreds of years in the past. Centuries ago.

Centuries ago. Like maybe in the year 1298.

Traveling through time was impossible.

A few days ago he would have said finding peace for his soul was impossible, too.

But the events of the past hour proved he was starting to find it. Instead of being overcome with feelings of inadequacy, he was enjoying quiet pride in what they'd accomplished. He felt contentment in knowing he'd done all he could, and accepting of the fact that he could not set everything to rights. That was God's job.

If a sour-souled, embittered man like himself could find peace, then maybe a woman determined to find her champion could travel through time.

And if that were so, he'd received the greatest gift of his life, while at the same time he'd been consigned to eternal pain.

He loved her.

He couldn't have her.

Sabrina knelt over the arrow. Her slim body swayed in

time with her rhythmic chanting. The words tumbled from her, rich and throaty. Completely incomprehensible. Barbaric. The way words might have sounded half a millennium in the past. The way she would be speaking them again, once she returned there with her champion.

Neil wrenched the elixir bottle out of his waistband. He tore the cork out with his teeth and then downed the fiery liquid in one long swallow.

Chapter Twelve

Neil's troops had been involved in their share of battles where they'd ended up on the losing side.

A stunned disbelief always gripped the soldiers in the aftermath. He could count on a certain number of men to hunker down with their heads buried in their hands, moaning *No, no, no* as if denying what had happened could change the truth of it. There would be some who'd keep staring out to where the victorious forces had withdrawn as if they expected them to come marching back to repeat the battle, with different results.

There was work to be done on a battlefield. Grisly work. Harder in some ways than what faced these folks who'd lost so much, but not so hard in others.

It was possible to treat the corpse of a fellow soldier with respect, with honor, but hold the essence of yourself aloof. Soldiers never acknowledged the inappropriate relief that often swept over the survivors, never admitted that they sometimes thanked God while they worked because it wasn't them lying stretched out waiting for the graves to be dug.

Neil didn't know if it was possible to feel that detachment while dealing with the wreckage of everything you'd worked your whole life to build. For these settlers' sake, he hoped so.

They displayed their own version of a defeated soldier's disbelief. Some of them walked from place to place murmuring the name of the structure that had stood there; some stood wringing their hands, while a few huddled on the ground staring at nothing. He understood their shock, because realizing the truth about Sabrina had dealt him a bone-shattering jolt. He was halfway tempted to shuffle on over to the hand-wringers and join in their aimless parade.

He knew from experience that would accomplish nothing. The tragedy had to be dealt with sooner or later. Sooner was better. There was only one surefire way to bring people out of shock, and that was to give them something to do.

"I want you women to begin going through the things you saved from the fire," he instructed. "Make several piles—kids' clothes in one, men's clothes in another, women's clothes in another. Make a pile for food, and another pile for whatever's left."

That got their attention. Some began nodding, while others crossed their arms against the idea.

"Everybody's things will get all mixed up if we do that. We won't know what belongs to who."

"Get used to it. From now on, whatever you have belongs to whoever needs it most, not whoever claims ownership. Everyone pitches in. Everyone shares."

One of the men began grumbling. "Me and my missus hauled every scrap of food out of our house before it burned."

"Good thinking." Neil gave him a nod of approval.

"Damn right. A hell of a lot more sensible than some people I could mention, who about broke their backs dragging a damned *organ* away from the blaze, and didn't bother saving anything else."

He jutted his jaw toward an ornately carved oak organ that tilted a little askew, close to the piles of salvage. Skid marks in the dirt proved how much effort had been involved.

"I don't see why I ought to share my food with Sam Stuart after he went and did something that dumb."

"Ain't dumb." Another man stuck out his jaw with a belligerent tilt. Stuart, the organ's owner, no doubt. "I'll bet there ain't another organ like it in all of Montana. Bet we can sell it for what we need to get a new stake."

"That's right." A woman joined the man. Husband and wife, judging by the proud way she tucked her hand into the crook of his arm. "We don't need your food. We can forage while we start over."

"Everybody's going to forage," Neil interjected while his heart gave an odd twist. The husband smiled down at his wife, who gazed back up at him with complete trust and belief. They'd lost everything, except each other, and a hunk of musical furniture. And somehow they'd held on to hope. "You'll need to forage for edibles, and I want you men to go out right now and do some hunting. Rabbits, birds, whatever you can find. Some wild boars, maybe. Or a bear."

"What about us, mister?" Neil felt a tug on his sleeve and glanced down to see a young boy staring up at him. A whole pack of children stood at his back. "What do you want us kids to do?"

Keep out from underfoot was all Neil could think of right off. But eagerness shone from the boy, and Neil knew it was important to him that he pitch in and help.

"Uh, horses," he said. "Water my horse, and the horses in the paddock. Feed them, too."

"Grain and hay burned up with the barn."

"Pull grass for them."

The children tore off to do as he'd bidden. He watched as the women reached the piles of salvage. They simply stood, looking, for so long that he began to worry they'd gone into shock again. Then one of them tugged a man's suit of long underwear from one of the heaps and spread it carefully on the ground.

"Here's the men's clothing pile," she said. They were soon busy sorting.

From behind him, someone cleared his throat.

The men hadn't gone anywhere.

"I thought I told you to go hunting."

"We decided we'd better stay here and see what you're going to do."

He wondered when they'd decided that, because he hadn't heard them say a word to each other. There must be something about living in a settlement, working on common ground, that drew men together, he thought, remembering how the men in Bamper had behaved in concert, too.

"I'm not going to do anything." He pointed to where Sabrina knelt, packing her cures and potions back into her waist pouch. "As soon as Sabrina's finished, we're leaving."

Eddie inched away from his fellow settlers. "Well, we was thinking that might be what you had on your mind. We're going with you."

"The hell you are."

"Ain't no reason to stay here. Ain't even sensible. Them Injuns won't be none too happy if they come back and find us still here."

"Well, I won't be none too happy if you follow me. Besides, you might not want to go where I'm going."

"Ain't too many places to go from here. You go south, you reach Bamper. You go north, you reach Fort Benton. We don't mind goin' to Bamper, but we're kind of hoping you're headed for Fort Benton. General Meagher's there. Seems like the safest place for us to go."

Meagher. Mention of the man made Neil clench his fists, especially when he noticed Sabrina cocking her head to listen to their conversation.

"Fort Benton's no more than a day and a half, two days at most, away from here. Road leads straight to it. I'm surprised your precious General Meagher didn't sweep on down this road and prevent that Indian attack."

"I'm kinda surprised, too," said Eddie. Some of his neighbors murmured their agreement. "The general sure knows how to put it to the Indians. We heard tell he took the army up north and cleared the Indians out of that whole section of the territory."

"Well, I heard tell he took the army up north and wasted a million taxpayer dollars." A couple of the men nudged each other. They all chuckled in disbelief. Neil's temper flared higher. "He wasted time and money, because the Indians are down in this direction. Burning this settlement, for example."

"General Meagher will be mighty upset when he hears about it, too. And I'll bet he'd be none too pleased to hear that you refused to give us a military escort, after what happened and all."

"Military escort?" He swore when he understood the man's meaning. "I'm no military escort. I'm a medicine man."

"Don't matter what you are. We aim to stick close. You strike us as the kind of fellow a man would like to have watching his back during a fight."

Neil's mouth dropped open. The whole group of them nodded and headed off toward the paddock.

Neil rubbed his hands over his face. Nothing was going the way he'd planned. The assignment that had started out so well had begun degenerating the minute . . . the minute . . . the minute Sabrina Desmond started breaking bottles in the back of his wagon.

He ought to grab her and toss her in the wagon and hightail it out of there before the settlers caught on to what he was doing. Something inside rebelled at the idea of running out on these men who'd decided he'd be a good man in a fight. He looked for her; she wasn't with the wounded men, both of whom had fallen into a drunken sleep.

She'd probably lost interest in staying close to him when the conversation drifted away from Thomas Meagher.

The peal of feminine laughter drew his attention to the women, and he found her. She'd joined them at their sorting. Somehow she'd managed to get them laughing instead of crying over the meager amount of salvage.

She didn't know he was watching her. She knelt on the ground and leaned forward, rummaging for something from the clothing pile. Her gown gaped away from her neck. The Druid's Tear bumped against the sweet curves of her breasts. Heat throbbed through him, reminding him of how those firm, luscious curves had felt pressed up against him the night before.

Her hair hung in tangles, its auburn glory muted with a faint film of soot. Thumb-size smudges dotted her cheeks, and a smear shaped like a comet streaked across her forehead. Her reddish brown gown looked dappled with black. Anybody happening along would have a hard time telling whether she was one of the women whose homes had been burned around them.

She didn't care how smudged and grimy she got, for all

her talk of squires and camp wenches doing the dirty work. She'd been pitching in with enthusiasm ever since they rode into this ruined settlement. No dainty tiptoeing, no nose-in-the-air theatrics, no moaning and whining about getting dirty. She'd forged into this group of folks armed with nothing more than the pouch of oddities at her waist.

Trying is the best anyone can ever do, she had said.

And now the women were laughing instead of crying. Sabrina herself shimmered with a happiness he'd never seen in her before. She seemed content, happier, with all these people around her. He thought back to what she'd told him about never having any privacy. He'd felt sorry for her, a little bit, but now he wondered if he shouldn't have felt a little jealous instead. He'd never been at ease amid crowds of people.

She probably didn't feel comfortable all alone with him, but she never complained.

She'd probably be thrilled if she heard the settlers wanted to tag along with them on the trail to Fort Benton.

The men had begun harnessing the horses. He ought to go over there and tell them not to bother. Ought to tell them firmly, giving them no opportunity to butt in with objections, that he didn't have the time or the energy to guide them to Fort Benton.

Sabrina's laughter rose loud and clear. One of the women reached over and gave her a quick, affectionate hug. Sabrina hugged her back. The two of them smiled mistily at each other like damned long-lost sisters.

"Aw, hell," he muttered.

He took a head count. The adults were easy: twelve men, including the wounded ones. Twelve women. They paired up. That made sense. No reason for unmarried folks to try to scratch a living out of this hard land. A swarm of kids—at least twenty. It was hard to get an exact count because they kept running around, and impossible to tell them apart with soot coating them from head to toe.

Mighty close quarters, to get all of them packed into the three surviving wagons. The wounded men might rest more comfortably in the back of his medicine wagon, where restless children and squirming adults wouldn't accidentally jar their injuries.

The women had finished their sorting. They chattered as they folded clothes and stacked the other goods in neat piles around the Stuarts' organ. All those things would have to be carried in the wagons. They couldn't afford to leave a single thing behind. They wouldn't have enough room, unless somebody who knew what he was doing took charge of the evacuation. Otherwise they'd never find space for an organ, an organ that probably did represent enough value to put a man and his wife back on their feet again.

It seemed important, somehow, to save that organ.

The women completed their work at the very moment the men finished harnessing the horses. They all swiveled in unison as if they'd been hypnotized and stared straight at him. Expectant. Needy. Looking to him to ease their loss, to lead them to something better.

He felt the old tightness in his chest, the all-too-familiar urge to bolt.

Sabrina spotted him. Though she still knelt, she straightened and clasped her hands in front of her waist. Without thinking about it much, he started walking toward her instead of running away.

"Neil—have you heard? They will come with us. Is it not wonderful?"

He held out his hand for her and helped her to her feet. A little shower of ash drifted off her head. She laughed and shook it away, which made the diamond bounce against her dress. Though soot coated the stone with an oily black film, he could see the sparks glittering within. The Druid's Tear, pulsing with the light of a thousand stars as it sent Sabrina, the chosen Desmond woman, on a journey that did not include him. Except as her driver.

"The food goes in my wagon." He dropped Sabrina's hand and started issuing orders for the evacuation. "Divvy up the rest of the stuff among those three. Try to balance the loads. The horses will have enough work hauling all of you around. We won't make much more than ten miles before nightfall."

Much daylight remained when Sabrina noticed the glimmer of water. "Look over there, Neil. Is that a pond?"

He cast only a cursory glance toward where she pointed. "Could be. Could be a mirage, too. It's hard to tell sometimes."

She settled back and watched to make certain it was not a trick of the eyes. A bird soared across the valley and swooped low, splashing in the water.

"It is a pond! A large pond. No doubt deep enough to submerge one's entire self." She could not contain her excitement. It was the first bathing-size body of water she'd seen since beginning her strange journey.

Neil hunched low, steadfastly refusing to look at her or acknowledge the pond.

She moaned low in her throat, and shivered, thinking how delightful the cool, clear water would feel sluicing through the grime that covered her.

"Are you cold, Breenie?" asked the child in her arms. "You don't feel cold to me."

"No, I am not cold. Women sometimes shiver in anticipation of pleasure." Neil sucked in a loud breath, which heartened her. He'd been sitting clench-jawed ever since they left the burned-out village, and had muttered many times that they would never reach their destination at the slow pace necessitated by so many wagons following theirs.

Not even the four children sharing their wagon seat had cheered his foul mood. He'd cracked nary a smile, even when the smallest child, little more than a babe, had wriggled beneath their feet and popped his head up between Neil's knees. So she had held little hope that he might swerve for the pond, but if he found it so hot that breathing was difficult, then perhaps he might be persuaded.

She shot a sidelong glance toward Neil. " 'Tis a hot day," she told the child. "A fine day for swimming, if one should happen across a pond."

She might have allowed a sigh to escape, but she did not mean to. Not really.

She felt Neil's attention upon her, drawn no doubt by the sigh. And perhaps because she was staring straight at the sun-dappled water, he looked at it, too.

"You want to stop."

"Aye."

"There's a good three hours of daylight left."

"Aye," she whispered, knowing he was right.

The child in her arms squirmed free. "You're too hot," he complained. He slid down between her knees, and then popped up again. "It's too hard down there." He crawled back up into her lap but did not remain; before Sabrina could catch him, he barreled onto Neil's lap. His knees must have gouged Neil's midsection, for he gave an agonized wheeze.

"Maybe we'd better stop." He sounded oddly hoarse.

"Oh, *thank* you!"

Her gratitude was so great that she placed a kiss, just a small one, upon Neil's cheek. A mistake. She loved the way the rough stubble of his cheek felt against her softness, loved the scent she inhaled with every breath. At once, the memory of the previous night's deeper, headier kiss filled her senses, making her crave more.

"Now *he's* too hot, too," the child complained. "Can we really go swimming?"

Sabrina caught the fidgeting boy and pulled him back onto her lap. She nudged the other children. "We're going swimming," she said. "Soon you'll be clean and cool."

Splashing and feminine laughter drifted through the trees. A bead of sweat formed at Neil's nape and trickled down his back, reminding him he was plenty hot enough without torturing himself by imagining what must be going on in the pond.

"You think they're naked? All the way naked?"

He wondered if he'd stated his thoughts out loud, and then realized it was another of the men who had spoken.

"Dan!" remonstrated Eddie. "That ain't no way to talk about our wives."

But to a man they darted secret little glances toward the trees that hid the pond from their view. A high-pitched giggle, followed by a throaty squeal, hinted at horseplay. Women, dripping wet, splashing water all over each other. Neil wondered if Sabrina knew how to swim, if even now she was treading water, all the way naked, with just the crests of her breasts showing above the cool water, with the rest of her body a sweetly curving blur beneath the surface.

Neil shifted his position. A couple of the other men did the same.

He'd gone hunting with the men, and they'd managed to scare up a few rabbits. While they were gone, the women had prepared a simple meal for everyone, and then bathed the children, who now lay sleeping under the wagons. Most of them were clad only in underdrawers. Their clothes had been washed in the pond and lay spread over bushes and shrubs to dry. And then the women had shooed the men away, making them promise not to look while they tended to their own grimy clothes and bathing needs.

"God-fearin' women don't never strip themselves naked," said Jim, the oldest of the settlers, and the biggest pain in the ass so far. "Not so's anyone else can see."

"That ain't so." Fred spoke loudly, and then blushed. He cleared his throat. "I've heard tell that some decent women—not our wives, of course—prance around buck naked in their bedrooms. I heard they think their husbands like it."

"I heard the same," said Eddie. He, too, blushed a deep brick red. "I heard they sometimes prance naked until they bear, say, a couple-three young'uns. Then I heard they stop."

"Why do you suppose they stop?" asked Dan, wistfully.

"I heard it's on account of they think their stomachs get too poochy and their, uh, upper parts ain't so sassy, so they're embarrassed to be seen. That's what I heard, anyway."

A collective groan of disappointment swept through them.

"Hell, someone ought to tell them that those men I heard about probably think those women I heard about look just fine, even if they do get a mite droopy."

There was a low, masculine rumble of agreement. Neil found himself rumbling along, and covered his surprise with a cough. He couldn't recall the last time he'd been with a group of men and felt as if he were part of the crowd. Neil Kenyon, captain, had by necessity of his office held himself apart from the men he commanded.

Not today. These men looked up to him a little bit, it was true, but only because they'd suffered a setback. Or maybe, he thought slowly, because he refused to accept the role of captain with them. Odd, how forgoing that mantle of authority left him both more vulnerable and more content. He understood these men whom he barely knew. He recognized the hunger on their faces, the longing in their eyes, the furtive movements they made to hide the physical reaction they felt at thinking about their women cavorting naked. Any man who looked at him would no doubt recognize the same things in Neil, as he sat there hankering after his woman.

His woman? Not his woman. She belonged to a champion.

Lucky thing for him that he'd sworn off women. He'd had a little lapse back there in the woods when they'd been alone, thinking he might change his mind about that, but he'd come to his senses in time. Before he could fall in love with the kind of woman who could make him believe that he would revel in watching her, in loving her, whether she was taut and supple in the early blush of womanhood, or whether her body had grown comfortable and familiar after long years of living and loving.

Somebody would grow old with Sabrina. It just wouldn't be him. Her champion, whoever he might be, held prior claim, and she was bound and determined to honor that claim.

"Say, Neil—you wouldn't happen to have an extra bottle of that painkillin' elixir, would you?" Patterson, the man with burned hands, licked his lips in anticipation.

"Maybe we could all use a little drink," Neil said.

He headed for the wagon, and Eddie just tagged along without asking. It felt nice to have someone come along to help without being ordered to do so. Maybe that was why Neil wrestled loose an entire case of elixir rather than rationing out a single bottle for each man.

He had to get her to Fort Benton. Make arrangements

with someone to care for her while she went off champion hunting and he fulfilled his mission.

Meagher figured in on both scores. How could Meagher be Sabrina's champion and Neil's nemesis?

He'd find a way to work it out, though, and then he'd get on with the life he'd planned to make for himself. A life alone, with no responsibilities, no worries.

No woman to prance naked in his bedroom. No men to be his friends.

Fort Benton lay straight ahead. He would see to it that they made it there tomorrow, before he started getting used to thinking that those things mattered.

Chapter Thirteen

The borrowed garments she wore filled Sabrina with such delight that she had barely been able to wait until Neil returned from the men's turn in the pond.

"Look, Neil." She spun in a circle like a girl, showing him how the gathered cloth belled out from her waist. She ran her hands down her sides. "This cloth—'tis called cotton. Not so hot as wool, nor as fragile as silk. I swear I can feel the breeze touch my skin."

His attention seemed fixed upon the contrivances called buttons that marched up the front of her blouse. He, too, must recognize the wonder of them. Oh, how she loved the feel and construction of these clothes.

"Are they not wonderful?" She skimmed her fingertips down and back up the row of buttons, each time nudging the Druid's Tear out of the way. "This blouse clings so tight—almost like a second skin. If not for the buttons, I would never be able to wriggle myself into it."

"Buttons come in handy," Neil agreed.

"And this skirt!" She hooked her thumb into the waistband and pulled it away from her belly. "See how cunningly the seamstress tucked and sewed. Material enough for five tunics has been gathered into the pleats for this waist. Do you remember how my gown fits me?"

"I remember."

"A straight fall from shoulders to ankles. A woman wearing such a gown simply cannot move with any speed, for the knees pull the front hard against the calves, and the bottom hem restricts the length of one's steps. But this skirt—the heavy gathers provide modest covering for my limbs, while underneath, my legs move with uncommon freedom."

She felt frisky as a lamb, unable to stop herself from cavorting, though she knew ladies did not disport themselves in such a manner.

"Sabrina, I'm real glad you like your new clothes, but maybe we ought to talk about some—"

"Like them? Oh, Neil, you cannot imagine how this feels. Every step sends the cloth sliding against my bare legs. My stockings are no doubt dry by now, but I enjoy this sliding sensation so much that I am inclined to abandon stockings altogether."

"Who needs stockings?" he said faintly.

She twirled again. "Nor do I wear a corset!"

"I can see that."

His voice had been growing progressively more hoarse. Concerned, she ceased her unseemly playfulness and studied him with a healer's eye. With some alarm she noted that his skin flushed ruddy rather than his usual tan.

"Do you ail?"

She reached up to press her hand against his forehead. Since he stood so much taller than she, she had to rise to her toes and lean into him a little, balance herself with one palm set against his chest.

These cotton garments did not provide as much insulation between his skin and hers. Though separated by a handsbreadth, his warmth penetrated with ease. The steady thud of his heart quickened beneath her hand. But she noted with relief that his forehead was cool to her touch.

"I'm fine," he muttered.

She sniffed. "I smell spirits upon your breath."

"That means you're standing a little too close."

He did not push her away, though. They stood joined by her hand against his heart, her hand against his forehead, and this was the most wondrous feeling of all, to be connected with the parts of him she admired most. His mind. His heart.

"Overindulgence in spirits flushes one's aspect," she said.

"Are you trying to tell me I look drunk?"

"You look . . ."

She could not complete the thought while he gazed down at her with no reserve in his demeanor. Humor sparkled in his eyes, in the curve of his lips. His hair curled at the ends, still damp from his recent plunge into the pond.

"All of us look a little drunk, I'd say." He nodded toward the opposite side of the clearing, where the settlers gathered. The men did seem uncommonly lighthearted, teasing their wives, tussling with their children.

Sabrina noticed the man called Eddie whisper something to his wife, Olive, and then the two of them, smothering giggles behind their hands like naughty children, darted off into the woods. A hunger started within her, lower than the pangs usually struck.

She did not think her hunger stemmed from the delicious scent of roasting rabbit wafting through the air. The cooking fires crackled, their light growing more prominent as the sun slid low toward the horizon.

"Shall we join the feasting?" she asked.

"It's just a mess of rabbits," Neil said. The low rumble of his voice vibrated against her ear, and she realized that she still leaned against him, still touched him where she willed. Her hand had slid down to cup the edge of his jaw without either of them knowing it, else surely he would have pushed her away. The tough tickle of his unshaven skin against her palm suddenly struck her as far more pleasurable than the sensations she'd been luxuriating in earlier.

She had no right to touch him so, or to take pleasure in it.

She moved away and twisted her hands into the abundantly thick folds of her skirt.

"I am reminded of Midsummer Eve. We celebrated it at Desmond just before I . . . came here. Feasting, and . . . and more." She could not bring herself to say *fornicating*. "There are not enough fires, though."

"We're risking too many as it is. Those Indians that attacked the settlement could still be in the area."

"Just as well. None of the ladies here have need of the Baal fires' magic."

"Baal fire?"

She wished she'd not mentioned the fires. "An ancient custom, still celebrated in some places. It is believed that a maiden will marry within a year if she dances circles around seven bonfires on Midsummer Eve."

He expelled a breath. "Then you're right. You don't need to go dancing around fires. You know there's a champion in store for you."

The full import of his remark did not overtake her until she'd allowed sorrow to have its way. But then a great rush of joy flooded the sorrow away.

"You believe me," she whispered.

"I believe you."

A fullness welled in her, something soft and wondrous that soaked up all the loneliness that had filled her for so long.

True love, she thought, must fill a person in just this way, all the time.

But even in the grip of exhilaration, a niggling fear wormed its way into her mind.

"Did you believe me before you indulged in spirits?"

He laughed, a rueful sound. "I indulged in spirits because I believed you, and it seemed like the best thing I could do was get good and drunk."

"Oh. Well. Then that is all right."

What did one do with such a gift as Neil Kenyon's belief when one knew she must seek another? Especially when he seemed so uncomfortable with his believing. She longed for him to touch her hair, to smile at her during this moment that affected her so deeply, but he forced his hands into his pockets and hunched his shoulders, looking embarrassed.

She wished she knew more of the way matters stood between men and women. Certes, some of the people surrounding them had married for love; others, she felt equally certain, had entered a union for mutual gain rather than love, exactly as she knew she must do. If only she could ask for advice.

Another couple stole away into the dark. One less woman available to dispense advice . . . or . . . a sign, pointing her toward the answer.

Yes.

Duty decreed she marry another. Destiny determined the champion she must bring back to her people. But she—*she*—could choose the man she loved, and offer him all she had to give.

"Neil." She reached for his hand.

"What the hell?"

His head snapped up. His arms crossed over his chest. His eyes narrowed. But none of his attention was directed toward her; if anything, she felt certain he had not heard her call his name.

She looked at what troubled him so, and saw nothing amiss. A half dozen men and women clustered around one of the wagons. Amid much whistling and stomping of feet, a blushing Lizzie Stuart was being hoisted into the wagon bed.

"What is bothering you, Neil?"

"I hope to God I'm wrong." But when a torrent of oaths interrupted his worry, she knew he believed himself to be right. "What the hell do they think they're doing?"

He gripped Sabrina by the arm and propelled them both across the clearing. They reached the wagon just as Lizzie seated herself upon a small stool in front of the large wooden furniture that had caused so much earlier contention.

She threw open a lid to reveal black and white toothlike objects. She sat upon the small stool that had been kept with the furniture and commenced pumping with her feet. She placed her hands upon the teeth, and Sabrina gasped when music poured from the furniture.

"That's a good 'un," someone cried.

"Stop this right now!" Neil yelled.

Nobody heeded his cry. A couple moved into the light cast by the largest fire. It was Dan. He held his wife by the elbow, and with his free hand tipped a bottle of Neil's elixir high in the air. Yet another bottle had been stuffed in his back pocket. All the men, Sabrina noted with a quick inspection, possessed bottles of Neil's potion, in varying degrees of fullness.

"This is a bad idea, folks, a real bad idea," Neil shouted, loudly enough to be heard above the music, to no avail.

Dan cast aside the empty bottle and began nodding his

head along with the music. His wife tapped her toe, and soon others in the group commenced clapping with the same rhythm as her toe tapping. Sabrina, caught by the music and the excitement, joined with them.

"Don't encourage them." Neil tugged her hands apart. "Listen to me—"

"And a one, two, three!" called Dan. He caught his wife in a strange embrace, holding one hand high in the air and drawing her close with an arm around her waist. Using quick, hopping motions they turned and twirled, her skirts swirling high against her legs. They laughed, all the while looking deep into each other's eyes as true lovers will do.

"Don't do this." Little volume accompanied Neil's request, as if he'd conceded defeat on the matter.

Sabrina knew he feared the Indian threat. Her woman's heart told her that more than worry over Indians caused the rigid tension in his jaw, the thinning of his lips. She remembered all he had told her of his doomed marriage. How it had begun with drinking spirits and dancing and stealing off into the dark. This night must remind him, vividly, of that time long ago, a time he considered one of his greatest lapses in judgment.

She had been on the verge of asking him to repeat what he considered a mistake.

Circumstance had certainly saved her pride. He had already admitted to being flown with spirits. If he had loved her while music kept rhythm with their movements, would his mind and heart have been there with her—or wandering with the ghosts of the past?

Soon other couples joined the dancers. The children crept to the edge of the firelit areas and sat watching, giggling and nudging one another with elbows as if their parents' exertions both amused them and made them proud.

"Say Neil—grab that woman o' yours and take a turn or two with us," shouted Jim.

That woman of yours. These people thought she and Neil belonged together, filled, as they were, with strong spirits—and stronger emotions firing their blood.

"If you cared about your women and children, you'd stop that damn-fool dancing and pick a likely spot for guard duty," Neil shot back.

Lizzie's music faltered. Some of the dancers dipped and swayed for a few more feet, while the rest stumbled to a quick halt.

Silence fell, swift and complete, as they all directed their stricken faces toward Neil. They drew together in the unconscious manner of a herd seeking safety.

"What're you sayin'?"

"You insisted on following me because you claimed you thought I'd be a good man in a fight. Well, I am. And that's why I'm reminding you that you were burned out by Indians less than twenty-four hours ago. Those Indians might well be in the area now. You built fires too big. If that wasn't enough to draw the Indians right to you, you're playing music like a circus drumming for an audience."

Lizzie clapped a hand over her mouth while tears brimmed in her eyes.

"No call to make my wife cry." Sam Stuart stormed over to Neil and stood before him, trembling, but wise enough to keep his fists at his side. Sabrina feared that in his black mood, Neil would not hesitate to ply his own, more powerful fists. "We was just havin' a little fun."

"Fun's over," Neil said. "Gather your families close, and try to sober up a little. I'll take the first watch."

He aimed first for the wagon, and wrenched the rifle out of its sheath without losing a step. He cradled it in the crook of his arm, his fist around the barrel. He should have had the weapon with him this whole time. He should have served as a good example, making sure these simpleminded settlers kept the danger of their surroundings in their minds all the time.

Instead he'd gotten them all drunk, himself included, because he'd felt the need to escape from his thoughts for a little while. Instead of keeping watch, he'd taken himself off with Sabrina and let her preen and flutter for him, while he pretended he had the right to watch her do it, which meant getting drunk hadn't solved a damned thing for him anyway.

The only thing that could have turned this night into a worse disaster was if he'd allowed the dancing to go on, and if he'd taken part. If he'd pulled Sabrina into his arms and danced with her under the stars, the way every ounce of his body had ached to do.

Just havin' fun, Sam had protested, and every man among them had nodded in support. Against him. Neil Kenyon, the bad-tempered grouch who had the nerve to remind them that they might be in danger.

The Indian threat was very real. But even if it weren't, he would have found some excuse to put a halt to the dancing. The men were on target in resenting him. They just didn't know the full extent of it.

So much for those brief moments of kinship he'd enjoyed. The sense of belonging, the tenuous band of friendship, had been just as fleeting, just as insubstantial, as the one moment he'd allowed himself to admit he loved Sabrina, before acknowledging she could not be his. As impossible as the one moment when he'd dared to think he might offer to be her champion, an idea so preposterous that it turned her diamond dark.

He lengthened his stride. He gripped the rifle so hard he wouldn't be surprised to find he'd crushed the barrel.

The rifle wouldn't be much good for shooting Indians, then, but firing a bullet might cause a backfiring explosion that would end his useless, mistake-riddled life.

"Neil! Please wait for me. I cannot keep up."

He didn't think anything could have stopped his head-long rush away from the camp. She proved him wrong. The sound of her voice wrapped itself around him and held him still.

He had charged off, figuring she'd stay behind. She belonged with the settlers in a way he never could. From the first minute she'd embraced them, not caring that their problems were beyond fixing. She'd given them all she had to offer without reservation, even though she knew she would be leaving them and could never be repaid. It didn't matter that all she had to give was a pouch full of frog spawn and skull moss. She'd dispensed her material goods but, more important, herself, with love and respect, while he'd doled out his contributions in grudging doses.

"You don't belong out here with me, Sabrina."

"Nonetheless, it is where I choose to be."

She came to him, the grasses whispering her passage. He felt her touch upon his arm, and some of the aching urgency within him subsided.

"You were retreating again."

"I'm going to stand watch." That was true, although it felt like a lie when he said it.

"I will go with you."

He looked down at her. They were close enough to the camp that firelight gilded her features and drew red-gold shimmers from her hair. Her quiet radiance paled, though, against the diamond gleaming at her breast.

"It's not a good idea for you to be out here with me," he said, keeping his eye on that damned stone. And damn if it didn't surge with a moment's dazzling brightness at his words, as if it approved of his effort to send her away.

"I am beginning to believe you think there are no good ideas in the world." She cocked her head up at him and tapped her toe. "Dancing is not a good idea. Merriment is not a good idea. Casting aside one's sorrows is not a good idea."

"Not under these circumstances. They've lost everything, Sabrina."

"Perhaps that is why they are able to frolic with such light hearts. For them, there is nothing left but possibilities."

"They're lucky," he said. "Some of us know for certain that what they desire most can never be theirs."

"Neil." He knew by the misery etched in her face that she understood what he meant. Her eyes sparkled with unshed tears. The Druid's Tear seemed to pulsate with approval.

He hated that diamond. He couldn't look at her without it winking up at him, reminding him that she would never be his.

But she stood at his side right now. She claimed it was where she wanted to be.

"Hide that necklace under your blouse," he said. "The diamond reflects the moonlight. Might give us away, if anybody's out there watching."

She complied. She loosened the top two buttons of her blouse and tucked the Druid's Tear beneath, and then buttoned herself back up again.

Neil began to wonder if he'd made yet another mistake in telling her to hide the stone away. Without it she seemed . . . not the barbaric Irish princess on a quest to find her champion, but a soft and sweet and incredibly delectable woman who'd chosen to walk out into the night with him. One ordinary woman who wanted to be with one ordinary man.

He settled them down on a small rise. The night was so dark that they would have to depend more on hearing than on eyesight. He glanced back and saw with some satisfaction that the settlers had at last taken his warnings to heart. The camp had gone quiet. Two of the fires had been smothered outright. The one remaining had been reduced to red-orange embers. Nobody had added more logs, even though the night was turning chill. The clearing lay dark, but not as dark as where he and Sabrina kept watch from beneath the trees.

He leaned back against a tree, balancing his rifle across his knees. She settled herself against the tree as well. Her shoulder bumped up against his. She angled slightly away from him, so that her eyes and ears searched the woods to his right, meaning he had only to keep watch over the woods to his left.

With two sets of eyes, two pairs of ears, they could do a better job, with less dread that they might be missing something.

The night air smelled fresh and clean. Occasional wind gusts struck cool against his face, but sharing Sabrina's warmth warded off the chill. Nice, sitting here, enjoying the dark, he thought, when you weren't all alone.

He realized eventually by the changing position of the moon that an hour or more had passed without him ever once growing bored, or uncomfortable from having his backside planted in the dirt.

It was the strangest—and best—guard duty of his life.

Chapter Fourteen

Sabrina found it all too easy to revel in her closeness to Neil and allow her mind to wander paths that had always before filled her with dread. Thoughts of what a man and woman might do together, in a bed, if they knew how to share laughter. Maisie had promised it could be wonderful. Sabrina believed it.

A poor guard she was proving to be, with all her attentions focused upon imaginary pleasures rather than the dangers that could be hiding in the dark. She cared more for the strong, steady thump of Neil's heart than any stealthy noises beyond the trees.

She resolved to do better, and as a start did her best to pierce the dark with her eyesight, but her mind filled the canvas of night with the image of Neil smiling down at her.

She forced herself to once more judge the silence of the night.

Utter quiet usually meant a foreign presence disturbed the night creatures.

A good night was never completely quiet; this night continued to vibrate with reassuring sounds. Small animals rustled through leaves and brush. Night birds pealed single notes of exquisite purity. Insects trilled songs that would not end until dawn.

"I don't think anything's out there," Neil whispered after a very long time had passed. "Not anything that's a threat, anyway."

"Then you stopped the dancing for naught." She kept her voice low, too.

He hesitated. "No, sweetheart. This is no time for dancing."

She wished her mind would not plague her with the memory of what he had told her, of how dancing had led to his union with another woman. She wished she could deny the spurt of jealousy that rose within at thinking he would never dance with her because the ghost of that other woman haunted him, warning him against dancing with someone else.

"Will there ever be a time when you can dance again?"

If he said yes . . . she did not know what she would do. She would be gone before his heart healed sufficiently to permit it. If he said yes, she would live out her days in Desmond Muir, wondering what sort of woman had quickened his heart. Wondering if he smiled his rare smile at her as he held her and spun her while music filled the air.

"I don't miss dancing. I'm not a very good dancer."

She could not believe that to be true. He moved with the easy elegance of a man who held complete mastery over his body. His long, lean length bespoke of much muscular control. She had no doubt he could execute any dance move he chose. Her throat tightened, knowing he'd deliberately misstated his reason for not dancing.

She had not the time to articulate her disbelief and concern, though, for the reassuring peace of the night was shattered by the sound of stealthy footfalls approaching their hiding place.

Neil tensed. Without making a sound, he moved with utmost care. He shifted his hold upon his rifle and drew it toward his shoulder. Neither of them breathed, holding still and silent to pinpoint from where the intruder approached.

"Psst!"

Neil's rifle swung toward the sound.

"Pest! Neil! You out here?"

"Yeah."

"Well, gimme a hint. I can't see anything, it's so dark."

Neil lowered the rifle. He made a cup of his hand over his mouth, and to Sabrina's amazement, he made a sound very much like the night birds whose song had lightened this night. He waited a moment and repeated the call.

He continued, perhaps a dozen times, until with a noisy rustling and crunching of twigs, a man came through the brush to join them.

He was little more than a dark, unidentifiable shape in the night.

"Who're you?" Neil asked.

"It's me, Jim."

"Not exactly a stealthy approach."

"I'm not exactly a sentry. Horses and cattle are more my line of expertise, and next to the way they paw the ground, I'm dancin' through these woods light as a ballerina. I'm thinking that if Indians are slinkin' around out there, it wouldn't hurt them to know a bunch of us are roamin' these woods, looking for them."

"A bunch of you?"

"Yeah." Jim cleared his throat in the manner of a man who'd been caught at a mistake. "We got to talkin'. Worse, the wives got to addin' in their opinions. They . . . I mean, we all agree you're right. We were actin' like idiots.''

"Can't take the whole blame on yourself," Neil said. "My elixir had something to do with it."

How easily he shifted some of the blame to his own shoulders. It was true he had dispensed his spirits to these men, but it was also true that none of them had been forced to drink it. He could easily have denied all responsibility.

Sabrina wondered if he could sense the pride she felt in him at that moment.

She heard movement, the slap of flesh meeting flesh in friendly camaraderie, and she knew Neil and Jim were shaking hands in the dark.

"I came out here to relieve you," Jim said. "You've been keeping watch for two hours now."

Two hours! She had known time had passed, but had not been aware of how much. She should not be so surprised. These hours she had with Neil were so infinitely precious, and they speeded by with distressing haste.

"I don't sleep much," Neil said. "I figure I can put in a couple more hours."

"We thought you might feel that way." Jim stomped over toward them, and with a little thump something fell at their feet. "My missus thought it'd be a good idea if you had some beddin' and a little food. That way you can stay on if you want, but if you get tired or hungry you'll have everything you need to make yourselves comfortable."

"Thank you, Jim," Sabrina said, so warmed by the thoughtful gesture that she doubted she would need the bedding.

"I don't know too much about this kind of thing, but I do know it helps to spell one another. I'll tell you what— I'm going to stake out a spot a few hundred yards through these trees. This might be a good time for you to take a break from watchin'. Try to nap. Then give me four-five of them birdcalls to let me know you're ready to go back on duty."

"We'll do that. Thanks."

Neil's voice struck her as uncommonly gruff, but not in a harsh way—rather in the way of a man whose heart had been touched.

Jim crashed off through the brush. They listened to his progress. Sound carried far through the night, and so it was a long time before she felt silence settle around them again.

"He stopped," she said.

"No. He's still going." Neil's whole body stood taut with the effort he put into tracking Jim, the way a soldier would listen. In so many ways, without saying a word, he reminded her he possessed a warrior's strength and skills. "Now he stopped. He's about four hundred yards to the northeast."

Four hundred yards seemed a great distance to her, enough to allow her to recapture the sense of privacy she'd shared with him. She stretched, suddenly conscious that she was still sitting while he stood. He seemed to become aware of it at the same moment.

"Take my hand. I'll pull you up. You're probably stiff from sitting in one place so long."

She came to her feet with a little bounce, and discovered she *was* a little stiff. Her knees threatened to buckle beneath her, but Neil must have anticipated the weakness, for his arm caught her around the waist, lending support.

The silence of the night, the intimacy of the darkness, pressed down upon them.

"Maybe someday," she whispered, "friends like Jim will help you learn to dance. I wish . . . I wish I could—"

She stopped herself before admitting out loud that she longed to be the one who could free his heart enough to let him want to dance again.

He lifted a curl of her hair, let it drop. "There's no music."

But there was a rhythm. It beat from her heart and coursed through her blood, and found an answer vibrating from him. She leaned more fully into him. His lower reaches pressed firmly into her belly. She moved her leg forward, and his leg moved back, a miniature retreat . . . but only for a moment.

He held himself very still. Very tense. And then he flexed his leg against hers, moving first one, then the other, forward . . . back. . . . Her limbs obeyed with such unquestioning familiarity that it seemed she'd been born to move in concert with him.

They were dancing. In the deepest black of the night, with no music save for the passion singing in their blood, they were dancing.

She felt a tremor shake him, and then a low, disbelieving laugh as he realized it, too. He did not retreat. He tightened his hold upon her, sure and strong. He spun her and turned with her. She could see nothing but the broad expanse of his chest; she could hear nothing but the beat of his heart pounding the tempo of their silent song.

Perhaps he was right, she thought with dizzy delight. Perhaps dancing did lead to nothing but trouble, for she felt the desperate urge to cast aside all her responsibilities and obligations and stay here dancing in the woods with him forever.

"I told you this wasn't such a good idea," he murmured, just before his lips captured hers.

She did not spare the time to contradict him. She showed him that his kiss was the best thing that had ever happened to her in her life. She twined her arms about his neck, holding him close, pressing herself more tightly into his surging heat.

He groaned and shifted his hold upon her so that his

hand cupped her bottom. He wedged her softness against the part of him that throbbed, hard and demanding, and roused such a sweet ache within her that she moaned with need.

" 'Tis not a bad idea, Neil," she managed.

"Sweetheart, you don't know what a bad idea this is."

She knew then that she could stop him. With but a word, or a gentle removal of his hands, she could put a dam against the tide of passion that threatened to engulf them both.

She knew she would not. She had craved this from almost the first moment she had met him.

She pulled down his head until his forehead met hers. She touched his cheek, and her fingers left trails of heat. She smoothed his hair back and traced the contours of his ear. He felt her lips against his forehead, and then a kiss against each eyelid, light as a breath of air fanned by a butterfly's wing.

"What are you doing?" He couldn't believe he asked that; he couldn't believe how hoarse he sounded.

"Your eyes and ears have worked hard this night."

Her mouth brushed his so gently he thought he might have imagined it, might have *wished* it, until she kissed him again. Light, delicate, there and gone quickly, as if she feared he might reject her mouth.

When she did it again, he moved to capture her mouth, molding his lips to hers, parting them until she parted hers and he felt the rush of her breath, tasted her against his tongue.

Something inside him crumbled, shattered, at the surge of need that exploded to life within. Need for her, hot and heavy, weighted his loins. He had to hold her, had to touch her, had to explore every inch of her and brand it with his hands, with his tongue, as his for all time.

He caught her head between his hands and claimed her

mouth. Tilted her back and tasted the skin at her neck, felt her life force pulse from the base of her throat. He ached to go lower and had to free the buttons that closed her blouse.

He reached for her warmth, for the silk of her skin, and found the Druid's Tear instead.

Even in this black dark it glowed with its inner, ancient fires. Until he touched it. The crystal glitter flared, and then went dull.

If the damned stone could speak, it couldn't say any clearer that he was not the champion Sabrina had been sent to find.

She made a soft, yearning sound. "Neil?"

He looked at the diamond and knew it had ruled her life. Knew she would follow its lead.

He broke the chain and threw the damned diamond into the weeds.

He didn't know how he unbuttoned her blouse, how he undid her skirt, how he stripped all away from her, but he did it. There wasn't enough moonlight to illuminate her the way he craved. He wanted more than the glitter of her eyes seeking his, more than moonlight glistening from lips moist from his kisses.

She was his shadow woman, there but not there, his to love for this night but with no memory burned in his mind for tomorrow.

He would take what he could.

She had begun this, with her talk of dancing. But now the rhythm of taking was his; he would finish what she had started.

He returned to her mouth, knowing he would never have enough of it, the lush pressure of her lips against his, the taste of her, the silk of her mouth as his tongue played with hers. He could feel her, so alive, in his possession of her mouth. Her pulse, the vibration of her throaty murmurs, the breath she shared with him.

His hands claimed her, too, while his mouth continued its tender assault. Her breast swelled against his hand, her nipple hardening for him, only for him. He swept his hand low, across the hollow of her belly, reveling in the shudder that welled from his touch and hummed through all of her.

She joined in the play, her fingers shaking as she fumbled with his shirt buttons. He let her take her time, each stroke of her nails against his skin raising exquisite shivers. He shrugged off the shirt while she explored his chest, twirling her fingers in the soft curls, shivering when she stroked his nipple.

She laughed, a triumphant sound, and placed her lips where her fingers had been, tantalizing him with a touch of her tongue against his nipple.

"That's exactly what I had in mind." He captured both of her hands in one of his and held them high over her head while his mouth plundered her tender skin. At the neck, where she had already accepted him, and lower, and lower again until his mouth traced the firm swell of her breast.

She moaned and twisted, offering more to his questing mouth. He took it. He would take all she offered this night; he would take more than she knew how to give, for this was his one chance.

He used his hands, his mouth, his tongue. He held her down when she tried to rise against him, lifted her when she shied away. All of her would be his for this night—all of her. The soft sounds she made inflamed him, each moan, each whimper, each pleading cry of his name striking his soul. Her pulse matched the rhythm of his, and then the two beat as one. The dual thunder deafened him to all else but the need pulsating within him.

She moved against him, her body firm. She tangled her long legs with his, twisting and shifting until she drove her center against the part of him that threatened to explode. He stilled her hip with one hand, and with the other taught her that a woman, too, could shatter with need.

He stroked her thighs until she parted for him, and he found her hot and wet, welcoming the invasion of his fingers with the supple lift of her hips.

He wanted to take so much more, wanted to give so much more. He moved over her, reveling in the way her body shifted to match his, the firm strength of her thighs pillowing his, the bold thrust of her breasts luring him into lowering his head and claiming them once more, each in turn.

Her limbs, long, slim, wrapped him, holding him close. She rose against him, slick and wet with the pleasure he'd already given her. So ready for him, her wanting matching his.

He could wait no more. His groan rumbled his pleasure as he slid his shaft into her heat, found her tight and trembling. She went still when he used his hand to guide himself inside her. He kissed her, knowing she would feel pain, helpless to prevent it, helpless to stop himself from causing it. "My lord," she breathed. He moved. Thrust. Exquisitely slow. And again. He felt the barrier, the proof of the virginity she had once asked him to examine, and even now, with his senses flown and his need thundering in his blood, he wanted to weep at the honor of her giving it to him.

Again. Not so slow.

He felt her give inside. Her hold on him tightened, tensed. He swallowed her sob into his kiss. Kissed her mouth, kissed her nose, kissed her eyes until she relaxed around him—but only for a moment. She kissed him back.

She wrapped those long, long legs around him, curled her arms around his shoulders. From deep within her began a shuddering contraction. She cried out in surprise.

"Neil!"

"Hold still, Sabrina. Sweetheart, you have to hold still or I'll—"

"I . . . I cannot." She lifted her hips. She tightened her legs around his waist, and a tremor shook her from head to toe. Her pleasure stole the last shred of control he possessed.

Need, aching and endless, consumed him, demanded he get closer, touch more of her, drive deeper into her. Her cries mingled with his while his body shook and heaved with the sweet release of claiming her, all of her.

It took a while for his senses to return, for him to realize that he was probably crushing her into the ground. He shifted, pulling her on top of him, sharing his warmth with her. He felt moisture against his chest and touched her face, finding the hot evidence of tears.

"Did I hurt you?"

"No."

"You're crying."

"Aye."

"Don't."

"I cannot stop." She trembled against him, turned her head, fashioned a tiny kiss against his chest. "I have found indescribable joy in your arms. Never did I think to love so well. But it changes nothing."

"Don't say that."

"I must. We both knew this. I most of all. But I could not deny myself this one night in your arms. Please tell me, please, that you will not hate me for this."

He tightened his arms around her until a soft cry from her made him realize he'd used too much of his strength.

But it wouldn't matter if he possessed ten times as much. She meant to leave him.

A flash from the dark drew his attention. He welcomed the distraction until he realized what it was . . . her damned Druid's Tear, winking triumphantly in the dark.

Chapter Fifteen

She hadn't spoken to him since he'd left her the night before.

Neil couldn't blame her. No woman could forgive a man who rose from lovemaking, gathered his clothes, and walked off naked without one word of explanation.

He'd kicked at her diamond, too, but only managed to stub his toe against the glittering treasure. He'd picked it up anyway, worried that she might not find it in the dark. Besides, he'd broken the chain again. It would have to be mended before she could wear it, before it could serve as a beacon, lighting the way to her true champion.

He'd been surprised to find her waiting at the wagon when he ventured back into camp the next morning. Even more surprised to notice that the way they were able to work together seemed unaffected by his frozen demeanor, her equally unreadable expression.

Seemed to him that they had both learned the knack

of getting on with life without showing evidence of their wounds.

He'd paced the night away, guarding the perimeter of their makeshift camp even though the other men had developed a fairly decent watch system. Tension kept him prowling. He'd kept telling himself it was his battle-honed instincts warning him that something threatened from out there in the dark.

A little voice in his mind had whispered the truth. Profound danger did wait out there, in the very delectable form of Sabrina Desmond. If he didn't keep circling the camp, he'd aim straight back to her and go down on his knees, begging for the chance to travel back through time with her. To live again through the futility of war for her. To make their one night together last for eternity.

What stunned him, what frightened him more than anything, was the realization that he couldn't go back with her. Not because he was afraid, as he'd been for so long, to suffer pain. He'd learned the real meaning of pain last night.

He could live with disappointing himself. Somehow, over these past few days, he'd come to realize that he was only a man. A curious freedom came from that realization.

But Sabrina truly believed she could bring the perfect champion back to her people. She also truly believed that a champion could do his job by saving one person, one scrap of land at a time. Neil didn't think she understood. She might believe that. He might believe that. But the people she ruled wouldn't understand. They expected her to come back to them with a hero.

He was no hero.

If she saddled herself with him, she would be the one to suffer the insults, the recriminations. She would suffer for his inadequacy.

And he loved her too much to let that happen.

"We must stop, Neil," Sabrina said after they'd been traveling for a good four hours.

"Impossible."

"The children must eat. Everyone is exhausted. The women must tend to their personal needs."

Typical that she'd mentioned the needs of others without admitting her own. He didn't know how lovemaking affected women from a physical standpoint, especially a woman who had never known a man. He shifted, uncomfortable with the memory of how he'd known he should be gentle, and yet he'd gone crazy with wanting her. He'd taken and taken.

"I picked up your necklace."

"I know. I watched you leave."

His conscience taunted him, demanding that he apologize. He couldn't apologize for loving her. He couldn't apologize for the agony he'd felt at hearing from her own lips that she would never be his.

"I fixed the chain. Seems I broke the same link as before."

She held out her hand. He fumbled in his pocket for the necklace and gave it to her. She studied the repair he'd done. He knew it was a clumsy job, but he'd done the best he could. "It'll hold," he said. "Just don't pull on it or that link will probably spread wide open."

"You are the only one who has ever pulled the chain, Neil."

His vitals clenched at remembering what had happened when he'd snapped the link the night before.

"Are you all right?"

"Why would I not be?"

"Well, because . . ." His body taunted him with the reminder of her long legs wrapped around him, her arms holding him close, her sweetness perfuming the very air he breathed. Children rode in this wagon with them, though, and he could not speak right out about the subject. "You asked me to examine you once before. Well, consider yourself examined. You were . . . untouched. It's all right if you admit you're feeling a little uncomfortable today."

Color flared in her cheeks. "And if I admit such a weakness—will you stop?"

"No."

"Why?" He hated hearing her plead. His proud beauty ought never to have to beg for anything.

"We're about ten miles from Fort Benton. It'll take us all day at the rate we're moving. If we stop we'll never make it before dark."

She sagged, and he automatically reached out to support her. She cringed away from him. He allowed himself to look at her, really look at her, for the first time since he'd turned away from her the night before. Exhaustion lined her face. The tender skin beneath her eyes looked swollen, as if she'd cried . . . but Desmond women did not cry. She'd probably spent most of the night rubbing away nonexistent tears.

The thin wail of a hungry child drifted from the wagons following them. The kids riding in his medicine wagon had stopped fidgeting a mile or two back, and had taken to staring at him the way a hungry dog riveted its attention on a person eating a big, thick steak.

Guilt gnawed at him, calling him the most inconsiderate man who'd ever lived. But he knew in his tactician's soul that stopping was not wise.

"This is the most dangerous point in our journey." He didn't have to explain, but he owed her at least that much. "If Indians are going to attack, they're going to have to make their move soon, before we get in sight of town."

"Indians, always Indians!" Again her color flared, and she displayed peevish temper for the first time since he'd met her. "Have you seen a single one?"

"No."

Henry Patterson thumped the heel of his foot against the wall of the medicine wagon. His voice, muffled through the wood, rose in demand. "When the hell are we gonna stop? I need to take a piss."

Sabrina swayed and slumped. She pressed her knees together. She didn't beg again; she didn't ask for more explanations, just sat there and grew pale with discomfort.

"Aw, hell."

Neil pulled back on the reins and stopped the wagon. He grabbed his rifle before levering himself down off the bench seat. "You men keep a sharp eye out," he called. "If anyone needs to go into the brush, go three at a time. Everyone else, stay as close as you can to the middle of the road."

He turned to help Sabrina down, but she'd already vanished from the seat. Gone. He knew she'd just hurried off to relieve herself, but finding the seat empty hit him with the force of a cannonball. After today that seat would always be empty. He'd sell the damned wagon, but in his head he'd always see that empty seat.

He gripped his rifle tight, wishing it were Sabrina he held between his hands.

People crawled from the other wagons, groaning when their feet touched the ground, placing hands against their backs. The children perked right up the minute their feet hit the ground; they commenced shrieking and laughing and running around like lunatics.

"Keep it quiet!" he ordered, but nobody paid him the least bit of attention. "I need you men to keep your guns ready and watch for any suspicious movements out there in the woods." One of the fellows waved halfheartedly in his direction, but Neil didn't notice any of the men obey his command. Too tired, most likely, from guard duty the night before. Like Sabrina, they'd allowed the absence of Indians to lull them back into feeling safe.

He was in charge again, by default.

How had he gotten himself into this mess? He'd started on this journey planning to keep his military status a secret, planning to avoid responsibility, planning to minimize all contact with troublesome human beings. And now here he was riding herd over a bunch of burned-out homesteaders who knew he was an army man. He had wounded civilians in his care, and hungry kids. He ought to feel plenty resentful that all this had been thrust upon him.

Instead, he cared. And in caring, he felt more alive than ever before.

He worried about these folks who had lost so much and faced such an uncertain future. He marveled at their fortitude and the hope they expressed despite their adversity.

He heard a thump from the back of the wagon and realized belatedly that he should have gone to help Henry. But when he got there he found Sabrina already there, halfway in the wagon, scooting back to pull Henry out into the sun. There hadn't been time for her to go off and tend to her own needs; she'd come straight here.

"Here, let me do that," Neil said, offering his arm for Henry to balance against. "You go off and do what you need to do. Make sure you take someone with you."

"Thank you." She didn't look at him, just darted quickly away. "Don't go too far into those woods," he warned.

The hand that gripped his arm seemed surprisingly strong for someone who had been burned so badly. Neil glanced down and saw healing skin, fingers that bent without pain. "That salve of hers seems to be doing you some good."

Henry flexed his fingers. "Seems to me you ought to

be selling her cures instead of the stuff you got in them bottles.''

"Her ingredients are a little hard to come by," Neil said.

"Well, she's like a miracle come to life, if you ask me. You're one lucky man to have a woman like that."

But Neil didn't have her. And he never would. He made a noncommittal grunt and took a quick look around the camp. None of the men seemed to be keeping watch. Some of the women had gone; he hoped they'd heeded his advice and stayed in groups. And over there—damn, much too close to a thick tangle of brush, Sabrina knelt, examining the man who'd taken the fire arrow in the shoulder. Again she'd put her own needs aside to see to someone under her care.

She'd removed her frog-spawn patch from the wound and was comparing it to the arrow she'd nurtured these past couple of days. A smile curved her lips, and sheer happiness shone from her, as if nothing in this world could have delighted her more than to know the man who'd been hurt was now on the mend. She bent close and whispered something, which made him smile, and which caused jealousy to twist ugly and coiled as a snake within Neil. She had taken a good long while to warm up to him, and now that he'd hurt her he doubted he'd ever see that smile directed his way again. He knew in his gut that she would always be on guard in his presence. It hurt to know he was responsible for dimming her natural impulsiveness.

He'd done nothing but hurt her, while she'd given him so much. If not for her he would be making this trip alone, closed within the shell of a disguise that had its roots far beyond accepting the mission from President Johnson. Neil Kenyon had begun weaving a disguise for himself years and years ago, when he'd taken a woman he didn't love to wife, when he'd watched in silent agony while men he could not save died around him. He'd thought the disguise was necessary, because a real man didn't admit his failures, didn't cry out loud when sorrow and agony rent his soul. But all a disguise did was trap those feelings inside.

Sabrina had come to him and made him realize that in hiding his failures, he'd buried his happiness as well.

She understood responsibility. She understood sacrifice. She reached out to help with a naturalness that had to be inborn, in the blood, the mark of a royal princess born and bred to care for those who needed her. She did not much care whether they were the Irish subjects she'd sworn to save back in the year 1298, or a bunch of poor, desperate homesteaders who didn't even have the sense to keep watch when ordered to do so.

She didn't care if she failed with them, or if she succeeded. She only believed in trying her best.

She had asked the same of him—that he try. Just try.

He had turned away from her last night because he believed she expected more. He believed that her pride demanded success.

She had never asked more than that he try. And she had given herself to him, and loved him, and taught him how to dance again.

Sabrina believed in him. She believed he could keep her safe, that he could lead men, that the pain he'd suffered in the past had tempered him the way a fire tempered an Indian's war arrow.

He had a choice to make. He could stand there secure in his disguise. Finish his mission, retreat into solitude, never love, never laugh, never dance again. Or he could claim the woman he loved and try his best. Just try.

No wonder her damned diamond kept dimming anytime he got too close. He'd been too blind to see the truth.

Something rare and wonderful swept through him, washing away the loneliness and bitterness that had ruled him for so long. He took one step in her direction. One. It was the hardest step he'd ever taken in his life. Step number two might be a little easier.

But he never got to find out.

The brush behind her moved and shifted, more so than the light June breeze could account for. An instinctive warning welled in his throat, but there was no time, no time to shout to her. No time to race across the distance separating them before the moving shape sorted itself out into a half-naked Indian. His brown skin had blended perfectly with the brush and trees. Leaves and feathers twisted through his hair. His face had been smudged with dirt or with soot. He swung a quick look over the camp, and his gaze came to rest upon Neil's, as if he'd instantly judged the others and realized no threat came from anywhere else. A taunting half smile curved his lips as he stepped away from the brush. With a quick, scooping motion he caught Sabrina by the waist, hoisted her over his shoulder, and disappeared once more into the forest.

The man she'd been tending simply blinked, as if unable to believe the woman who'd been kneeling before him had vanished without a sound.

But there was sound aplenty coming from Neil. A sound not unlike the howl of an anguished wolf poured from him as he pounded to the place where she'd disappeared. He didn't care how many people he stepped on, how many he shoved out of the way as he ran. He hated them, every last one of them who'd blinded him with their need, who'd ignored his warnings and left it to him to take care of them all.

With every agonized breath, with every long-legged stride, his conscience taunted him with the truth. While he'd been standing there daring to think he might be right to claim the happiness she promised, fate had proven he had no right to dream of such things. Once again in his life he'd proven that he was unable to hold on to what had been placed under his care.

Sabrina's breath had been knocked from her when her assailant slammed her over his shoulder. Her struggles, pitiable from lack of air, gained no quarter against the arm he held banded around her waist. Surely coopers did not forge rings of iron around barrel staves any tighter! His shoulder dug into her belly with every step. His hair, a long, heavy hank of midnight black woven with all manner of feathers and painted twigs, brushed against her nose, rank with the scent of rancid bear grease, making it even more difficult to take in air.

Thorns and twigs clawed at her while her captor ran through the brush. These garments she had been loaned, this wondrous cotton, would surely be ripped and torn beyond repair.

She pummeled at her captor's broad, reddish brown back. Between grunts of heavy breathing, she thought she heard him laughing. Laughing! He dared touch her person, dared damage her borrowed clothing, and he laughed!

She left off pounding her fists and pointed her toes. Her borrowed boots weighed fearsomely heavy upon her feet, and for this moment she was glad. Her first two kicks struck against strong, knotted flesh—his thighs, no doubt, the muscles working hard with the effort of carrying her away from Neil at such speed. Her next kick landed squarely amid much softness. The grunting merriment ended with a pained gasp. She had found her mark, and she followed it with two more quick blows. She braced herself, and sure enough he collapsed into a heap. She thudded free of his hold, dropping bottom-first into the dirt. He cast her a malevolent glower before he rolled away, cupping his manhood. He curled into a whimpering ball of pain.

She felt light-headed from lack of air, and falling so hard had knocked even more breath from her. She could not indulge such weakness, but though she struggled to escape it seemed she moved through oceans of mud. She had crawled no more than an arm's length away from him when she felt his hand encircle her ankle. She tried kicking back at him, but he twisted her leg in a painful manner that all but paralyzed her, and he pulled her back toward him, wiping out her pitiable progress.

Neil had caught her by the ankle when he'd first found her in the back of his wagon. Odd that such a memory should surface now as her stomach scraped upon the ground. His grip had been firm and determined, but he'd made no effort to cause pain or to punish. This man who'd caught her glared down at her with fury while deliberately maintaining his hurtful grip. A simmering hatred exuded from him and promised much more unpleasantness to follow.

Neil, my champion, where are you? she cried silently. But even as she ached for him, she knew she had only herself to blame for her predicament. He had warned her to stay near the middle of the road, pleaded with her to keep others around her. And she had ignored him, certain he was being overcautious.

She'd been certain that he did not want her, and she was desperate to put distance between them before she humiliated herself by throwing herself into his arms.

He must feel he had failed her. She knew he was the sort of man to take such things to heart. The story he had told her of his dead wife and child, his guilt over losing men in the honest heat of battle—all these things revealed a man who cared too deeply, who could not accept that some matters were out of man's control and solely up to God.

Death stared down at her in the form of this red-brown-skinned savage. She might well die here in these woods, at her captor's hands. Would God be so vindictive as to doom the Irish people because she had failed to live, failed to marry the proper man and return to her proper place and time with the Irish champion? Desolation swept through her, and she realized that she was just now understanding the despair that must grip Neil when he remembered those things he perceived as failures. A low moan welled within her. She understood now, all too well, how wrong it was to believe that so much responsibility could fall upon such insignificant shoulders. And she understood as well how impossible it was to turn one's back upon those obligations.

Her captor mistook her moan for a sign of capitulation. His snarl twisted into a smile and he pulled her another inch closer. Within kicking range. She mustered every bit of strength she possessed and planted another kick into that spot she had found before. His hold upon her melted. His eyes rolled back in his head in a manner she might have found comical if she weren't so frightened at the moment. She scrambled backward like the skittering sea creatures that she'd heard lived in the sands along the Irish coast. Her captor made no move to follow, and exultation swept through her.

Until she backed into naked legs.

With sidelong glances to her left and her right she realized that at least ten Indians surrounded her. She'd escaped from one only to fall into the hands of many. She shivered. She brought up her knees and curled her arms around them and pressed her face against her legs.

"Sabrina!"

The very air vibrated with the violence of his call.

Loud crashing and slashing sounds heralded his arrival. Four armed settlers stood at his back. The brush had torn at his hair and his skin, leaving him wild-haired and bloody. Battle lust burned in his eyes. He appeared every inch the champion, exuding danger and violence. Neil lifted his rifle to his shoulder and squinted along its length.

But the men who held her prisoner did not quail before his mighty charge. One of the Indians wrapped her hair around his hand and pulled her head high, baring her throat. He held a knife against the soft, pulsing hollow of her neck.

She wanted very badly to appear brave and strong. But a small whimper escaped her throat.

"You can't shoot," warned Eddie. He placed a comforting hand on Neil's shoulder. "Even if we take out one apiece, they'd cut her throat before we got them all."

Neil paled. With a barely discernible tremor shaking him, he lowered his rifle. The knife at her throat went away, but whoever held her hair maintained his grip upon her.

"Let her go," Neil said.

Her captors whispered among themselves, and they formed a circle, trapping her within the forest of their legs. Then one of them stepped forward. "She healing woman. We need."

"We need, too."

"We have."

"You stole her."

The Indian shrugged. "We have. Not yours no more."

"I'll buy her back from you."

The Indian who spoke with Neil turned to his fellows and barked something harsh and indecipherable. Some murmured with interest. Some laughed. The man whom she'd kicked staggered toward the group, shouting what sounded like strong denials while casting glances toward her that promised he would gain his retribution upon her.

"What you give?" demanded the Indian who could speak English.

"Money. Whatever you want."

The Indian laughed.

"Alcohol."

"We keep her. Woman good other things."

The one who held her twisted her hair and drew her to her feet. The pain radiating from her skull sapped all her strength, turning her humiliatingly pliant. She prayed that Neil understood she could do nothing against the agony.

As a unit they moved backward, keeping her in their midst. She saw Neil shake with fury and impotent rage. Terror raced through her blood—terror and outrage of her own, that these Indians somehow roused all his old wounds.

Knowing it was futile to struggle against so many, she did so anyway. She snarled and struck out blindly with her hands and her feet. They put a stop to her threat by simply sweeping her feet out from under her while releasing her hair, sending her thudding into the dirt. Once more her breath deserted her. She lay there, dazed, while everything seemed to fade around her. She could hear nothing but the sound of her heart pounding. Loud, so very loud, louder than it had ever sounded before . . . until she realized that it was not her heart making such a racket, but a very real drumming against the earth that she could sense because she was pressed so close into it.

And soon the Indians noticed it, too. With consternation, they began milling and shouting in their guttural tongue. One stooped and began winding her hair again; his cohorts shouted until he blessedly let go of her. Her head began to clear.

A horn blared, sharp, and lacking the depth of the herald

that announced knights riding into battle, but a clarion call nonetheless.

"Damn, Neil, if it don't sound like the cavalry's riding to our rescue," marveled one of the settlers.

Within no more time than it took to blink her eyes, it was possible to hear the snorting of horses, the creaking of saddle leather. The horn sounded again, producing a variety of notes. Within another moment the first of the mounted soldiers burst into the woods.

A bullet cracked; the Indians took to their heels.

Soon the small clearing was filled with nervous horses, with grinning soldiers. She struggled up to a sitting position and had to brace her hands against the ground while dizziness caught her in its grip. Her surroundings seemed to spin around her. One moment her vision beheld naught but mounted, victorious soldiers. The next, she saw what her heart wanted to see: Neil Kenyon, walking toward her.

Soldiers. Neil. Soldiers. Neil.

Soldiers.

One of the soldiers, whose garments boasted even finer medals and embellishments than the one Neil kept hidden away, dismounted from his horse. He removed his hat and brushed it against his legs. He loomed before her, reaching her before Neil, who paused, stricken at the sight of this great personage standing before her.

He crouched down low to bring his eyes level with hers. A bushy mustache graced his lip, and fine, curly hair sprang out all over his head.

"Are you all right, ma'am?"

She nodded.

He smiled widely, and offered his hand to her. "Brigadier General Thomas Francis Meagher. Former acting governor of this fine Montana Territory. It's happy I am to be of assistance."

Chapter Sixteen

Thomas Francis Meagher.

Neil stepped back and studied the man through hooded eyes. Tall enough. A little heavy through the gut. Older than he'd expected the Irish champion to be, maybe mid-forties.

His dark hair was peppered with gray. His hand looked large but too soft to wield a champion's sword, and here and there Neil thought he noticed the brown blotches of age. He imagined that the parts of the man hidden by the uniform drooped and sagged from too many fancy dinners and too many nights telling tales over bottles of whiskey.

The thought of Sabrina's exquisite body, her long legs and slim arms wrapped around this man, made his skin crawl.

The thought of her making love with any man other than himself did the same.

He couldn't afford to let passion cloud his thinking. He shook those thoughts away and studied the man he'd been sent to neutralize. Meagher strutted with the confidence of a hero. The deference shown by his men appeared honestly earned. Soldiers spotted fakes a mile away and seldom granted them the respect he sensed coming from them toward their general.

Meagher basked in it all. Accepted the honor, the respect, the admiration as his just due. Maybe it was—he'd saved Sabrina while Neil could do nothing but lower his weapon in impotent fury.

Meagher helped Sabrina to her feet. She swayed a little, and he steadied her with a hand at the small of her back. She stared up at him, smiling. She ran her hand down her hair, smoothing it; she brushed dust and forest residue from her skirt, tidying herself—the way a woman might primp when her beloved unexpectedly showed up for a visit.

Jealousy gripped Neil, hard and hot and malevolent.

The settlers who'd followed him into the woods walked past him as if he weren't there, moving to stand in the reflected glory of Thomas Francis Meagher. The man exuded power and authority, and they seemed to drink it in with more appetite than they'd shown for Neil's elixir.

Meagher surveyed the area, his expression smug with satisfaction. His gaze lit upon Neil and hesitated no more than a fraction of a second before moving on, dismissing him as of no importance.

Sneer all you want, Neil thought. *Let her look at you like you're a gift handed straight from her Druid gods. I'm going to bring you down. . . .*

A tremor shook him. His mind tormented him with the image of that Indian holding a knife to Sabrina's throat, and himself unable to save her. Try as he might to hate Thomas Francis Meagher, he couldn't do it. If not for his timely arrival, Sabrina could be dead. Or worse.

Knowing this did not make it easier on his pride to walk

across the clearing and thank the man for accomplishing what Neil had been unable to do. The irony mocked him. It seemed a lifetime ago that he'd thought about taking that first step toward Sabrina, to tell her he understood what she needed and was willing to do his best for her, willing to try.

Maybe it had been a different lifetime, because now everything had changed again. There was no more hope in his soul. No more impetus to try. From now on he need do only what he must, and right now that meant putting one foot in front of the other until he stood at Thomas Meagher's side.

Retired general. Former acting governor. Current pompous ass. The man simpered and preened for Sabrina's sake, and she seemed completely taken by his posturing. She gazed up at him with dazed delight, as any woman would if she'd just been saved from the brink of death. Worse than that was the glow that suffused her, as if the thousand stars she claimed hid within her Druid's Tear had somehow transferred themselves to her. The damned stone hung around her neck. The stone that went flat and dull every time she moved toward him, every time he touched her, almost pulsated with brilliance while Meagher held her.

Sabrina seemed to agree with the diamond. She stared up at Meagher as if she'd found, at last, the champion she had been seeking.

She hadn't spared Neil a single look since Meagher's arrival.

Neil cleared his throat awkwardly, both to cover the pain of that realization and to gain Meagher's attention. It didn't work in one case, but did okay in the other. Meagher frowned sideways at him, annoyance clear upon his features.

Neil stuck out his hand. "Thank you. Sir," he added, almost choking over the address.

Meagher shook his hand. Only half his attention seemed focused on Neil, and Neil understood, for he'd often looked down upon civilians with the same lack of interest. "Glad we happened to be following old Thick Wolf Pelt's trail. 'Tis troublesome they've been. I've spent a goodly time these past months discouraging Indians from raising commotions."

"Neil tried his best," Sabrina said. Her speech seemed a bit slurred, as if the mere presence of Meagher turned her drunk with delight.

"He did his best, I'm sure." Meagher spoke with false joviality.

"He held the Indians at bay until you came."

"Well, and I'm sure you'll be recalling me saying, we *were* on their trail." His tone was merry, but edged with steel, hinting that he did not care to share one shred of credit for the rescue. "We'd have caught up with you sooner or later."

" 'Twas brave," Sabrina insisted. "Not so easy for four men to face down a dozen. Easier for so many soldiers."

Meagher's smile thinned. "Four against a dozen, true, but none of those savages had a gun." Sabrina seemed ready to speak again, and he hurried to interrupt. "But I'll not be denying any man's bravery. He distracted them for a couple of minutes."

Neil didn't know which was worse: hearing Sabrina try to manufacture a hero's role for him where none existed, or listening to Meagher's condescension.

"I'm grateful," he said.

"Can't say I'd be blaming you," said Meagher. "I'd be sore-hearted to lose a pretty little wife like this."

Neil weighed his options. He knew the settlers believed

he and Sabrina to be man and wife. So, obviously, did Meagher. But if Meagher was the champion Sabrina sought, it might not suit her to be thought permanently hitched to Neil Kenyon.

It would be easy to continue the deception. He just had to murmur some sort of noncommittal agreement, and Meagher would hand her over, one man returning another man's property.

Yes, he could make it very easy for himself, very complicated for her.

But she wouldn't stay with him.

She believed in him. She trusted him to do the right thing. To do his best. When a man loved a woman, doing his best meant sacrificing himself so she could realize her dreams.

"We're not married," Neil said.

"You're not?" Meagher's head swiveled with quick interest, while around him, the settlers gasped with disbelief.

"But Neil, you rode in together. You slept out there in the woods together." Jim's face reddened.

"Like brother and sister," Neil lied. "Sabrina and I are business partners. We each have our own, uh, medical specialties. Nothing more."

He fancied that his denial caused some of Sabrina's glow to dim, but maybe that was all in his mind, for she made no objection. And any loss of excitement on her part was more than made up for by the brightness lighting Tom Meagher. He grinned down at Sabrina. He raked her with a lustful glance that no man had the right to use with a decent woman.

"Not married, a pretty little Irish lass like you. Well, sure, and that's the most interesting news I've heard in a long, long time."

* * *

Much whispering took place among the husbands and wives when Sabrina and her rescue party returned to camp. The women eagerly welcomed back the men who had accompanied Neil, but after quick kisses and reassuring touches, the men had pulled their wives aside and whispered things that turned the women's eyes wide with shock and dismay.

Sabrina felt as if all eyes were upon them. Different. Measuring and judgmental. Because Neil had told the truth about their unmarried state, and for some reason they all blamed him for traveling with her.

The soldiers circled, urging everyone back into their wagons. The prospect of a true military escort seemed to lend heart to the settlers. They shifted the loads in their wagons, repacked bundles. Sabrina did not understand until it came time to leave. She paused to check on Henry and found his pallet gone, the aisle between the crates of medicine bare.

"Over here!" he called, waving from a newly made space in one of the wagons.

The wagon seat lay empty, no mischievous children to climb between her feet and crawl over her lap. They, too, had been reclaimed by their families and packed like chickens bound for market in the back of yet another wagon.

She understood. They did not want the taint of unmarried lovers to stain their families. She tipped her chin high. No shame would color her skin, she vowed, for she felt nothing but pride and love for the man who ruled her heart.

She had one foot on the step, the other dangling in midair, when someone tugged at her skirt.

"You can't ride with him, Sabrina." Lizzie Stuart tugged again, and Sabrina had to come down from her unsteady perch or tumble to the ground. Her head still ached from the fall she'd taken earlier at the Indian's hands. She did not relish another.

"My place is with Neil," she said.

"Humpf." Lizzie cast a hostile scowl toward Neil, who walked in their direction, unaware of the shifting of the settlers' loyalties. "I'll bet that's the way he'd like it, all right."

Lizzie sounded much like Maisie. She gripped Sabrina's arm with the same sense of purpose. Still a little dazed and unsure on her feet, Sabrina could not summon resistance as Lizzie propelled her away from Neil's medicine wagon and toward the cart that held the organ and the three Stuart children.

They stormed straight across Neil's path. His eyes met hers, held, and then shifted away. He issued no challenge to Lizzie's command of her. He made no objection.

What little strength had seeped back into her limbs deflated at realizing he would not claim her. How could she have forgotten the way he'd abandoned her after making love? She must have mistaken the agony in his expression when the Indian held that knife at her throat. She had believed he bled for *her*.

Not so, she realized with dull comprehension. He had held the opportunity to declare his love for her, and he had cast it aside. *Brother and sister,* he had said. *Business partners. Nothing more.*

Always, always, she failed to heed the warnings he issued. Always she believed he sought to shield a wounded heart. She had been wrong about him all along.

Thomas Meagher appeared pleased with the riding arrangements. He shouted commands that set his men into motion, and the settlers obeyed him with more alacrity than they'd shown Neil. Once all were moving to Thomas's satisfaction, he dropped back from the head of the group and paced his horse alongside the Stuart cart.

He smiled down at Sabrina. Magnificence radiated from him, from the proud tilt of his hat to the golden splendor of the medals gracing his chest. His horse, the finest of all, moved with a high-stepping gait, as if proud to carry such a hero upon its back.

"I'm hoping you'd not be minding a bit of conversation to pass the time, lass," he said, with a cocky grin that told Sabrina he expected her to be pleased with his company.

"We sure don't," Sam Stuart said.

Meagher cast him a faint smile, but returned his regard at once to Sabrina. He seemed oblivious to their blushing and simpering. Almost as if he was so accustomed to obeisance that he no longer noticed it.

Or perhaps she wronged him. Perhaps in the way of a true champion he did not realize when awe was directed his way. Her understanding of men and their motives had proved to be sorely lacking of late.

"You're looking hale," he said. "No lasting damage from the savages, eh?"

"A bit light in the head," she said. "Nothing more."

"Then I'll be sure to include an extra thank-you in my prayers to the Almighty this night. I sense a divine hand in the events of this day."

He seemed predisposed to believe in miracles. Maybe there was an element of divine interference in all that had happened. This opportunity had surely been arranged by the gods, to journey through such a wild land and have the territory's most important person virtually to herself, to question him and do all she could to determine whether he was the champion she sought.

She could do little, however, but stare longingly behind her at Neil. He no longer led their small caravan, but drove at the rear.

He rode alone, the way he'd been when she'd come to him. The way he'd wanted to be. The way he'd said he intended to remain.

She could not tell whether it suited him, for a frightening blankness had taken over his features. His eyes revealed nothing. His expression was void of all emotion. He had claimed there was nothing in his heart, and that awful emptiness seemed to prove it was true.

How could a man who had held her in his arms, who had given her so much ecstasy, turn away so thoroughly if he truly cared? She knew the answer. He could not. A man like Neil cared from the depth of his heart. If he so easily turned away, it meant that his dalliance with her had been the very mistake he'd tried to avoid. A mistake, an indulgence, brought about by dancing, the lingering effects of strong spirits, a loneliness that demanded temporary slaking.

She had faced death twice this day. Physical death, as with the Indians. The other death was harder to bear— the death of her silly notion that she might have found love.

But one thing would not die, and that was her obligation to her people. She had been sent on this journey to find the Irish champion, not to indulge her foolish whims about love. The man who might be the very champion her people so desperately needed rode alongside her at that very minute while she sat there yearning for that which she could not have.

How right her mother had been to raise her without indulging in such weaknesses. She was Sabrina, lady of Desmond Muir, the one chosen to restore the Irish spirit. The Druid's Tear had spoken, coming to life for her after countless generations of Desmond women tried and failed to fulfill the prophecy.

She called upon the strength that had sustained her

through all those lonely years. She stiffened her shoulders and tilted her chin with pride.

"You are an Irishman, General."

"Born and bred." He cast her a grin. "Not a day goes by that I don't miss the homeland."

"Then why have you come to this place?"

"Ah. That would be a long and interesting story. Would you be caring to hear it?"

"Nothing would make me happier," she said.

"It's a bit of a bad boy they thought me. Not my countrymen, mind you, but that hag of an English queen. Victoria. Sentenced me to death, she did!"

Sabrina hoped her face reflected the appropriate astonishment.

"Called me a troublemaker. Said that as long as I lived on Irish soil, there could never be peace between the two countries. Well, as you know, lass, to the English, 'peace' means Irish capitulation. Never would I stand for it, and to their credit, they never doubted my determination."

"You are not dead," Sabrina pointed out. "Did the English queen change her mind?"

"In a manner of speaking. My countrymen raised a hue and cry over my execution such as had never been heard before. Victoria commuted my sentence to transportation to the penal colonies. That hellhole known as Tasmania. Almost rather be dead than spend my days so far from the Irish sun."

"Did she set you free?"

"I should say not! Made my escape, I did. The lads said it couldn't be done. Tasmania's bound by wild seas, you know, and I had no choice but to swim my way free. Others had tried before me, but none succeeded. But here I am, living proof of what Irish determination can accomplish."

She had found her man.

A soldier dropped back and leaned over in his saddle,

saying something in low tones to Thomas. He nodded, and then turned back to Sabrina as the soldier returned to his place in the formation.

"They'll be needing me at the front," he said. He touched his cap in a gesture of respect. "It's conversing more, you and I'll be once you're settled in town."

She turned to watch him ride away. Her champion. Her heart should soar with gladness; instead, it felt hollow and lacking in spirit.

No matter. The soldiers seemed to sit straighter as he thundered past them. The horses seemed to lift their hooves higher. The Stuarts glanced at one another and shook their heads, awed. It mattered naught if her spirit withered and died. Thomas Francis Meagher had spirit enough for them both.

Fort Benton's adobe walls stood tall and solid, with the sunlight gleaming dully against the rough surface. The area surrounding the fort teemed with people. Neil knew that the fort itself had been home to fur traders until just a year or two earlier, and the army had not yet decided whether to occupy the fort itself or continue to expand the small town that had sprung up around its perimeter.

The soldiers goaded their horses into a gallop as they neared the town, leaving the wagons and carts to follow at their own pace. The townsfolk scarcely acknowledged the soldiers, but interest spread almost visibly when wagons rumbled into view. By the time their small caravan rolled to a stop on the main street, a sizable crowd had gathered.

They weren't interested in him or his wares, though. The sight of new families brought the happiest cries, the loudest shouts of welcome. He went around the back to help Henry out of the wagon before he remembered he'd been shunned as a pariah. No matter. The empty space beckoned, offering a temporary sanctuary. He climbed inside, pretending to take stock of his inventory. He didn't need to do that. Most of it had disappeared down various throats. It didn't seem to matter. He couldn't really regret the way it had gone, even if it meant most of his life savings were wiped out.

He could hear the excited buzz of conversation, the amazed cries that greeted the stories told by the settlers. The walls of his wagon insulated him somewhat, dulling the sound. It was almost as though a transformation had begun. For a few days he'd been part of that group, one of the men, someone they turned to for help and advice. He hadn't wanted their trust or their dependency. And now it was melting away.

Loneliness tolled inside him like a huge, ponderous bell that could not stop ringing once its weight was set in motion.

He wondered if he could just crouch there in the dark, hot confines of his wagon and never have to see anyone ever again. Never have to move among crowds of people who belonged to each other, knowing that he was alone. Never have to look at a woman and remember the hurt and confusion that had clouded Sabrina's eyes when he'd told Meagher that they were no more than business partners.

But he couldn't hide away. He'd come here on a mission, and in order to complete it he had to compile information on Meagher. He had to investigate incidents that could lead to the destruction of the man who had saved the woman Neil loved. If he succeeded, he'd have to arrest the man who might be the Irish champion. Meagher had to be the one Sabrina sought. She'd come looking for a man who could save an entire nation. Back there in the woods, Neil had proved he couldn't save one woman from a band of half-starved Indians.

It would solve his problem, he realized with sickening despair, if he simply let nature play its course between Meagher and Sabrina. If Meagher was the Irish champion she was meant to marry and take home to her people, then let them go do it. Removing Meagher from Montana was the goal, and if he ended up back in damned 1298, happily married to the most alluring, fascinating woman ever born, and found himself ruling the country he loved with such passion, then Neil could consider his mission accomplished.

And then he could just go off into the mountains as he'd planned. With nothing. While Meagher had it all.

Fury smoked within him. They weren't so different, he and Meagher. Both of them had fought in the War Between the States. Meagher had no doubt lost men under his command. Why hadn't Meagher slumped into a bottomless slough of grief and regret?

Maybe . . . maybe because Meagher didn't care about anyone but Meagher. Sabrina had been trying to tell him this all along, that only a man who loved too much and too well could know such despair at loss. He'd dismissed her advice.

But what if she was right?

Then that meant that striking out for the wild high places wouldn't do a thing to ease the ache in his heart. Solitude and peace wouldn't fill the emptiness inside him. Turning his back on the world wouldn't change the essence of him, any more than turning away from Sabrina had stopped him from almost dying when he thought she might be stolen away by savages.

She had seen inside his soul with a clarity he'd never managed. And instead of being repulsed, she'd loved. His blood pounded, fired by the memory of her breath sighing into his, of the delicious yielding of her strength beneath him. He'd held happiness in his arms and lost it.

There would be some who would say that the memories would sustain him in the years to come. That he'd look back and be happy that he'd grasped those few moments of joy.

If anyone dared say that to him just then, he'd smash his fist into his face.

The memory of one hour's loving wasn't enough to sustain him for a lifetime. It would take a hell of a lot more. Like a lifetime of loving. That was impossible. He was just an ordinary man who couldn't work miracles. An ordinary man who stood no chance against the ancient power of the Druid's Tear. All he could do was love Sabrina. Love her, and make sure that her dreams, at least, came true.

A curious peace washed through him. He held power over Meagher—incomplete power so far, but soon enough he might hold enough evidence that would condemn Meagher as a traitor. Once he gathered enough, he could arrange a private meeting with the man to convince him that disappearing from Montana would be in his best interests, so that if he had even the slightest notion of turning down Sabrina, he'd have to think twice.

Remembering how Meagher had reacted to Sabrina, to her beauty, to her Irishness, Neil didn't think he'd have to do all that much convincing.

Chapter Seventeen

"Well, don't you look pretty today, Sabrina." Lizzie smiled as she fussed with the collar on Sabrina's blouse.

Sabrina gave her a halfhearted smile and tried not to pull away from the unwanted touch.

It was difficult to recall how she had endured living in Desmond Muir, with her maid forever hovering over her, twisting this, tweaking that. Neil had seemed somewhat wistful when she'd explained the numbers of people sheltered within Desmond's walls, and truth to tell, she had found it difficult at first to adjust to this less crowded time. With Maisie, they had been only two women in a small house of three rooms. With Neil, she had known the wonders of a man and woman alone beneath the stars.

Here, in Fort Benton, she lived with the Stuarts in a small shack of only two rooms—crowded, with their three children and the two adult Stuarts. Everyone had assured her she was lucky to find shelter at all. At one time she would not have minded the company, but something had happened to her. She no longer felt the need to see others, to touch others, to have them do the same to her, the way she had in Desmond Muir. Within her own walls, she had required that contact to replace the love she'd never known from her parents, and to serve as a reminder that she sacrificed herself to the Irish champion for the sake of all those people.

She had learned since then that only one touch was required to banish all loneliness, all doubts.

"You seem a little nervous, hon." Lizzie gave her collar another tug.

"A soldier stopped by earlier. He says Mr. Meagher will call upon me this evening."

Lizzie's hand stilled. She cleared her throat, and then stepped away. Consternation furrowed her forehead.

"Is that why you're all dressed up? Evening's a while off, yet."

In truth, Sabrina had dressed in her borrowed best because she had determined she must see Neil. She had expected Lizzie to object to that plan, not to the news that Thomas Meagher planned to visit.

"I thought you admired Mr. Meagher," said Sabrina. "Why do you appear so troubled?"

Lizzie rubbed her hands along her hips, and then clasped them together in front of her. Her face reddened. "It's your own business. But you ought to be careful, honey. It's bad enough folks know you were traveling with that no-account medicine quack."

Sabrina bristled. All of Fort Benton seemed to regard Neil with barely concealed derision. The settlers had over these past few days drifted into doing the same.

"Why has everyone turned against him? You did not consider him no-account when he helped you after the fire."

"Maybe that's just it," Lizzie said. "Sometimes folks get

embarrassed when somebody's helped them and they can't offer anything in return."

"He expects nothing from you."

"Well, it doesn't help that he stalks around town like a grizzly who left his right paw in a trap. He turns folks skittish. Half of them are afraid to buy his medicine. I don't know how you tolerated traveling with him."

"He was ever the gentleman and champion with me," Sabrina said softly.

But she could not let her thoughts linger in that direction. "Tell me why Mr. Meagher's visit worries you."

Lizzie caught her hands and peered earnestly at her, her kind face creased with concern. "You know folks tend to be a little on the forgiving side out here on the frontier. Especially for a pretty gal like you. Men are so woman-hungry that they'll overlook just about anything a gal does, providing she stays pure afterward. But honey, you're pushing tolerance a little too far when you start keeping company with a married man."

"Married man?" Sabrina tilted her head, confused.

"Mr. Meagher."

"He's *married?*" Sabrina's question ended on a disbelieving squeak. "He cannot be married!"

"You didn't know? Honey, he's been married twice. First wife died a while back. But for the longest time he's been married to a fancy society lady. I heard just this morning at the general store that she's coming out here to join him any day now."

"He cannot be married." Sabrina found it so difficult to breathe that she might as well be wearing a corset. She reached out a hand to support herself against the wall, and Lizzie grabbed it and helped her lower herself into a chair. Sabrina sat frozen with disbelief while Lizzie fanned her with the flap of her apron. Sabrina's distress seemed to have restored Lizzie's good opinion of her.

"He is a mighty handsome fellow, I'll grant you that. There's something about a man in charge, ain't there? Course, the trouble with a man in charge is that he tends to think he can have everything his own way. No doubt he figured on entertaining himself with you for a few days until his wife gets here."

"Wife." Sabrina did not know how she managed the word through lips gone so numb.

Lizzie abandoned her apron flapping. "Maybe I ought to get a cold compress for your head. I didn't realize you were so taken with Mr. Meagher. I figure him old enough to be your father. Truth to tell, even though you two seem to have parted ways, I thought you were real sweet on your Mr. Kenyon. There was something about the way you looked at each other that made me think you two had found something really special. . . . Well, your love life is none of my business."

Lizzie's agitation finally pierced Sabrina's distress. "Oh, you have it all wrong, my friend. I do not care about Mr. Meagher in a . . . a love-life way."

But telling the truth had been the wrong thing to do, for now Lizzie's attention sharpened, and, too late, Sabrina bit her tongue. What could she do now—admit to Lizzie that she believed Thomas Francis Meagher might be the Irish champion, and she had traveled across six centuries to find him and take him back? Impossible. Neil was forever cautioning her to guard her tongue, and once again she came to value his warnings after the damage had been done.

Her frozen silence served her well, though, for it seemed Lizzie mistook it for a weak attempt to cover her true feelings. She patted Sabrina's hand. "There, there. I know you don't have romantic feelings for him. It's always a shock to hear a man's married."

"That is true," Sabrina said, remembering how stunned she had been when Neil had told her he'd once been wed.

"I can send a note and tell him you've changed your mind about seeing him," Lizzie offered.

"I . . ." The breadth of her dilemma confused her. She had known she must spend time alone with Thomas Meagher to determine if he were truly the champion she sought. She could not understand why the gods had chosen to complicate her quest in such a manner. Unless Thomas was not the champion. But if he were not . . . then she did not understand why she had been sent to this place, or what she was to do next.

You were sent because you wished for a miracle, a small voice within her whispered. And find it she had, in the form of one Neil Kenyon. But he was not the champion. He had told her so. A woman who loved him, truly loved him, would not ask him to perform the impossible. He would try. And he would fail. And his soul would shatter forever, never to heal.

She craved him with a fierceness that did not bear examining. He alone understood what had brought her to this place. He alone understood how duty drove ordinary people to attempt extraordinary things, even when failure and loneliness were the only likely results. He alone might help her muddle through the mystery of Thomas Meagher and determine the right steps to take.

Without Neil Kenyon, she was totally alone in this strange world. But that was not why she ached for him. Even if she were back in her own time, surrounded by everything familiar . . . even if she had married and her own children clung to her skirts . . . even if she stood with the champion upon the balustrade and witnessed the miracle of the Irish people triumphing over the hated English, her heart would endlessly ache for him.

"I will see Mr. Meagher," she told Lizzie. "But first I

must seek Mr. Kenyon's counsel on ... on another matter."

Lizzie's face crumpled. "Oh, honey, don't go trying to make one man jealous by telling him about the other. I have to tell you, you just ain't got the poker face needed for that kind of foolishness. You're a gal who has her heart writ plain upon her face."

"Fear not, my friend. I will do nothing foolish." She rose from the chair and gripped Lizzie in a quick hug. "Everything will turn out the way it must."

"The arrow was *poisoned,*" the soldier repeated, for what Neil felt sure was the twentieth time. He flexed his shoulder toward Neil. "I need me some poison remedy, not some overpriced Energizing Elixir."

"And I'm telling you that if the arrow was poisoned you'd be dead instead of standing here arguing about the price of my medicine."

"Like you know so much about battle wounds."

"I've picked up a little experience here and there."

The soldier snorted with derision. "Maybe I ought to go tell my commanding officer that we got us a regular Indian-fighting expert out here hawking patent medicine."

Neil gritted his teeth rather than tell the insolent young idiot that his commanding officer could certainly use a man of his own experience. He supposed he ought to be glad that he'd perfected his disguise enough to hide the air of military demeanor that had clung to him longer than he'd expected. He doubted there was a single soul in Fort Benton who suspected the truth about him.

But the success of that part of his plan had turned out to be a tainted victory. Folks accepted him as a medicine peddler, which meant they thought him a slick, untrustworthy character out to trick them out of their money. They didn't seek his company, and they weren't exactly eager to confide all their secrets about Thomas Meagher to him.

Two privates had accompanied the arrow-shot soldier. They'd propped themselves in the shade and had been watching the argument with amusement. One of them stirred. "C'mon, Hartley," called one. "Let's go find a saloon. A few good whiskeys and you'll forget all about that poisoned wound."

"It's not poisoned," Neil ground out as Hartley shrugged his shirt back over his shoulder.

"Not poisoned, but 'tis a fearsome imposture." The female observation stopped all of them cold.

Neil stood riveted in place while Sabrina walked up to Hartley and deftly flicked the shirt back down off his shoulder. She studied the puffy hole where the arrow had gone in. She gave a quick nod. "Aye, an imposture."

"See that," said Neil. "Not poison. An imposture."

He wondered what the hell an imposture might be. He wondered what she was doing there when he'd tried so hard to avoid seeing her. Well, it hadn't been hard, considering she seemed to be doing her best to avoid seeing him. He wondered why he was so damned happy to have her near that he could feel the grin all but split his face.

"You're the healing woman," Hartley said with reverence. "I got this little scratch chasing down them Injuns what grabbed you."

"I am forever in your debt," said Sabrina. "To my endless delight, I find that Mr. Kenyon and I can help you."

"He wants three dollars for that elixir of his."

"Three dollars."

Sabrina had never seemed cognizant of—or much impressed with—the value of Neil's inventory, but she cast him a questioning brow after Hartley named the inflated price he'd been charging in an attempt to make up some of his lost savings.

"I guess I could let him have one bottle at my cost," Neil said. "Two dollars and fifty cents."

"Two dollars and fifty—" Hartley's objection ended with a delighted yelp when Sabrina traced her fingers along the ridge of his shoulder and over the unharmed plane of muscle. "I guess I'll take two bottles."

Hartley's friends edged closer. "I'm feeling a little low myself," said the bigger of the two. "Stomachache. Would you need to touch my belly to see what's ailing me, ma'am?"

"Touch is essential to the healer's art," Sabrina said. "You may remove your shirt."

Though only one lout had complained of a stomachache, both soldiers shucked off their military blouses and stood there grinning like half-naked fools. "You will need potions," Sabrina said after giving each hairy stomach a quick pat. She sent a sidelong glance back at Neil. "I have herbal mixtures that must be mixed in elixir. Much elixir."

Hiding a smile, Neil dangled a bottle of elixir.

The soldiers dug into their pockets. "Will two bottles apiece be enough?"

"For the first dose," she said. "Then I will need to check your stomachs again, and you may require yet more potion."

"Why don't you boys go sit under those trees again, with your backs up against the trunks," Neil suggested. "You never can tell how hard those potions of hers are gonna hit you. I'm not lying when I say you've never had anything like the concoctions she mixes up."

"She'll come over and check on us once we finish these, right?"

"Right."

She stood next to him, watching as the soldiers settled

in the shade. It felt right having her there, with the top of her head just reaching the ridge of his shoulder. He didn't know how he would ever stop looking at her if he looked at her straight on, so he stole little peeks at her, sideways. He'd never seen the dress she was wearing. It didn't fit her all that well, a little too loose everywhere as if it belonged to a larger woman . . . or maybe she'd lost weight over these past couple of days. He'd taken his own belt in a notch.

She wasn't wearing the Druid's Tear.

"Where's your necklace?"

Her hand went to her throat. "Sam holds it in safekeeping for me."

"He must realize it's very valuable."

"He thought so, until this morning. I slipped it over my head right before coming to see you, and it . . ." She paused, but Neil finished her sentence in his mind: the stone's fire had died the minute she headed in his direction.

"Sam fears it might not be a diamond at all, but a simple moonstone. Of little value."

He had to ask the question that circled endlessly through his head. "Still shines up a storm when you're aimed toward Thomas Meagher, though, doesn't it?"

"I . . . I do not know. I have not seen him."

"You haven't?" Exultation swept through him. "Why not, Sabrina?"

"It is no concern of yours," she said.

She was dead wrong about that, but he didn't know how to tell her without admitting all the ways he'd been a fool. "I was just hoping you might've found out a few secrets about him. If you do, be sure to pass them along for my investigation."

She moved away, showing where her allegiance lay.

She'd done her hair up the way the townswomen wore

it, in a sort of loose puff around her face with the length caught up in a knot at the back of her head. He spotted the pin anchoring it all in place. One quick tug and he'd send her hair tumbling down over her shoulders, the way he liked it.

He jammed his hands into his pockets.

"Thanks for stepping in to help with those soldiers."

"They did seem disinclined to do anything you asked."

"One more little piece of evidence that proves I'm not your champion," he said with false lightness.

"Aye. The champion must inspire unconditional fervor. Men must willingly do all he demands."

Neil didn't care for the turn their conversation had taken. He wanted to tell her that he used to inspire men, that they'd followed him unquestioningly, until he'd lost his taste for battle. But admitting that wouldn't raise him any higher in the championship stakes.

"I still don't have the sales technique honed down real well," he said.

She seemed content to make polite responses. "I am happy to assist you, since I owe you far more than I can ever repay."

"You don't owe me anything." She seemed about to protest, so he changed the subject. "What's in that stuff you plastered on Hartley's shoulder?"

The smile she gave him was a true Sabrina smile, one that twisted his heart into a knot that might never work free. Her eyes sparkled with mischief. "Since he annoyed you so, I took the liberty of mixing some ground snails into the skull moss. The snails help smooth a contentious nature."

"Uh-huh. And the potion those two are drinking?"

"Fine hairs plucked from fried mice," she said. " 'Twill help curb their lustful natures. Everyone knows mouse hair helps with bed-wetting as well."

He burst out laughing, and had to spin away from the soldiers. He doubted they noticed, though, because they were rapidly getting drunk. It felt good to laugh. He hadn't laughed for a long time before she came. He hadn't laughed after she left. He wondered if he'd ever laugh again once she was gone for good.

That thought quieted his laughter.

"What brings you here, Sabrina?"

Before she could answer, Hartley called for another bottle of elixir. If they kept downing the bottles at this rate, and at this price, Neil would earn his nest egg back in no time. He passed out bottles and collected money from the three men.

"You need to check my shoulder again, miss?"

Sabrina knelt next to him and rested her hand on his shoulder. "You will heal well now. Take better care next time you ride into battle."

"You don't need to tell me that. You got to tell General Meagher to have a better care for his men's health. He gets you so riled up and ready to fight that you don't pay much attention to the danger."

Neil stilled. He didn't think Sabrina had deliberately provoked this conversation, but it was exactly what he wanted to hear. He hadn't managed to gain the confidence of any of the military men so far.

"Meagher shouldn't be leading you into battle at all, from what I hear," he said, hoping he'd injected the right amount of disinterest into his observation. "He's retired from the army, right?"

"That don't make any difference. Montana needs every able-bodied man fighting to keep her free. Never met a man so set on freedom. You listen to him for a couple of minutes and you're ready to fight for freedom yourself, even though you're free already."

Sabrina drew in a sharp breath, and it tore right through

Neil's heart. He knew that the champion she sought had to value freedom above everything.

"Keep Montana free from what?" Neil asked. "Free from Indians?"

The soldiers blinked owlishly at him. "Beats hell out of me," said one eventually.

They'd passed too quickly from sober to drunk, Neil realized. He wondered what the hell was in those bottles of Ebenezer's Energizing Elixir. He hoped they were too drunk to grow suspicious of his interest in Meagher.

"Now," remonstrated Hartley, "he did have us fighting Injuns up north a couple months ago."

"Didn't get any."

"Was a hell of a campaign."

"Weren't no Injuns, Hartley."

"Maybe not. But them Irish fighting songs he taught us went real good with beer." Hartley cleared his throat and began singing in a clear tenor.

Sabrina, her hand pressed against her mouth, her eyes wide with wonder, hummed along. "Mr. Meagher taught you that song?"

"Yeah. Said it was old, real old."

"Singing that song before battle lends men the courage of heroes."

Hartley lifted his bottle of elixir in an unsteady toast. "That's exactly what he said. God bless General Meagher. Wonder if he'd drink some of this with us?"

"You bet he would," Neil said.

The soldier wagged a reproving finger. "Now, don't be so sure of that. The general turned down a reception in his honor back in New York, all on account of he said he can't drink and enjoy himself when his native land still suffers from sorrow and sub . . . sub . . . subjection."

"General Meagher said that?" Sabrina said with awe.

"I'll drink to General Meagher's favorite toast." His

friend lifted his bottle, too. He cleared his throat and lowered his voice. "Montana's not Ireland, but we can make it seem close."

"Meagher's a patriot," Neil said, his throat tight. "He doesn't go around making toasts that smack of treason."

Hartley giggled. "Well, Meagher was acting governor when the old U.S. of A. tried to annex Montana as a state. Didn't happen, did it? Montana still stands alone."

The conventional wisdom in Washington had decided that Montana's application for statehood failed because it had been rushed, cobbled together by inexperienced politicians led by Meagher as acting governor. What if, instead, the failure had been deliberately designed by the shrewd hand of one who'd meant to sabotage the effort?

Neil's mind raced, wondering how much of this information he could trust. The men were drunk, which could mean a couple of things. They could be making up this behavior of Meagher's. Or they could be telling the truth. If what they said was true, then the rumors that had reached Washington were also true. Meagher, under the guise of patriotism, might be secretly undermining efforts to grant statehood to Montana. How could a man who'd fought for the Union work clandestinely against his government?

Sick at heart, Neil glanced at Sabrina, and found her glowing with joy.

And no wonder. These men had just told her that Thomas Meagher was a true Irish patriot, who valued freedom above all else, who managed to keep his tiny kingdom independent while a larger, more powerful ruler tried to take it over.

Hartley wheezed out a few more words of his song, and then his chin thudded against his breast. A wavery snore sounded from one of his friends, while the other simply keeled over onto his side and curled up like a baby. Sound asleep, the lot of them. He'd get no more information from them.

"I guess you've found your champion, Sabrina."

"So 'twould seem. But . . . I am unsure."

He laughed bitterly. "Obsessed by freedom. Men will follow him anywhere, even if they believe he's determined to turn part of United States soil into Irish territory. Teaching American soldiers to sing Irish battle songs. He sounds tailor-made for you."

"Aye, and I will meet with him this evening, and explore his suitability. I would by now be convinced he is the right man—save for one thing. He is married, Neil."

Distress turned her pale. Jealousy clawed at his gut, whispering that she wanted her champion so badly that she'd give herself to a married man if that was what it took.

"How am I to bring him to Desmond as my husband if he already belongs to another woman?" She asked the question so softly that he thought she must be asking it of herself.

He knew she'd been looking for a champion. Knew that champion couldn't be him. Which meant he'd known she had to go back to her own time with another man. And yet hearing her so calmly state she expected to act as a wife to Thomas Meagher got to him so badly that he couldn't think straight. His head was a jumble of images, of diamonds winking malevolently, of florid, middle-aged Irishmen staring with lust at a young beauty, of Sabrina so sure and determined that she must bring the champion home to her people.

The legend of the Druid's Tear said that the stone would come to life when the chosen Desmond woman began the journey that would lead to the champion.

Funny how in his jealousy-crazed, addled state, he couldn't recall her telling him that the legend said anything about marriage. Only that she would bring the champion home.

"Sabrina—who says you have to marry him?"

But he had been silent too long, wrestling with his thoughts. She had already turned and walked away.

Chapter Eighteen

The rest of the day sped by all too quickly. Sabrina helped Lizzie put in a small garden to replace the thriving one abandoned at the burned-out settlement.

"Durned Indians could've waited until we harvested the early vegetables," Lizzie grumbled. "Or burned us out before we did all that planting. Now we won't have any onions this year. Won't have potatoes. I reckon we'll be good and sick of beans and squash come next spring."

Come next spring . . .

By next spring, Sam vowed, the Stuart family would own new, richer land. Selling their organ would give them a stake, but these vegetables Lizzie meant to grow in the too-small patch of ground behind their rented shack would have to form the bulk of their diet if they meant to avoid spending that stake. Winter would be hard and comfortless, with dull fare and poor shelter, and only the hope of spring to see them through.

Lizzie, undaunted, believed in that future.

Sabrina would never know if Lizzie's faith was justified, for she would be back in Desmond. Not just back in Desmond, but long dead, her name, perhaps her entire existence, lost to the mists of time, while Lizzie and her family worked toward a new dream.

Her hand trembled on the hoe.

"Where does it come from?" Sabrina asked. "Your spirit?"

"My spirit?" Lizzie slammed the edge of her rake through a dirt clod.

"The inner fire that drives you. Do all those of your blood possess such strength?"

"Far as I know, only my brother and sister share my blood. Our family's a regular mishmash of nationalities. A little English and French on my mama's side. Papa contributed German and Polish and Russian. I'll bet there's a drop or two of your Irish in us as well."

Sabrina worked her tool free from a clump of matted roots. "One of your ancestors must have done something to give rise to your spirit. Some wondrous deed to lend you the courage to continue on in the face of adversity."

"That's just ordinary living, Sabrina. Getting by. Looking ahead. Hoping for better but making the best of what you get. If you're calling that spirit, well, I guess it has to come from within a person, not from what someone else does *for* them."

The notion struck Sabrina speechless.

"Take you, for instance," Lizzie continued. "There you are, a girl on your own. Got yourself into a business partnership. When that didn't work out so well you made friends and now you're ready to start a new life, just like me and Mr. Stuart. Seems to me you got a bucketload of spirit yourself."

Sabrina hacked at the hard earth while she considered Lizzie's observation. She, Sabrina of Desmond Muir, had spirit? Where had it come from? There had been no Irish champion in her ancestry.

Her hands blistered but she did not pause in her work. The sun beat down, scorching the back of her neck. Flies, drawn by sweat, pestered her until she swatted them away, and half the time she struck herself, depositing smears of dirt against her skin that dried and made her itch.

She had never known this type of physical discomfort. Such tasks had always been managed by servants in Desmond. There was something steadying about tearing into the ground when one's thoughts were all muddled. The sting of blisters, the tired ache of muscles forced to work in unfamiliar ways, reminded her that she possessed a living, breathing body with needs of its own. A body encasing a strong spirit.

It was one more thing to puzzle over.

Confusion beset her at every turn. The man she loved was free to be her champion. She knew how badly she had hurt him. Her own heart still bled from the agony of watching him walk away from their lovemaking. But he could live with the pain of spurned love. She did not believe he could survive failure. And so she had let him walk away.

The man she would accept as the champion was not free. Her instincts would not let her dismiss him out of hand. Something told her that Thomas Meagher was the one. She could not ignore that inner voice. She had been born and raised to find the one who would inspire it.

Lizzie's words gave her hope. Maybe the champion wasn't doomed to failure after all. Perhaps her people already possessed the spirit, and did not realize the strength they held within—because they had been schooled to expect a champion. Certes, she had been raised believing such.

If she held the Druid's Tear aloft and dazzled them all with its shimmering glory, and announced that the man who stood at her side was the true champion, they would believe. It mattered not whether their spirit was newly forged, or merely awakened. Her duty was to bring it to life.

She must provide a champion.

If failure was not a certainty, then could Neil be the one? Or must it be Meagher?

Lizzie groaned, interrupting the endless circle of Sabrina's thoughts. She stood and placed a hand at her back. She looked up at the sun.

"Goodness, Sabrina—your visitor will be here anytime. Don't you want to get cleaned up a little?"

She paused and pressed the head of her hoe into the earth. Lizzie had worked just as long, just as hard, and showed the evidence of it. Dusty hair. Smudged clothes. Hands roughened from hard work. And yet Lizzie need not primp herself to greet the man who was her champion. Sam would take quiet pride in his wife's dishevelment, knowing it meant she'd worked hard for the good of their family.

Neil had seen Sabrina at her dirty worst before, when they'd helped these settlers after the fire. She'd felt no need to clean herself and wipe away all traces of her labor. She had felt Neil's eyes upon her and sensed the heat of his desire, no matter her appearance.

But for the champion she had chosen, she must appear clean and tidy. She knew this. She remembered Thomas Meagher's proud aspect, his carefully fashioned garments, and knew such things were important to him.

She'd once thought so, too. Every time she'd imagined the champion, she'd pictured a glorious man bedecked in shining warrior's garments leading a thousand men into battle.

She'd seen, though, that sometimes a champion could wear nondescript blue britches and faded cotton shirts.

He would take his place at the watch whether or not others followed. He would not expect his woman to wash away the evidence of her work; nor would he expect her to find him less magnificent with the marks of his particular battles dimming his glory.

Her thoughts swirled again. Had she chosen right in selecting Meagher?

She shivered. She had made her choice. Only time would tell if she'd chosen well, or if she'd cast aside love for no purpose.

"I am sorry to leave you to finish this yourself," she told Lizzie.

"I'm sorry, too. You know how I feel about you meeting with Mr. Meagher. You'd best be careful what you say around him."

"I will not call him 'my lord,' nor will I ask him to examine my virginity," Sabrina promised.

"On second thought," said Lizzie, "I think I'll just come along in case you need me."

Thomas, with a grand sweep of his hat, bowed from the waist as he entered the shack. He turned to Lizzie. "I'm obliged, madam, that you have given me the pleasure of visiting your, er, lovely and gracious home," he said, with a nod of his head.

"Humpf. I'll be right outside. I'm leaving this door propped open. Sabrina, honey—you can give me a holler if you need anything."

Thomas stared with some puzzlement at Lizzie's foot-stomping departure, but when he swung his attention back to Sabrina, his face was wreathed with smiles.

"I'll not be knowing why yon lady's back has gone up at the sight of me, but you certainly are a pleasure for this weary soldier's eyes, my dear."

He seemed so fond of flowery phrases. She feared her steadily improving, but still inadequate, grasp of English might fail her if she tried to match him.

Two people united with one purpose should not have such difficulty understanding each other. She had always known what was in Neil's heart, no matter how loudly he yelled, how hard he tried to divert her in other directions. He'd understood her equally well.

Understanding, unfortunately, did not a champion make.

While preparing to meet Thomas, she had tried once more to wear the Druid's Tear. The diamond had shone with a brilliance never before achieved. So brightly did it flare, she could barely notice the broken link that Neil had so inexpertly mended.

There was no mistaking the Druid's Tear's choice. There was no avoiding her duty. Thomas Meagher was the champion she sought, and she must be direct with him.

"It troubles Lizzie that you are married," said Sabrina.

Redness flushed Thomas's skin more quickly than an eye could blink.

"I am troubled by it as well," she admitted. "Very troubled."

"Are you now?" His shoulders straightened. He tugged at the lapels of his coat, and with a cocky tilt of his head, he smiled.

"I truly did not expect to find you wed to another."

"Ah, well, dear lady, 'tis lonely without a mate."

"I know," she whispered.

"Truth to tell, 'tis best this is out in the open between us. Mrs. Meagher and I have lived apart for some time. 'Tis true she's coming to join me—she's in Helena right now, resting a bit before tackling the last part of the journey. She'll not mind, I assure you, if I spend a certain bit of time in the company of an Irish lass. Are you understanding that there's meaning beneath what I'm telling you, Sabrina, my lass? We share common blood, which gives us a greater understanding of each other's . . . needs."

"You would not seek me out if I were not Irish?"

He seemed to weigh his response very carefully. His glance swept over her quickly, the way she'd noticed Neil studying terrain for signs of danger.

"You're a tempting morsel, my dear, Irish or not. But I'd be lying to you if I didn't admit there's some truth in what you're saying—your voice carries the sound of the homeland. And I'm so hungry for it that I'm drawn to you like a bear to honey. I've never before strayed from my vows, even though Mrs. Meagher's . . . sweetness . . . runs dry ere the bear's appetite is slaked."

He winked at her.

She wished he would speak more simply. Neil had never confounded her so.

"You are very fond of Irish things."

"Irish things. Irish people. The blessed homeland herself. There's not a day goes by when I'm not missing the glorious green that doesn't seem to exist anywhere else. When I'm not craving the breath of salt air against my skin. When I'm not aching to bask in the heat of a good peat fire and slake my thirst with a pint of the rich golden Irish ale that nobody in this place can manage to brew properly."

"Why do you not return if you miss it so?"

"Ah, well, that would be asking to have my head severed from my neck, now, wouldn't it?" He grinned and gestured toward a chair, indicating that she should sit. She complied. He took the chair opposite her and leaned forward. "I'm not regretting one single minute of the trouble I caused for the sake of Irish freedom. They'll not be forgiving me for that back in England, and most here don't know the whole of my rebellion. They wouldn't understand. They don't know the meaning of a noble cause. They think a skirmish that lasts a few years makes a war.''

''I have heard you fought very valiantly for the Union.''

''You heard right.''

She remembered Neil's suspicions about Meagher.

''I have heard that now you fight against the Union.''

He frowned at her, and she bit her lip. She hadn't meant to phrase the comment so clumsily.

''Some think you are the reason Montana did not earn statehood.''

''That's a dirty lie.'' Sincerity rang from his denial. Instinct told her she could trust him on this. Neil must be told. She would have to tell him Thomas Meagher was not guilty of the treason Neil suspected.

Perhaps she could find answers to others of Neil's questions as well. He had only that morning expressed that very hope. She could give him the gift of knowing Thomas Meagher was innocent, so he need not deem his mission a failure when Thomas went away with her.

''Is it true you wear the uniform of a general under false pretenses?''

He smiled, but it was a false twisting of his lips, and the piercing regard with which he held her told her he'd grown displeased with her questions.

''And who exactly would be spreading such filthy tales about me?''

''I think them quite wonderful tales. Ireland has ever sought to hold itself apart from the rule of England. I know little of statehood, but any effort to retain sovereignty gives me hope that there is a purpose to Ireland's endless struggle.''

He shot her another assessing gaze, and then nodded, as if to himself. Passion lit him, the passion of a man who would stand against all odds.

''These settlers don't understand. They hold their destiny in their own hands. I love and respect the Union with all my heart—but we Montanans must gain certain concessions before taking the plunge. This is a land of newcomers. None of the people here have centuries of love for this land singing through their veins, as we do for our beloved Ireland. They're thinking only of what they might gain from statehood. They're not thinking of what they could lose. Maybe it takes a lifetime of fighting the English to understand what's at stake."

"You fought the English?"

"Name me a true Irishman who doesn't relish killing Englishmen above all else."

"Oh, *why* do you have to be married?" The words burst from her before she could contain them. She would never learn to guard her tongue. "I felt so certain you were the one, and each moment I spend with you tells me I chose well."

Thomas took a quick peek at the open parlor doors, and leaned closer to her. He cleared his throat, and yet he sounded rather strained when he spoke. "And what would the two of us be doing if I didn't have a wife, sweet lady?"

"I cannot bring myself to tell you." She congratulated herself for controlling her tongue before blurting out the truth about her quest to return to Desmond Muir with the Irish champion. "You would think me a brainless fool for spinning such wild hopes and dreams about the things the two of us could do together."

He reached out and caught her hand and clasped it between his. He felt warm and solid. Big, strong hands, capable of wielding swords, of holding banners aloft, of waving men into battle. Very nice hands, even if they lacked the magical fire that set her blood to boiling.

His pulse pounded, though. Every inch of him seemed eager and alert.

"Tell me."

Aye, there was a definite touch of hoarseness in his voice. She wondered if he required a throat-soothing potion.

"Sweet Sabrina—when you dream dreams that include me, what do you imagine we might be doing?"

" 'Tis too grand to put into words, Thomas." She pressed a hand against her heart to guard against spilling all her secrets in her usual thoughtless manner.

"You must give me a wee bit of a hint."

He had spoken of his words meaning more than they said. Of their common blood granting them a deeper understanding. Maybe it *would* be a good idea to work her way up to the truth in small steps, rather than startle him with the full magnitude of the challenge she meant to present him. Perhaps he would be able to deduce the astonishing truth from a few hints.

She closed her eyes, making a picture in her mind of the glorious battle for freedom that he might lead. Her people would fight to the death behind the true Irish champion.

"Screaming—good screaming, from the excitement and the ecstasy of satisfaction finally gained after endless yearning. Bodies bending and twisting but never tiring, determined to wring every bit of pleasure from the moment so long denied. I have no doubt the very earth would shake."

His jaw had gone slack. His eyes seemed unfocused, dazed with a strange combination of lust and awe. He understood! No doubt he was overwhelmed by the realization of the honor that would be his. She must have done a better job of portraying the battle scene than she'd thought, for he certainly seemed enraptured of the notion.

She heard a movement from beyond the doors and feared Lizzie might overhear. She leaned close to Thomas so that her lips just brushed against his ear. "Our names would be linked, and spoken with awe throughout the course of history, Thomas, if only you were free to come with me."

He lost his breath in a wheezing gasp. Sabrina pulled away, worried by this new symptom of ill health.

He made an impatient sound of denial. "When?"

"Never. You are married. 'Tis impossible."

"Suppose I were no longer married." He said it so calmly, so easily, that a chill skittered down her spine. She had imagined Robert dispensing with her with equal ease once he'd secured all he wanted. Men were avaricious, covetous of power, regardless of when they were born. But she was no better. If it meant securing the Irish champion for her people, she would live with the sin of causing a man to set aside his wife.

She recalled the accusations Neil had made against Thomas. Meagher's enemies disappeared, Neil had said.

"Would you make your wife disappear?"

He burst into laughter. "Ah, but you have the Irish flair for melodrama, my sweet. And the typical Catholic revulsion toward divorce, hmmm?"

"Divorce?"

"The legal dissolution of a marriage."

"You can do this? Without causing Mrs. Meagher to suffer?"

"I daresay Mrs. Meagher's pride might take a blow, but there would be compensations. She's a strong woman and can do well on her own. But we get much too far ahead of ourselves. Divorce is a serious business. I'd need to . . . get a glimpse of what's in store, so to speak. Make sure what you have to offer is worth disrupting my very comfortable life."

She would have to take him to Desmond Muir to show him the richness of her heritage. In this time she had naught to show him but the Druid's Tear. He might find himself sufficiently dazzled by its splendor.

She touched a hand to her breast, exactly where the shimmering stone would fall once she donned the chain and resumed the journey that would bring home the Irish champion. "I believe you will be overwhelmed by what I have to offer."

His eyes darkened with anticipation as they fastened on the hand touching her breast. "When?"

"Soon."

"How soon?"

She did not know. There were many things to consider. She would have to tell him the whole story, but she could not do so here where Lizzie might overhear. And if he agreed, well, one could not simply wish upon the Druid's Tear and disappear while people stood watching. "As soon as I can contrive a way for us to be completely, utterly alone."

"Leave that to me."

"You will not harm Mrs. Meagher?"

He chucked her under the chin. "A tender heart to go with your soft skin. There are all manner of ways to rid myself of those who annoy me. Some pleasant, some less so. If it pleases you to go gently with Mrs. Meagher, then that is how it shall be done."

She felt no satisfaction. "This does not rest easy on my soul."

"That's why you need me," he said. "There's nothing I won't do in pursuit of a noble cause such as ours. You will learn to do the same."

He spoke the right words. He stood with the graceful ease of a warrior. A leader who inspired confidence in his men; a man who understood that sacrifices must be made for the sake of the cause. She had found her champion. She did not think it appropriate to burst into tears.

"Tomorrow." He lifted her hand to his lips and planted a soft kiss just above her fingers. "I'll walk you through town and show you the potential of the place."

"Potential—whether or not Montana becomes a state?"

His gaze narrowed. "Would there be a reason, now, why you keep coming back to that particular subject?"

"No . . . no."

He studied her, his entire demeanor stiff with suspicion.

"I am just very nervous about what we plan to do," she said. And the tremor that shook her was not entirely feigned.

Her shivering served to ease his tension a little, but just a little. "I possess a temper to match my Irish blood," he said. "You'll not be wanting to give me cause to suspect your motives. My enemies—supposing I had any—would confirm the truth of what I say—supposing they were around to say it."

"I swear you are exactly as I prayed you would be," she said.

"What we have said here today, all of it, remains only between the two of us."

"It can be no other way."

"Tomorrow, then."

"Aye," she whispered. "Tomorrow."

Chapter Nineteen

"Easy now, easy!" Neil called as the crowd of soldiers pushed and shoved to get close to the medicine wagon.

He was getting better at this. Soldiers had come running when he'd opened the back of his wagon no more than ten minutes earlier. They'd started waving money at him before he'd even spouted off three lines of the speech he'd finally memorized.

He'd spent every free moment since arriving in Fort Benton studying that stupid speech, in the hopes that filling his brain with useless drivel would wipe out the memory of Sabrina walking away from him.

So far it hadn't worked.

"Six dollars," he barked at a soldier holding up two fingers.

"Hey," complained the soldier. "Hartley told me a bottle cost two and a half dollars."

"Hartley got a special deal."

"Oh, just shut up, Elwood," muttered another soldier.

"It's still a hell of a lot cheaper than the whiskey at the saloon."

So that was why he'd suddenly developed such a large clientele. His selling technique hadn't improved at all.

"Price just went up to four dollars," he announced.

"No fair!"

"Then go to the saloon and get a better price."

Such a storm of grumbling greeted his announcement that a person wouldn't be blamed for thinking he'd gotten caught up in a thundercloud. But the soldiers handed over their money and Neil doled out the elixir.

When he'd filled all the orders, the soldiers left and he stared down in disbelief at the sheaf of greenbacks fanned out in his hand. He'd recaptured every bit plus more of the cost of the elixir he'd given for free to the burned-out settlers.

Sabrina had been right. Casting benevolence increased one's wealth. This money was the only kind of wealth he'd held important. He made a fist, crushing the money. Nothing but fancy paper. Couldn't tell one bill apart from the other. Once he'd spent them, he'd remember neither the bills nor the goods they purchased.

He'd remember until the day he died that night when he'd swilled elixir with men who'd looked upon him as a friend. When he'd danced a little. When he'd held a miracle in his arms. He'd been a rich man, truly rich, for a day or two.

Sabrina. Her image danced through his mind, and he had to blink twice, three times, before he realized that she wasn't just a figment of his imagination, but was really walking down the street.

On the arm of Thomas Francis Meagher. Meagher's aide fawned a pace or two behind them. The three made a small but regal parade as they strolled in his direction.

Meagher caught sight of him, and a smug little smile curved his lips.

I stole your woman, said that smile. *I already have one of my own, and now I have yours, too.*

Without really knowing what he meant to do once he got there, Neil crossed the road to stand in their path.

She walked with her head bowed, unusual for her, and he missed the proud, bold tilt of her chin. "Sabrina."

She lifted her head and he saw that she knew exactly who she would find standing there.

"Good afternoon, Neil," she said.

"Sabrina," he repeated, just for the pleasure of hearing her name spoken aloud.

" 'Miss Desmond' might be more appropriate." Meagher shifted his hold on Sabrina, turning it purely proprietary rather than courteous. "I see you brought your money with you. Might as well be shoving it back into your pocket, my man. Miss Desmond and I have already come to an understanding."

He could tell by the confusion upon Sabrina's face that she didn't understand she'd just been called a whore on the main street of Fort Benton. Meagher's lackey smirked.

Neil shook. She looked cool and pretty in a borrowed skirt and shirtwaist. Her hair had been pinned up to reveal the graceful curve of her neck. He knew by touch the natural slimness of her waist, but she looked so small now that he'd bet every dollar held in his hand that she was wearing a corset.

She'd worked so hard to adapt to the ways women were expected to behave in this century in which she did not belong, and now the man she thought was her champion insulted her in public.

Despite his own shortcomings, he would have done better by her, he realized with a jolt.

He *would* do better for her.

"Pistols at dawn," he bit out the challenge.

Meagher stared at him in puzzlement for a moment, and then burst into laughter. "Good Lord, and you think you'd be challenging me to a duel?"

"You heard me."

"Even if I consented to take part in such foolishness, I'd not be lowering myself to duel with the likes of you." He ran his gaze over Neil in a derisive manner. "Go back to hawking your quackery, peddler."

Neil dropped the money into the dirt and shifted into a crouch, ready to spring.

"Neil! Don't!" With an anguished cry, Sabrina placed herself between him and Meagher. "He will make you disappear. He truly does such with those who annoy him. This was one of many secret things he explained to me."

Neil closed his eyes and groaned silently.

"Dear lady." Meagher's voice had turned low and ominous. "I'm thinking you're not the simple lusty wench I took you to be. You assured me all those questions you plagued me with were innocently spoken."

All those questions . . .

"Sabrina doesn't always phrase her statements the way she really means them. Isn't that right, sweetheart?"

She flinched, leaving no doubt she felt betrayed by his weak effort to save her. Her chin tilted up, sending his heart sinking.

"I chose my words and questions most carefully. I regret none of them. I thought . . . some people . . . might be interested in what I learned. Very interested."

"Sweetheart, listen—you weren't asking Mr. Meagher to admit to anything that could be damaging to him, right?"

"Wrong. Those are exactly the questions I asked him. I found his answers most illuminating. I—"

"That's enough." Meagher jerked on Sabrina's arm,

startling her into silence. "You and I will discuss this matter. Privately."

He motioned to his assistant, who promptly stepped forward. Meagher whispered something to him; the assistant smirked again.

Neil didn't like the looks of this. "Let her go."

Meagher ignored him.

"Confine this young lady in the blockhouse inside the fort," he instructed his aide. "Don't let anyone know she's there. Bring the key straight back to me." He handed Sabrina over with the distaste he might accord the transferring of a roach.

"Let her go," Neil repeated, taking a menacing step toward Meagher.

"Or what?" Meagher cocked a brow. "You'll be knocking me on the head with one of your medicine bottles? I can have you arrested. One cry from me, and every soldier within earshot will come running."

Arrested, locked up, he'd stand no chance of helping Sabrina. Neil reined in his hatred.

"Neil!" She called his name. Her eyes were wide with terror, her face white with fear as the aide gripped her arm and guided her toward the fort.

She had roused Meagher's suspicion with questions— questions she would never have thought of asking if Neil hadn't allowed his jealousy to show.

He'd placed her in serious danger simply because he'd been hurt and angry. He knew she spoke without weighing the consequences. He knew she held a somewhat sketchy mastery of the language, knew her attempts at saying important things often backfired. And still he'd pretended the only reason he was interested in what she'd done with Meagher was to see if she'd pass along information to him.

She'd leaped heart-first into interrogating a man so

crafty that the United States president had sent a battle-hardened captain in to do that very thing.

He'd cut himself away from her because he was afraid to love her, afraid that he wouldn't be able to take care of her. And look what had happened as a result.

She continued to look back at him over her shoulder, but she did not call him again.

"You hurt her, you'll answer to me."

"Hurt her? Now why would I be doing that?"

"You're locking her up. Secretly. Not as a prisoner, which would give her certain rights and protections. I don't think that means you intend to ply her with roses and champagne."

"Ah, but there you'd be wrong. You see, the wee lass stirs something in these old bones. One minute I thought we had an understanding, and the next I found her expressing all manner of reluctance. A day or two in the blockhouse won't hurt her. Not much to do in there except think over her options and make up a pretty story to explain her behavior. 'Tis grateful she'll be when I release her. Very grateful, I'm hoping."

Neil's dropped greenbacks fluttered in the wind, and a woman and then a child caught sight of them. With nervous, guilty looks, they raced from one fluttering bill to another, collecting them and stuffing them inside their clothes.

Neil watched and marveled at how little it meant to see his money disappear. At the start of this journey, he'd held recouping his savings as second in importance only to carrying out the president's mission.

Now the money meant nothing.

The mission be damned.

Sabrina had chosen Thomas Francis Meagher as her champion, and that meant President Andrew Johnson didn't get him. Not if Neil Kenyon had anything to do with it.

The trouble was, now the tables were turned. Meagher had Sabrina in his control. If she tried explaining the legend of the Druid's Tear, he'd probably laugh it off, believing it to be a bizarre, featherheaded lie concocted to explain her unseemly interest in Meagher's activities.

She had told him that one had to believe with all one's heart in the legend in order for it to come true.

The champion of the Irish people turned his back and started walking away.

Neil could do the same. Retreat, the way he always did when situations got out of his control. Right now, the only way he could see to help Sabrina would be to try to convince Meagher that time travel and magic were possible. He couldn't even convince burned-out settlers to watch for Indians, or pain-racked soldiers to buy medicine.

Meagher wouldn't hurt her. She would eventually convince Meagher of her sincerity, the way she'd convinced him.

He could walk away. She'd be fine. Eventually.

"You ever make a mistake, Mr. Meagher?" Neil called.

"I daresay I have." Meagher paused and glanced over his shoulder, wary but interested. "And you?"

"I hope to God I'm not making one at the moment."

Something of his desperation, his determination, must have conveyed itself to Meagher.

"I'm listening."

"You're an Irishman, Mr. Meagher." At the man's curt nod, Neil continued. "What would you say to you and I partaking of a bottle of my elixir, while I tell you a tale that involves Druids and magic and time traveling . . . a tale that tells the secret behind the eternal optimism of the Irish spirit?"

"We Irishman love our tales—whether they be about

leprechauns or fairies or anything of a magical nature. Belief in the mystical is bred into our bones."

So far, this was going more easily than Neil had expected. He didn't care to stand there in the middle of the street shouting out the legend of the Druid's Tear, though.

"If you're the man I think you are—more important, if you're the man *she* thinks you are—you'll find this tale extraordinarily interesting."

"So it involves the lass."

"Her name is Sabrina," Neil shot out, his rage rekindling and almost making him lose his careful control. "Lady Sabrina of Desmond Muir, one of the most pivotal border estates in Ireland."

Meagher's interest waned visibly. His lip curled in a sneer.

"Is it now? Well, suppose I was to say I know every inch of Ireland and I've never heard of Desmond Muir. And suppose I was to say I don't have much interest in drinking with you or listening to your tales."

"If you were to say those things, I guess I'd have to say you are indeed making a mistake." Neil walked closer, forcing Meagher to turn to face him. "I might have to say that President Johnson has sent an investigator here to Fort Benton to look into your affairs, and that the investigator has turned up some interesting incidents just begging to be explored."

"An investigator? If there were such a fellow, I'd warn him that Montana is a wild and dangerous place, where accidents befall even those who are careful."

A threat, not so thinly veiled. Something to add to his arsenal, if it came to that.

"President Johnson is well aware of the danger. That's why, if any investigator he sends fails to make a report, he stands ready to send another in his place. And another, and another if need be—until the job's done."

"Well, the dear president would just be wasting his time, wouldn't he? It would be a stupid fellow who left damaging evidence about for all and sundry to discover."

Meagher crossed his arms over his chest, but the pallor bleaching his ruddiness betrayed him.

"Hell, he could be smart as the devil, but if the investigator dedicated his life to the task, he'd be bound to find a small slip here or there." Neil pretended nonchalance. "Maybe the investigator wouldn't bother looking at all, and would make an 'all clear' report to the president, providing . . ."

"Providing what?" Meagher bit out.

Neil no longer cared who might overhear. He was tired of couching his words in hypothetical terms.

"Providing you listen to the tale, and do your damnedest to believe it no matter how outrageous it sounds."

Meagher boggled. He tapped the side of his forefinger to his mouth, gesturing for quiet. "Got a bit vehement there, my man," he said, barely above a whisper.

"There's a great deal at stake. You stand a chance of being ousted from power in utter disgrace."

"I'm aware of that." Meagher seemed strangely calm, as if he'd been expecting this threat to his power. Or maybe he'd been through something like this before, during his past exploits, and simply understood the value of weighing his options. "Your President Johnson has already seen to it that I'm no longer acting governor. There's none so proud as an Irishman, and none so keenly aware of the subtleties of power. Perhaps 'tis why the lass touches me so—when I'm with her, I get the sense I'll find what has always eluded me, because of her."

Neil knew the sensation intimately. It clawed at his gut to hear another man admit the same.

"Hear me out, Mr. Meagher. I guarantee you won't feel you've wasted your time. If things go as planned, you might find . . . let's just say your wildest dreams just might come true.''

Meagher sighed, and then sent Neil a rueful, thoroughly engaging grin. To his utter disgust, Neil found himself liking the man.

"Ah, Mr. Kenyon, as I said—we Irishmen love our tales, especially if there's a happy ending. And I'm finding a drop or two of your elixir would not go unappreciated after all.'' He clapped an arm around Neil's shoulder. " 'Tis eager I am to hear about Druids and magic and traveling through time.''

Chapter Twenty

This newest prison Sabrina found herself occupying was the most difficult of all to bear. One chair furnished the room; naught else. The air struck chill and damp, no doubt because the two-foot-thick walls kept the sun at bay.

She had explored the room's possibilities while the sun stood high. Narrow windows stood too tall for her to see through, and so she dragged the chair from one window to the next. She peered down at the slice of town thus framed, seeking Neil's wagon, but unable to find it. She prayed it was because of the angle of her view.

He could have left the town altogether, without saying good-bye.

He could have been deemed an enemy, and . . . disappeared.

Her new burst of shivering could not be blamed entirely upon the cold.

Daylight faded into dusk. Dusk darkened into night. Nobody came to speak to her. She climbed her chair again, and rose to her toes and craned her neck to see if she might expand her view just a little, but Fort Benton had stilled with sleep, the houses drawn shut, the only sound the "all's well" hails of the sentries keeping watch against Indians.

She stepped down from the chair. Sat in it. Wrapped her arms about herself in a futile effort to get warm.

It was almost like being back in her chamber at Desmond Muir, she realized. Chilled from without, chilled from within. No maid inside this chamber with her, it was true, but guards were posted somewhere without to see to it that she could not escape as she waited, waited, waited for the champion.

At long last, she heard noise from the outside corridor. The clanking of keys. Footsteps. Men—more than one. The aide who had locked her in told her no one save Thomas would know she was here; no one save Thomas would come to her after she had learned her new lesson.

She whirled away from the door and took no comfort in the sight of the moon sailing high. Near midnight, she reckoned. Beyond the time when someone should have come for her, if his purpose was noble.

They spoke, low and rumbling words that were indistinguishable to her. Something about the tenor told her they were friends, or at least easy with each other, and confident that no one would challenge their presence in that corridor, at her door, so late at night.

She jerked at the sharp snick made by the releasing lock.

"Sabrina."

Two voices called her name. She turned and saw them both illuminated by the light of the lantern Neil held high.

She put a hand to her head, certain she must have suffered a fit. She blinked to clear her vision. But naught was wrong with her. In front of her stood the man she loved. And next to him, the man she'd chosen as her champion. In accord.

To one she wanted to run. To the other she must go.

Her limbs would not obey, and so she stood there, shivering in the chill.

Neil moved no closer, but she felt his regard steady upon her, probing, examining, reassuring himself that she fared well. The numbness within her, the chill, edged away as she felt wrapped in that visual caress, warmed and cherished. Loved. She read the truth of this in his eyes, in the softening of his lips, the lips that found saying words of importance so difficult.

Thomas Meagher looked upon her with something like awe, his expression that of a miner who sought iron ore and found gold instead.

"You told him," she said to Neil, scarcely daring to believe it. How difficult it must have been for him to tell so convincingly a tale he'd found hard to believe. How difficult to hand over to another man the woman he himself loved.

He nodded. "We brought your necklace, Sabrina. He's ready to go with you. But something's wrong."

Neil reached into his shirt pocket and removed the Druid's Tear. He held it by the chain. The stone swung back and forth, milky and opaque, lifeless and dim as it had been when hanging around her mother's neck.

"The stone never lives for you." Her throat ached to make the admission. "Let Thomas hold it."

"We tried, dear lady, but I'm not averse to having another go at it." Thomas wrapped his huge hand around the stone. He held the fist he'd made to his forehead and closed his eyes, his lips moving in prayer.

He opened his hand. The Druid's Tear lay dull upon his palm, almost gray.

"You are not the champion?" she said in disbelief.

"I *am*. Sweet Jesus, I want to be. I've spent my life searching, hoping, never finding what was exactly right . . . it seems everything I've done has been in preparation for what you need of me."

"Aye. That is what I believe. Let me see it." She went to them. She wanted to touch Neil but dared not for fear she would never be able to let him go. She reached for the Druid's Tear and caught the chain, while Thomas stubbornly held tight to the stone.

At that moment, with her hand and his linked by the Druid's Tear, the diamond burst into life, so dazzling that she had to shield her eyes against it. A shimmering rainbow of color swept the comfortless room. Greens and golds and reds and oranges reflected off the faces of the men, while she felt as though blackness would engulf her.

"It is exactly as the legend decreed." Her voice had taken on the dullness abandoned by the stone. "I am the chosen Desmond woman. Without me, the stone will not accept you as the champion."

"No!" Neil caught her and pulled her against him, breaking her hold on the chain. His heart hammered against her ear. She wrapped her arms around him and buried her face in him, glorying in the feel of him, the scent of him.

"Sabrina." She turned reluctantly at Thomas's anguished call. The Druid's Tear had dimmed again.

"I have to go," she murmured.

"I know." Neil took a shuddering breath and stepped away from her, leaving her bereft. "Not here. Sentries are posted outside. They saw me walk in with Mr. Meagher. If he disappears now, there will be too many questions asked."

"And all the blame for my disappearance would fall upon you." Thomas nodded in understanding. He frowned in thought. "I have it—the steamship *Thompson* is docked right outside on the Missouri. Nobody's aboard. I often use the officers' quarters to tend to paperwork. Nobody will question if I go there now."

"We have to smuggle Sabrina out of here without their seeing her," Neil said. "They'd ask questions, since nobody knows she's here. And I'm sure you'd prefer it if they didn't see the two of you going aboard the ship together."

"Aye, 'twill be hard enough on Mrs. Meagher without her being told I've run off with another woman. Please don't take offense, lass," he said to Sabrina. "I've been married to the woman for twelve years. The least I can do is leave her able to hold her head high with a widow's pride, rather than giving people the ammunition to call her a scorned woman."

"You must write her a letter with your officer papers," Sabrina said. "Explain matters to her."

"I doubt she'll be understanding the full of it. But I'll try."

"The soldiers know you and I came in together," said Neil. "We'll leave together and distract them with some conversation while Sabrina slips out behind us. Once she's clear of the fort, you can go to the ship, and I'll be on my way."

He spoke with the confidence of a tactician accustomed to making battle plans. She wondered how he could be so unaffected by their impending separation. They would never see each other again, ever.

"Engage those lads in conversation," Meagher advised. "Talk to them for a good while after I'm gone, so they can testify later that I went off alone."

"Talk to them." Neil laughed without humor.

"Perhaps you can sell them a bottle of elixir," Sabrina whispered, her heart aching.

He gave her a crooked smile, and she fancied she saw

the light of the Druid's Tear reflected in his eyes. That would be impossible, unless tears welled there, unshed.

Perhaps Desmond women were not the only creatures who never allowed themselves to cry.

He touched the curve of her cheek, and then traced gentle fingertips all over her face, as if he meant to memorize her features.

"I'm out of the medicine business, sweetheart," he said. "Lost my partner."

Neil let Meagher do the talking while he stood there in an agony of helplessness until Sabrina stole out of the blockhouse gate. She kept to the shadows and darted around the corner, safely out of the soldiers' range of vision.

"Cigarette?" the soldier asked.

"Thank you, lad, but I think I'll be heading over to the *Thompson* to do a bit of paperwork. I'll be saying good night to all of you now."

"Good night, sir."

Neil watched Meagher follow Sabrina's trail.

"How about you?" asked the soldier. "You want a cigarette?"

"No."

"Well, then."

"Well."

He stood there, paralyzed. *Make conversation,* Meagher had said, so they would remember him. Neil figured this approach might work just as well—an oversize, miserable man standing silent as a rock with his hands jammed in his pockets while the soldiers wondered why in the hell he didn't just go off and leave them be.

He counted seconds off in his head. After five minutes he felt pretty sure Sabrina and Meagher would've climbed aboard the *Thompson*. He counted another five minutes to make sure. No cry arose, demanding identification for an unknown woman boarding a ship.

He found he could move then.

" 'Bye," he said to the soldiers.

" 'Night."

He could move, but not too fast, because he wanted to run after Sabrina and make her stop, make her stay. He kept his legs forging in the opposite direction, aiming for his wagon. Each step was as agonizing and slow as if he waded through thigh-high mud.

"Don't go." Talking to himself. When for all he knew it was already too late. The damned Druid's Tear might've whisked them away within seconds of climbing onto that ship.

"Don't leave me." He didn't bother lowering his voice, even though he knew sound traveled far during the night. He was already something of a pariah in this town. They might as well add *lunatic* to the list of reasons for not liking him. Which they would surely do if they spotted him walking around, talking to himself, saying things he'd never thought he'd say.

It hit him with the force of a hammer blow that he'd never said them to Sabrina.

Never asked her to stay. Never told her he didn't want her to go.

He somehow found his wagon through the haze of fog that gripped him as he realized the full extent of his stupidity. It probably wouldn't have changed anything for him to say those things to her, but it would have meant something to her. She would have known how profoundly she'd changed him, how she'd found a man who walked and talked but had no heart and turned him into someone who was willing to try.

It would have meant something to him, too. He'd never

thought it possible that he would want to say those words. She alone was responsible for making the impossible come true.

He'd never told her. He'd held her glorious body in his arms and loved her and never told her.

He climbed into his wagon seat and slumped, his head hanging down almost to his knees.

"Two o'clock and all is well," the sentry called, soft and reassuring.

All was not well. Rage at realizing just *how* not well robbed him of all caution.

"Come back to me," he yelled. "Don't leave me."

He felt like an idiot while his desperate cry reverberated in the night air. He wondered if the sentry would come running, and how he would explain himself.

Whomp.

The wagon shuddered as if it had been hit by a cannon-ball.

"I'm in no mood for this," Neil called a warning. He'd had to add another hasp and padlock to the wagon since the soldiers had taken such a liking to his elixir. This wouldn't be the first time they'd tried breaking past his defenses.

He heard a scuffling from inside his wagon. The groan of wood as someone bumped into a crate; the tinkling of glass bottles shifting in their cases.

He'd heard those sounds before, every one of them. The day Sabrina had mysteriously appeared in the back of his wagon.

Hope burgeoned in him, too strong to hold back. He was off the seat and around the back before he managed to pull the keys out of his pocket. His hands shook so hard he didn't think he'd ever manage to undo those locks, but he did, and he practically ripped the hasps out of the wood from the force he used to yank them open. He pulled the doors apart and they went slamming back against the sides of the wagon.

Moonlight flooded the interior.

Nobody was inside.

He caught the roof for support, and sagged forward. He was back where he'd started. Hearing things. Imagining things. Before he knew it, he'd forget everything he'd learned from her, and she would never know how magical she had made these past few days of his life.

"One minute." He harangued the heavens at the top of his lungs. "I'd trade my life for one more minute with her. One minute to tell her I love her."

Well, his imagination was already acting up but good, because it seemed that off in the farther corner of the wagon, a shimmering started and gradually sorted itself into the ghostly shape of the woman he loved. Beautiful, but insubstantial as mist. There and not there, the shadow woman he'd loved in the woods.

"I love you," he told the shadow woman. "I'll always love you."

The mists swirled, seemed to settle and thicken.

"I didn't want you to go. I didn't want you to leave me. I would have tried, Sabrina."

"I know." Ghosts spoke in echoing song, it seemed, creating a musical blessing that rang straight through to his soul.

"If I had one minute with you, I'd tell you everything you wanted to hear."

"One minute would not be long enough. 'Twould require days. Years. Nay—a lifetime."

She walked toward him. Touched his face. Cool, like a nighttime breeze, and then warmer and more substantial. The shadow woman stood taller than he, and she had to bend to place a soft kiss on his forehead. She let her face rest against his and he felt something hot and wet trickling against his skin.

"Now I know you're not real," he said. "Desmond women never cry."

"It seems I am no longer a Desmond woman. I believe this means I am now a Kenyon woman." She moved away a little and opened her hand. On her palm rested a single link from the Druid's Tear chain, a link that had twice been broken and poorly mended, and now lay twisted, gaping open where the mending had failed.

She put a hand to her head as if she were feeling a little dizzy. "You were always ripping that chain from my neck and rending it apart."

"Just twice," he said.

Someone came running in the night. Neil glanced behind him and saw the sentry coming at him, full speed, his rifle clutched in one hand. He skidded to a stop. "Oh, it's just you."

"Just me," Neil said, loneliness swamping him.

"Is he bothering you, ma'am?"

"Nay."

The sentry nodded, and left.

It took Neil a moment to realize what had happened. The sentry had seen Sabrina. Talked to her. Received a response.

He turned back, and she wasn't a figment of his imagination.

He reached up and caught her around the waist, felt the slim suppleness, felt her sway and knew he didn't have a solid grip. "Come a little closer, sweetheart; I'll get you down from there."

"Oh, Neil, I feel as if I have been falling for a lifetime. You are certain you will catch me and keep me safe from harm?"

"Forever."

She leaned into his hold. He pulled her close, letting her slide down the front of him, reveling in the warm, solid feel of her.

She ran her hands along his chest as if to reassure herself that he was no shadow man. She clasped her hands behind his neck and pulled his head down for a kiss—a long, tender, exquisitely hungry kiss that roused all his appetites and promised to take a lifetime to satisfy.

"How?" he managed to croak at last.

"I did my best to do my duty," she said. "We each held a portion of the Druid's Tear and wished to be back at Desmond Muir. I could not wish with all my heart, for my heart was here, with you. But it did not seem to matter. All proceeded as before. Thomas Meagher and I entered the swirling blackness. I felt myself falling, and knew utter despair. And then . . . the chain broke."

"The chain broke."

"Aye, at this link I am holding. I thought I had been judged unworthy and would spin forever in that black abyss. You cannot comprehend my desolation . . . worse, even, than knowing I had been consigned to hell for all eternity. And then I heard you call to me."

"You heard me?"

"You asked me to come back to you. You asked me not to leave you." A smile trembled on her lips, and then she shot him a sly, mischievous glance. "You are always yelling, my lord."

"Once we're married . . ." he began.

His throat tightened. More words he never thought he'd say, and now he wanted to say them so badly he couldn't get them out fast enough. "Once we're married, you'll be surprised at some of the things I'll always do."

Epilogue

A bell tolled, sonorous, matching the somber mood of the crowd gathered along the riverbank.

Sabrina reached for Neil's hand when three mounted soldiers, exhaustion lining their faces, cantered toward the major awaiting their report. Their uniforms clung wetly, and their horses' coats were muddied to midchest, showing that man and beast alike had forayed repeatedly into the river while conducting their search.

They dismounted and joined the major for a quick consultation.

The major turned away, and made a sign of the cross.

Whispered *No*s and muted sobs rustled through the crowd.

The major motioned with his hand and the bell tolled again.

"I have an official announcement," he said once the reverberations quieted. He pulled a paper from his pocket. He opened the folds, stared at it, folded it up again. He removed his hat and tucked it under his arm, and then pinched the bridge of his nose. "Sorry," he muttered.

He let a moment pass before he once more unfolded the paper, and then began reading.

"Several nights ago, General Thomas Meagher advised the blockhouse sentries of his intention to spend the night aboard the steamship *Thompson* for the purpose of tending to paperwork. He has not been seen since. There can be no question that he boarded the *Thompson*. He left a stack of letters on his desk, all addressed in his own hand. It is presumed that at some point during the night, he took a walk on deck and slipped somehow into the Missouri River."

"That's a dirty lie!" cried a man. Affirmations from the audience seemed to encourage him on. "General Meagher's surefooted as a goat. He went on a mountain-climbing expedition to Central America. He wouldn't trip and fall off a ship that ain't even moving!"

The major continued with his prepared statement, shouting to override the objections.

"Army personnel conducted a massive search of the town of Fort Benton, the fort itself, and surrounding areas. There is no sign of the general. All of his worldly possessions remain in his quarters. It is assumed that General Meagher has drowned."

"No!" Cries of denial swept through the crowd.

"General Meagher wouldn't drown in a shallow, slow-movin' river like the Missouri! He swam hundreds of miles in the *ocean* to escape prison."

The major crumpled his paper and gestured toward the dejected soldiers. "I'm no happier to be reading this statement than you are to be hearing it. These men just came back from a thorough search. They were our last hope. They hunted fifteen miles downstream, covering every inch of the riverbanks, examining any . . . debris . . . caught in the river. There is no sign of a body."

"That means there's a chance Mr. Meagher's still alive," called a man.

"If he is, we'll find him," promised the major. "There's word that a reward is going to be posted. Could be as high as ten thousand dollars."

The amount of the fortune being offered stunned the crowd into silence.

They remained as they were for a while, silent, holding something like a vigil for a man who had touched their lives. Eventually some fashioned a sign of the cross, as the major had done. Others let their shoulders slump.

One by one they drifted back to their homes, their families.

"They will miss him," Sabrina said.

"They won't forget him."

"They will grieve, but they will go on. A strong spirit lives within these people of Montana." She reached for Neil's hand. He enfolded it within his, and then embellished the connection by pulling her into the curve of his arm. She rested her head against his chest, listening to him, feeling the rise and fall of his body against hers.

They had loved one another so often and so well these past days that they'd all but forgotten to sleep. Exhaustion, and repletion, should fill her; instead, desire stirred within.

"We will like it here," she said. "This is where we belong."

Author's Note

Thomas Francis Meagher—Irish patriot, Civil War hero, noted politician who served as both secretary and acting governor of the Montana Territory—vanished without explanation on July 1, 1867, from the docked steamship *Thompson*.

A massive search, and the posting of an astronomical ten-thousand-dollars reward for information concerning his disappearance, failed to produce any results. His disappearance remains a mystery to this day.